10 Past
DARK

10 Past DARK

SHANTANU KULKARNI

PARTRIDGE
A Penguin Random House Company

To order additional copies of this book, contact
Partridge India
000 800 10062 62
orders.india@partridgepublishing.com

www.partridgepublishing.com/india

Contents

For Shilpatai and Himani

Acknowledgements

There are things we want to tell. But we never say these.

These are not secrets.

Secrets, we share. But some of those feelings which are yet to be dressed in words, which are juggled between dreams and a conscious, wakeful, alert mind just don't come out. We get lost in the midst of a crowd, amble absent-mindedly, and don't recall what we were thinking when we try to. And all this while we make our best attempt to tell ourselves we have a perfectly normal life. Punching in code, compiling instructions for machines—those don't understand stories, but just ones and zeroes.

But we are wrong. Those dream crumbs which are born in the darkest attic of the body don't just shrivel and wither away. They wait for us, lurking behind other thoughts, selecting the dreams they want to attack, ripping us out of sleep.

These stories are those restless thoughts. Once I decided those thoughts must be put down on paper, I allowed myself to be carried away. And this helped me release all the bottled-up exasperation. The characters in the stories gave me their parts as I started rambling with words. They came with absolutely no plan or order; there were nights they haunted me, terrified me, and at times delighted me. They allowed me to slide unabashedly into my own subconsciousness, observing the known things do the unknown.

Many people supported me to write the stories I used to tell. They gave their valuable suggestions, their 'ahas' and 'oh' remarks, corrections, and a lot of encouragement. I am especially grateful to my sister and my wife, without whom this would have never existed. My wife bore patience with me in my state of being one of the characters of my story followed by my weird absent-mindedness. Most of my writings were after dark, after everyone slept, except her, who listened to my raw thoughts and gave her 'umhmms'. And most of the times, those 'umhmms' transformed the stubborn ideas into words and eventually stories. My sister was always the first to read the manuscript (in the middle of the night). She would wait for the email and read it regardless of the time at her end. I was never the first one to read the first draft; it was always her. And she was the one who believed that there would be few more people around the world who would read these stories and a book is a possibility.

Among the first readers were a few of my very good friends. They forgivingly read some of the first drafts and didn't complain. Gurvinder, Imran, Carol, Anuj, if I hadn't got encouragement from you guys, I wouldn't have kept going. Shilpa, thanks for connecting me to Vani; she was the first person to read it critically.

And Marie, a big heartfelt thanks to you for all the editing that made this bunch of words readable.

The Wanderlust Nurse

Nothing really changed here for a long time. Shilhur is still just a speck, hardly noticeable on the state map of Maharashtra, the typical in-between village, off some seldom travelled highway. People hardly came here with their free will. Most people here are either because they lost their way and didn't find a way out (yet), or were born here. The continual exodus of the young in search of better lives had left this village a place of the ageing generation, who were mostly entrusted to care of their grandkids.

Today was more or less like what it had been yesterday, dry and hot. The sky looked pale behind the dull brown stunted mountains. And the place wore the usual silence. Even the birds weren't chirpy in this place. There were not many left anyway. Probably vultures and eagles were still around. They were as silent as the other residents of the place and stayed put on dry tall betel nut trees on those stunted mountains. In that speck of a village, under that blanket of silence stood a lonely shed: the rickety clinic of Dr Ghanshyam, the only clinic in the radius of twenty, or maybe even thirty, kilometres.

Inside the clinic was no different. There was a shroud of silence here as well. But this was different. This was of the screaming silence types, the one of heartbreak (the break that makes you know the location of the heart in the body). Silence which barges in uninvited, unannounced, sneaking in without the background beats or reverberating drums or crescendo of sad violin notes just tells you the address of the heart in the upper cavity of the gut, otherwise a granted place.

Two men stood in the clinic room. One of them stuck his chin on his chest, watching his feet, rather gazing through them, through the

1

floor, actively avoiding eye contact with the other person. The other was following the fine dust motes, which shimmered and danced in the crisscross soft bars of sunlight flooding through the chinks of the door. The air in the room was stuffy, laden with what was going on in minds of those two people.

Finally, Ghanshyam cleared his throat and spoke in a choking voice, 'You serious?' He said that and felt sudden pressure at the base of his throat. He leaned forward and tried gulping the lump that stuck in this throat and said, 'Last evening when you told me you would be leaving, it seemed like a passing thought. I thought that sleeping on it would make everything right and a good morning would bring us back to the usual business.' He stopped and took a deep breath followed by a big sigh. 'But here you are with your bags and stuff. You think this is a bloody joke? You come and go as and when you please?'

Silence.

Ghanshyam continued, 'You were more than an assistant, always a friend. And this is how you get back to me? Sudden announcement, and bye?'

Silence.

'Money didn't keep you here for all this time, I knew that. Nearly from the time you came here. I know what I pay. There is something else, has to be. Don't know what that is that keeps you here, or kept you here for all this time. Never bothered to find out, as long as you were happy and I had no problems, the patients were happy, they felt loved, what else does a doctor need? Everything was perfect till last evening. What changed suddenly? What are you looking for? Anand . . . this abrupt leaving is ridiculous, stupidity!'

Ghanshyam didn't remember the last time he felt sad. There was a sense of something hanging in there, something looming between Anand's eyes, and Ghanshyam could feel it, but did not understand. Why now? Why this suddenness, when the world was perfect? Anand was for granted; that he could leave one day never crossed his mind. He was waiting for a response to his reproaching, which was more of a pleading, but there was no change in Anand; he was still looking through the floor. The dirty brown dust-coated windows of his clinic filtered the soft morning sunlight, backlighting Anand, almost creating a halo around his head. Ghanshyam could see Anand's silhouette, not his expression, and this frustrated him. He did not know if Anand was as sad as him to leave or was just indifferent. 'For God's sake, Anand, say something! Your silence is torturing me. I am a bloody doctor, have some respect, don't make me plead like this!' Ghanshyam almost cried.

Anand looked up to face Ghanshyam. Their eyes met for the first time since their conversation started this morning. Ghanshyam saw the light bounce off Anand's flooding eyes. It gave him some kind of satisfaction, that Anand was also not happy to leave him and that place. He felt he still held a chance to stop him. And so he changed his tone and played emotionally. 'Think about the people here who love you, who need your care. I might be able to run this clinic without you, and maybe treat a few problems, but will never be able to heal as you do and probably not save as many lives. These people need your love, Anand, they need to be healed, please stay . . . don't go!'

A pregnant silence reigned, a silence in which the questions hung heavy like the floating dust motes in the room.

Eight years ago, when Anand came to Shilhur looking for a job, the scene was different. Ghanshyam had refused even the thought of needing an assistant. Having an assistant meant he had to pay somebody from whatever little he made and train him as well. Anand was desperate for the job. A meagre pay was okay for him.

'Sahib . . . please allow me to help you, I can read and write, I can do dressings, I can do bandaging for your patients . . . I will do whatever you ask me to, all I ask is just one chance, sahib.'

'Sahib . . . sahib' went on as Ghanshyam was tending his patients. Patients in the room felt sympathy for this young boy, though he didn't really look as desperate as he sounded. Looking healthy, with neat clothes, a clean-shaven, serene, and peaceful face, he hardly seemed like a case of desperation. Nevertheless he had sincerity in his eyes; he didn't look like a fraudster, not exactly handsome, but with something appealing about him, something that stood out. But, Ghanshyam could not decide what it was about him that arrested his attention. He remained unmoved through all those pleadings of Anand. He was telling himself not to be fooled by those compelling, earnest eyes; this person was just another village bum looking to make some quick money.

The 'sahib . . . sahib' in the background was getting on his nerves though. And Anand didn't look to be a fellow who could be insulted and driven out of the room with shouting and abusing, so he made him stand in the corner of the room and wait.

Just then a few villagers rushed in the clinic with hoo-ha; they were carrying a profusely bleeding old man. He was holding his temples with both his hands as blood ran over his face. The ruckus was because this old man was the head of the village and while he was putting the roof on his house, perched on the bamboo ladder, somebody had pushed him and run away. Ghanshyam felt it was a good time to put Anand to the test. Failure was guaranteed and he would be driven out for good.

'Look here, we are lucky today, we have amongst us today a very good nurse.' He pointed towards Anand and spoke to the harried villagers. Others in the room stood surprised looking at each other's faces. Ghanshyam winked at one of them and gestured them to keep mum.

He asked Anand to clean the old man's wound and make him ready for the examination. In the next few minutes, the villagers who saw Anand pleading a few minutes back, stood there in silence watching him perform the art he was saying he was good at. A few murmured amongst themselves if indeed he was some famous doctor's assistant. He cleaned the blood with spirit and cotton swabs. He felt the nose of the old man to see if it was broken, lifted his eyelids to see how bloodshot they were. He tenderly ran his fingers in the old man's thick hair to check for any bumps. By the time Anand was done, the old man was completely calm and soothed. While Ghanshyam was preparing the medicine, Anand described the details of the wound like a professional. All through the cleaning of the wound, Anand looked perfectly at ease, as if he did this all the time. Ghanshyam couldn't believe that a person could bandage that well. His right-hand fingers moved more like an artist's. The left hand held the other end of the bandage and rolled it around the old man's forehead. Ghanshyam, awestruck, was watching every small detail, how Anand forgot the world around him, and the old man became his world, how his unrelated talks pacified and the old man didn't realize that the solution stings when the wound is cleaned with it, how his left-hand fingers bent at unusual angles rolled the bandage and made a perfect knot. Ghanshyam, who was usually chatty with his patients, stood quiet, lost in his thoughts, just nodding as they left. He knew that not taking Anand after his open exhibition of skills would not go very well with the villagers, and especially when the headman was so happy with him.

He was convinced Anand was not what he seemed; there was more to him than what everybody saw. Who was he, a con man? Why would a con man come to his clinic? There was hardly anything to take from him, then why?

'Ahem.' Anand cleared his throat to get Ghanshyam's attention.

'Oh, yeah,' Ghanshyam responded, a bit startled.

'So, can I get a job, sahib?'

'Who are you? You are not somebody desperate for money. With this expertise, you can get a good job in cities. Why here? Why with me?'

Anand smiled, and walked a few steps towards Ghanshyam. 'Many questions in one breath. I understand though.' And then he paused, giving out a slight sigh, as if thinking, making up an answer that would satisfy Ghanshyam.

Ghanshyam didn't really want all his questions to be answered. Nobody wants that. Living with questions, with a few doubts, with self-built hypotheses is the way we have learnt to live. The mysteries, the unknowns make life interesting to live. When things are answered easily, we create newer doubts and newer mysteries, and those are usually damaging.

'Does it really, really matter, doctor sahib, who I was before meeting you? Are you ready to put your trust in the words I say or you will run a background check on me? I know, most likely you will not go to the length of checking my past. It might be rather difficult. Easy thing would be, sahib, to trust your instincts. They will not lie. If you think I can be trusted, trust me and hire me. I won't let you down. And yes, people call me Anand.'

The one who was begging and pleading for a job a few minutes back had found a sudden confidence. Maybe he realized that show in front of the villagers confirmed his job.

'You are not from here.' Ghanshyam was not yet ready to leave.

'No, sir, I have travelled some distance to reach here.'

Ghanshyam noticed the change of *sahib* to *sir*. 'Why here?'

'I like this place.'

'Nobody likes this place,' Ghanshyam said and moved across the room, bored of standing in the same place, not really expecting any good answer. 'Tell me, how do you know all this? You look young enough not to know.'

Anand uttered with a little laugh, 'Practice.'

Anand looked just some years over thirty at that time. Ghanshyam kind of realized for now he would have to keep Anand. He told himself, at the age of fifty-four, he was not getting any younger; with an assistant like Anand, if he agreed to work for low pay, he could hope for some relaxed time. If he didn't like him, he would find out a way to take him off. For now, he would explore what he had just received.

'You are yet to have your lunch, I am sure about it. Come with me. There is the lock and key of the clinic, lock the door, though it is just a suggestive thing. I still lock the door so that patients know I am not in. We will go to my home. Did you find a place to stay?'

That was eight years ago. In these eight years, the scene of the clinic had changed. There was a cleaner, better curtain to partition the patients being examined, and two small beds, one for the patients with Ghanshyam and the other for somebody to lie down on while they awaited their turn. There were a few chairs too, not just the wooden bench they had for so long. The clinic itself looked cleaner and more organized. As for Ghanshyam, who hated dependency, he was completely dependent on Anand. In just the first month of Anand joining, he had completely impressed Ghanshyam and more importantly won the hearts of the villagers. Many days, it was Anand who was running the clinic, and Ghanshyam enjoyed his new-found time for self-indulgence. Ghanshyam had not married. He felt wives were not dependable. After his medical education from a nearby university, he had settled into a cosy life in this, his native village. He earned more than enough to have two square meals and the great goodwill of village folks. And now with Anand around, he realized the time was at its best. In these eight years as Ghanshyam moved to his sixties, it seemed Anand stayed as young as the day he had come. Though at times Ghanshyam did see a kind of restlessness in Anand's eyes, he had not bothered to question it. About Anand's personal life, he had said he was a widower and never mentioned anything about having a child. He did not wish to marry again. Ghanshyam also agreed with Anand that women were root of all issues and he should not get married again and should concentrate on his clinic.

Perfect eight years.

Last evening as they were closing the clinic for the day, Anand told Ghanshyam that he would be leaving the clinic and the village tomorrow. Ghanshyam had joked, 'Yeah, in search of a girlfriend? We will talk about it some other time. I am tired and want to go home.'

This morning, Anand came with a duffel bag full of clothes and hugged Ghanshyam. It was then, that Ghanshyam realized Anand was serious about what he said. He just did not know how to survive without Anand. And he was sixty plus now, he did not have enough motivation or energy to find somebody new to assist him or rather take care of him like Anand did. He had taken Anand was taken for granted, more like a son. And now suddenly, all the comfort he was used to was moving out of his life.

'This is it, sir. The time has come to make a move.' Anand finally said something.

Ghanshyam felt a sudden pressure at the base of his throat. The awareness of loneliness! Eight years back, there was no Anand, and life had no complaints. But this thickness in the last eight years made everything heavy; it was the fear of solitude, not love for Anand.

'What do you mean, *the time has come?*'

'It means the time has come for me to go.'

'Why, Anand? Did I do something or say something? Why are you going?'

'Nothing you did, sir, has made me take this decision, it is just that I know that my time to leave this place has come and I should go. I will always remember our eight years together very fondly.'

'This doesn't make any sense, one day suddenly you announce you are going, and you actually go!'

'I realize that, sir.'

'So, stay.'

'Can't do that.'

'Let me at least get prepared then. You cannot walk in here at your will and go whenever you feel like. I am running a clinic; there should be a sense of responsibility. I will let you know when it is a good time for you to go.'

'There cannot be any more right time than this. I have thought over it for some time, the time has come, and I must go.'

'What is this *time has come, must go,* and all that? Where are you going, what is the urgency? You know what, tell me where you are going, and I may allow you. I might come to meet you someday.'

'Sir, I am a wanderer, I don't know where I am going, and so I cannot possibly tell you what I myself do not know. I'll walk a few miles, hitch a ride, catch a train, maybe swim a river and reach my new home. I just don't know where that place would be.'

'Oh, that sounds so dramatic. Is this some plan to serve humanity? Use your knowledge to help people across the country?'

'Sir, don't embarrass me. I am a simpleton, putting things that I know into practice.'

'No, you are not! You are hiding something. You have been hiding all along. I knew it but never asked you, but I think the time has also come to tell me about yourself. Why did you come here in the first place? You said you don't have any relatives, you don't even know your parents. But then who is that woman whose photo you carry in your pouch? Yes, I saw you once tenderly moving your fingers over a woman's photo. A fragile and old lady in the photo, is she is your mother? Who is or was she?'

'Sir, thank you for all your help, but I must leave.'

'No, I am not going to allow you to go today, even if it means that I run by your side till the end of the village and gather a huge crowd.'

'Sir, I beg you, please don't make it any more difficult than it already is.'

'Only on one condition, you must share with me your secret, tell me who you are, from where you came and why you served me and all these villagers selflessly.'

'There is no secret! I am a wanderer who worked as a nurse, in a village about 200 kilometres from here. I left that village like I am leaving this one. I get an urge to move after couple of years, in fact here I stayed the longest.'

'You can fool the naïve villagers, not me—from the way you work, you have had a lot of experience. It takes years of experience to know the medicine combinations you know, it takes years of knowledge and reading the way you talk to the villagers. You could not have learned it at the age of thirtyish. I am not a fool, I know you are much more than a nurse. I could make it out working with you in the first month itself, I never spoke about it, as your skill helped me. But today, if you are going away, I need to know everything.'

'Sir, please let me go.' Saying this, Anand got up, wiping his tears, and started walking towards the door and climbed down the three steps outside the clinic.

Ghanshyam darted behind Anand with a childlike ferocity, forgetting he was on the other side of his sixties. His knee buckled on the third step, making him land on his right ankle for his sprinted fourth step, bending it sharply. He lost his balance completely and banged his head with a loud thud on the door column and came crashing down the three steps outside the clinic, head first. Anand turned back sharply to stop Ghanshyam's fall, but he was already down with his face down on the ground. Bleeding nose, ugly gash on his forehead, and twisted ankle. Anand was trembling as he picked up Ghanshyam like a child and brought him back in the clinic.

'Marvellous, a bit in a horrible way, but good!' Ghanshyam commented as Anand softly placed him on the bed meant for waiting patients. 'Don't go . . . I request you.' Anand was busy as he mixed a carefully measured dose of some strong, pungent painkiller and gave it to Ghanshyam to drink.

'This will settle you. And don't talk, Dighu.'

Ghanshyam started to say something when a searing pain shot through his temple. 'Aaah . . . this is bad.'

'Don't talk,' Anand said curtly. He cleaned Ghanshyam's wound and face, bandaged his forehead, and propped him up.

Ghanshyam tried to sit up fully, but could not. 'I am going to die, aren't I? So don't leave me like this.'

Anand looked in his eyes and smiled, his own eyes now were more than just a little moist. 'We both know you will not die, certainly not because of this. The concussion is bearable. So let me go. Though I feel terrible to leave you like this, I must go.'

Anand settled the doctor comfortably on his bed, adjusted the pillow on his back, and fetched him a book to read. 'Don't move, don't exert yourself, in a few minutes, someone is sure to come by and can help you, a good bed rest will set everything right. You don't have any cracks or fractures.'

Ghanshyam stared at Anand, and smiled as if recalling something. He knew he could trust Anand's judgment.

Anand started leaving; on his way out, he paused for a moment, thought of looking back, but controlled himself and stepped out. At the threshold of the door, he lingered. Both of them were silent for a few brief moments that seemed almost never-ending to Anand.

'This old man will remember you for the rest of his life, tell me who you are, why you came here, and why are you going now.'

Anand turned back and looked at the doctor.

Ghanshyam gave a faint smile and extended his hand. Anand came back and took Ghanshyam's hand in his with a caring and warm squeeze.

'Sir, my story only disturbs people. But if this is so important for you, I will go with what you want.'

'Good. Tell me in detail about yourself.'

Anand looked at him as if reading something on his face and then got up and walked a few paces away, turning his back on the doctor. 'Sir, there are stories that lie buried deep in hollows of time, and that is where they should be kept. You are a doctor . . . it is difficult for you to see what lies beyond your conventional science. Crossing the chasm of what you were taught as truth, tangible and understandable, happens only in tales for you. You would call these the blind beliefs of superstitious idiots. That there exist other realms, with happenings that would creep you out and send shivers up your spine are but scary fantasies or movie plots to you. I do not know how you could begin to believe what I am about to tell you. About one thing I am sure though, the end is distressing.'

'Try me, Anand,' the doctor said, putting aside his book.

'This world is an old place, older than our science tells us.'

'For God's sake, stop the footage and start speaking sense. Once you are done, you may leave peacefully.'

'Peacefully,' Anand laughed. 'I hope so, I really hope so,' he murmured.

Anand took a long pause, looked out of the window, and then slowly, deliberately turned to face Ghanshyam and spoke in a soft hushed tone. 'Let me start with my experience of time. It is a myth that time is a healer. For a few unfortunates as me, who have an overabundance of time, it is no healer. It is a bloody cheater. The name my parents gave me was Ulhasrao. Our family name was Chandre. It was the date of October the 16th, 1685 when I was born.'

'Did you say sixteen hundred eigh-huh-tee five?'

'Yes.'

'Yeah, right! And I am Aurangzeb. What makes you think I asked for time-travel tales?'

'No? Well then, that is your choice. I can walk away if you don't want to listen. In fact I would be rather glad.'

'Ha! Go on, your story has an interesting flavour, fake as it seems, I want to listen. A story like this deserves whisky. Why don't you shut the door, put the closed sign and let's hear this unbelievable tale of yours. Get me the bottle from the drawer below, you can make one for yourself.'

'You should know better that. With a concussion like that, you are not supposed to have alcohol.'

Both of them looked at each other and gave a soft grunt of laughter, as if they remembered an old joke.

Anand obliged him. Ghanshyam sipped his whisky, relaxed back in his bed, and gave over all his attention to Anand. 'Go on,' he said waving his glass towards Anand.

'At that time, the British had not yet overrun the country. I was born in a wealthy family. We were zamindars, in the part of India now known as Vadodara in Gujarat. I was like any other rich boys in my neighbourhood, arrogant and short-tempered.'

'That you are even now,' Ghanshyam chuckled.

Anand ignored the comment. 'I was not very educated. Other than basic reading and writing, I did not know much. We had a tutor called Gopalrao somebody, I don't remember the last name, probably it was Shinde. He taught me basic mathematics and Sanskrit. As a young boy I was a womanizer and alcoholic. I had slept with many women before I got married to a girl twelve years of age. I was twenty-three at that time, late by our standards, and people felt I might never get married. My wife was younger than kids of a few of the married women I slept with. People feared me as I went into the villages to collect taxes. We had a very young king then, Sayajirao Gaekwad III. Our family being Maharashtrian, we spoke the same mother tongue as the royal family, so we were on good terms with the royal circuit. I was around thirty-three years old when my father told me to go to talk to Raja Jaimal of

Jaipur, on behalf of our king, about allowing free trade and friendship between the two kingdoms. It was a good opportunity for me to go to Rajasthan, as one of my friends, Mir Singh, was staying in Alwar, not very far from Jaipur. Mir and I had met at an auction for Arabian horses years ago in Rajasthan. Both of us were instantly thick as thieves since we both fancied the same things, women and alcohol. I reached Alwar, enjoyed a couple of days compensating for the monotony of married life by indulging in all the salacious pleasures which I had missed.

'I was a day late starting for Jaipur. The evening before I was to go to Jaipur, Mir had thrown a party and there was abundance of everything we revelled in. It was late by the time I was ready to leave Alwar, but since I had to reach Jaipur the next morning, I had no choice but travel through the night. I was drunk but felt I could maintain my balance, and as long as I could get some sleep in the tonga, I was good to go. Mir arranged for a horse carriage to take me to Jaipur. Just around midnight, as we left Alwar, the carriage began to rock furiously as it bumped on the uneven stony road. I told the tonga-wallah to slow down, but he just muttered something under his breath and kept driving like crazy. I knew he was venting out his anger on me. Mir had forced him to take me to Jaipur in middle of the night, which according to him was an ungodly hour. The tonga-wallah had resisted making the journey and had come up with one excuse after another to delay our departure to the morning. But Mir, who had probably more alcohol in his veins than blood, lost his temper. He rudely shouted at him, reminding him that he was the master and the tonga-wallah would do as he was told. When he still saw some reluctance in the tonga-wallah, he slapped him hard across his face, and then went so far to kick him so hard on his butt that the tonga-wallah flew and landed with his face in the mud near the carriage wheel. I had rarely seen the kind of hatred, and thirst for revenge, that was visible in the tonga-wallah's face when he got up and wiped the mud from his eyes. The way he spit out the soil from his mouth was like spitting at Mir.

'We travelled through the shadowless roads, bumping wildly on the uneven barren road. Not a soul we encountered since we left Mir.

Both of us didn't speak to each other, probably cursing each other. I was cursing because just in the first three, four kilometres, I could feel each bone in my body rattle in that damned rocking tonga. He slowed the speed as we entered what looked like a forest, but then I don't know what got into his head, he was manic again. I could see only the back of his head, which he kept on bobbing as he yanked the reins of those horses, and the tossing of the carriage resumed.

'The forest was not dense, but enough thick to make the wind howl. In that darkness, there was no way of knowing what lay ahead of us in that bloody deserted place. As we moved deeper into the forest, our tonga was being thrown in every possible direction, I was holding the side rod of my seat with both my hands as if my life depended on it. I shouted at the tonga-wallah to slow down, but either he didn't listen or pretended not to. Finally, I took out one of my sandals and threw it at him, striking his nape. But before he could react to that, we struck very hard on something. I crashed full face on the front of the carriage and the tonga-wallah was thrown off or maybe he dived, I don't know. It took me a couple of minutes to recover, my nose was bleeding and there were a few cuts and gashes on my face. I jumped down from the carriage and saw the wreck. The left wheel was out and the right one was still rotating on the broken axle. The tonga-wallah was lying flat a few feet away. As I came around, what struck me were the bloodshot eyes of the horses, there was horror in their eyes. They were trying to rip away from the tonga. And when they saw me, something happened, they completely freaked out as if they saw a ghost. The cry they let out tore through that black night. It still reverberates in my ears and sends shudders through my spine. They leapt on their hind legs and ran, dragging the one-wheeled carriage. Their neighing was echoing long after they were out of sight. After so many years, I have forgotten many things, but those bloodshot eyes, blood dripping from slits near their noses where the reins dug in, those screams still haunt me.

'Thankfully my nose was okay, it had stopped bleeding. I walked to the tonga-wallah and softly kicked in his ribs to see if he would get up. He did not. His mouth, chin, and cheeks were smeared with blood.

But with the horses gone, he was not useful for me. I was not sure if I should stop there or continue. Stopping there with this unconscious tonga-wallah didn't seem like a good option. And after the echoing of the horse cries had stopped, there was an eerie silence. Resting there would have meant I would have dozed off, and that was the last thing I wanted to do in that place. I felt the only thing sensible to do was to keep walking slowly till sunrise.

'At Alwar, I had been told legends of Bhangarh, of the witches of Bhangarh and had been told to keep away from that forsaken place. They said it had been cursed. I was going to walk right through Bhangarh in middle of the night, alone.

'What curse? And did you believe all that?' Ghanshyam asked.

Anand turned back to him, appearing startled. He had nearly forgotten he had an audience.

'The story they told me, I laughed at it. It was folklore, more like a B-grade flick. But that night, there in the wilderness, yes, I believed it. It was a place inhabited by the dead who did not die but were not living as well. The story said, about some hundred or so years ago, that was when I heard the story, Bhangarh was a great and prosperous city, abundant wealth, and happy people with a perfect benevolent king. The king had a ravishing daughter, Ratnavali. She was a legendary beauty. When she came to the king's court and watched him from behind the intricate lattice walls, people would wait for just one glance from her. The king had not allowed many men to look at her face. They said, one fateful day, a black magician, Singhia, came to the king's court and he saw Ratnavali's eyes. He fell for her charm and the only thing he wanted was to have her for himself. To accomplish the hunger of his loins, he began to keep a watch on her courtesans and noticed that Ratnavali used to send her maids to fetch aromatic bathing oils from the market. One day, he cast a spell on the oil so that anyone who used that oil would be drawn straight towards the magician and satisfy his carnal desire. However, the princess' trusted maid was a practitioner of the dark arts and she sensed his deeds and told Ratnavali about it. Ratnavali threw the oil at a huge boulder that lay across the fort and her maid cast a counter-spell on the oil, and the stone was hurled towards Singhia, bringing about his inevitable doom. But as he lay there dying, he uttered his final curse: Bhangarh would die, everybody would suffer, a huge storm would come and soon the city would not see the sun again. And his words rang the death knell for Bhangarh; a huge dust storm followed that destroyed and decimated the entire city, which was left bereft of its people and structures. Even today the enigma continues; it is said that the spirits of those who died an untimely death, in the fortified ramparts of the city, still roam the streets of Bhangarh, as night descends on this accursed land.'

'Yes, typical folklore,' Ghanshyam interrupted again.

'Very recently, I heard the Indian government has put a signpost there forbidding people to go in Bhangarh after sunset. I am sure, you believe in the Indian government.'

Anand continued, 'I did not have a wristwatch then, but approximating with the speed and time we started, I estimated I was near or in Bhangarh. The plains had long gone and the bumps of the Aravalis, the mountains of this area, had been acknowledged by the cart. I was sure by then, the tonga-wallah did not wish to pass through Bhangarh and that was the reason for his reluctance.

'I continued walking, slowly, eyes wide open, trying to see as much as I could. I did not know which direction I was taking, just kept following the pathway through the trees which seemed the closest thing to a road. The tree just above my height were losing their definition and merging with the blackness of night. It was getting colder, the winds getting stronger, a dog howling somewhere ahead, a bat or owl screeching just overhead. There were silent cries in the air, cries I could feel but not hear. Was I the only one there? Though I tried to be quiet, taking careful measured short footsteps, trying to stay as unnoticeable as I could, I felt prying eyes on my back. Every time I looked back, something that was of the colour of that night scuttled and hid itself. The darkness then stared back at me. Something else was out in that night, watching me, following me, slinking hungrily behind me, mocking my fear. The only thought was if I held myself together and kept walking for an hour or so, I might pass through Bhangarh and could find a village where I could possibly get some local assistance.

'Something in my heart kept telling me there was something sinister, mean, vengeful about this whole place. Drenched in my sweat, I kept moving, it was lot scarier to stop. Stopping would mean being aware of where I was, and that was the last thing I wanted to do. I don't know how long I walked before I heard those sounds. A few minutes? Hours? I had lost track of time. It was then that I heard those scratchy whispering sounds, like dozens of iron nails scraping the paint of an old wall, but not quite, these sounds were harsher. These sounds had language, but not the one I could understand. I tried following those voices. Were they from the same person or a couple of people talking? Were they really voices or just some nocturnal sounds? I was scared, the black trees towered over me as if they were watching me, smelling my fear and smiling. Then suddenly, I felt the voice called my name. Ul-haaa-sssss . . . the 'ssss' had a hissing tone. Ul-haaa-ssss . . . Those sounds changed everything. I might not recall clearly what happened yesterday, but I recall every detail of what happened that night.

'It was a faint and sorrowful sound, almost human. Like a grunt of agony. It came across the path I was walking. It gave a sting of fear in my heart. I stood there frozen for a few minutes allowing that fear to take over me and pass through. I tried to reason with myself that a human sound in this wilderness was a sign of hope rather than fear. Maybe the village was around the corner. Everything around me was of the colour of the night, some things were darker than few other things, but dark it was. I started moving towards the sound. Upon walking a few steps and peering through the thorny foliage, I saw at a distance of fifteen or twenty feet from me a lady under a tree. I tried squinting and opening my eyes as wide as I could a couple of times to make sure there was actually a person there and not something else. It could have been an eye trick, a visual hallucination around the desire to see somebody in that dark place, a semi-delirious state from the alcohol in my blood and the bang on the head from the fall. I kept looking and I felt there was a slight twitch in her head and an involuntary shiver ran through my body and left all goosebumps on my arms.

'She was barefoot, with thick silver anklets. She was sitting with two hands down on the ground, and her face away from me and her feet pointing in my direction. She was dressed in a typically Rajasthani outfit. Her skirt was red, or it looked like red in whatever light my eyes could gather, or I just imagined it to be red. Her blouse was also of the same colour. She had rich ornaments on her body. While I watched her, I felt as if everything around me was silent. Everything including the insects, the birds, particularly the noisy bats, and the wind were watching her. Instinct told me to run as far as possible from that scene, this was the sinister thing that I kept feeling in my bones for some time. But I still stood there, frozen to rigid immobility, contemplating on what I was seeing. I was about to take a step back, when I heard her sob. She moved her hand over her face, twirled a tendril with her fingers and tucked it behind her ear, and then in a sudden jerky motion, she looked at me. And in that moment our eyes met. I wanted to run away, expecting to see the face of an old, shrivelled witch, but instead it was a face of exquisite beauty, her skin so fair that it glowed in the night. Her dark wavy hair outlined her face, going way below the shapely pair of round shoulders. The almond-shaped eyes were as dark as the night, but still shone like the moon. You should know that women those days were not skinny as they are now.

'She extended her hand towards me as if asking for help. I thought it would be stupid of me to fall in the trap of her beauty. I was sure this was some kind of witch magic, so I started taking steps back. She spoke with a sob in her husky whisper: "Sir, I am a newly-wed bride going to my parents' house on the third day of my marriage."

'I knew this was the custom. The brides go back to their parents' home on third day of marriage. As she continued, I stood there mesmerized by her beauty, entranced by her dry voice: "I was being carried in the palanquin by four of my servants. We were going peacefully, the men were singing some bridal songs to keep themselves awake, but then suddenly an hour ago, there was a deafening sound of horses as if they were crazy. All the men looked back and I too poked my head out of my palanquin to see what that noise was about. And from nowhere there was a pair of horses with blood in their eyes, the edges of their mouths dripping with red bloody lather. They were dragging a carriage with one wheel. The entire thing was looking so scary that the servants threw my palanquin and fled. I am very scared in this jungle all alone. Please, O noble sir, I beg you to help me." I saw to the left that there was indeed a broken palanquin, which somehow I had not seen till she told me about it.

'She went on with her story: "Because of the fall, both my knees are bleeding." She showed me by raising her skirt above her knees. They were actually bleeding. There was a small pool of dark liquid under her knees, probably blood. Her blouse was torn on the right side, and there were gashes there, the way it would happen if a person falls on that side. But then, my mind kept on screaming, this is the arena, I should not get involved. I started walking backwards. I could see the swell of large teardrops forming in her eyes. I still kept walking away from her. But for me to leave such a good-looking girl alone was a big sacrifice. At this time I felt I was still a bit high, I was already visualizing her with me on a soft warm bed. Her captivating beauty seemed out of this world. A girl so beautiful exists only in imagination. For a few seconds, I asked myself was this real or was my mind playing tricks on me in this wilderness? Her story seemed credible. I knew about the horses. I don't really know the real reason that held me there, humanity towards a poor girl all alone in that forsaken place or her being so seductive. I suppose the latter. I stopped and took one single small step towards her. And that still stays as the biggest mistake of my life. As soon as I did that, her body twitched in a strange way. This made me uncomfortable and I started moving backwards. Not looking at a tree trunk that I hit while moving back, I tripped and fell flat on my back and momentarily closed my eyes.

'The next instant, my heart missed a beat, I saw something came flying onto my chest. The remains of my senses were probably lost then. In a blink of an eye she was on top of me, her curly wavy hair on my shoulder, and she was bending down on me, with her legs apart on my torso. I shouted with all my might, but the intended scream never came out of my throat, all that came out was a feeble fading whimper. The only sound that filled the air surrounding me, a sound which even today rings in my ears and makes me miss several beats and keeps me awake on many, many nights, was her laughter. Or probably it was her growl, a chilling, primitive sound. Her eyes had the raw savagery. As she laughed, she opened her mouth and kept on opening it. Her face changed, it elongated. The lower jaw just kept on opening and must have opened like five to six inches and a wet, thick, red tongue dangled on my face. It smelled of rancid, rotten meat, of death probably. I should have died of heart attack that night, but probably I was destined to live, endure a curse for all my doings. With all my might I pushed her; she or it had not expected this move, it just happened as a reflex when that blob of a tongue touched my face. She fell sideways, and as I started running with all my might, she pounced on me and missed me, but after her face-down landing, she dived, caught my left hand. Her hand . . . it was not a hand which tapered off with fingers, it was like a claw, with hideously curved thick nails. And when it touched my skin, it was like a scalding hot iron pressed against me. It stuck there, on my arm. But in those moments of white-knuckle fear, I didn't succumb, my survival instincts made me fight. I swung to my right and with all my might kicked her hand that clung to me. She was already down from her missed landing on me. I gave another kick on her hand, followed by one on her shoulder that held me, and I heard a snapping sound. That was when I saw her face, the look of surprise, probably she never thought that I would give a fight. She thought that her scare factor was enough to get her prey. And I don't know what made me fight that night. But I did. Her face . . . the lower jaw was as if loosely attached to the base of her ears on two screws, her long red tongue was still dangling, her eyes were nearly out of the socket like ugly white balls popping out of dark holes. I was nearly dragging her, with her holding my arm. I stopped, I don't know why, but I stopped, saw her dangling eyes and then kicked her rabid face. She rolled over to the other side, and I tore free and bolted like crazy, screaming my lungs out. Jumping over the clumps of weeds, pushing through the thorny low-hanging branches, through cuts and bruises, I ran. I ran the life-saving run. At every second I felt I would feel the scalding hot claw tear my back and pierce my lungs and melt my heart. It didn't happen. The last time, I summoned enough courage to look back, I saw she was still behind me, her entire body withering, convulsing. She was getting thrown back every step she took towards me, as if there was some kind of invisible perimeter which she was not able to cross. She let out a slew of the ugliest curses, her dry voice reverberated across the forest. "Give it back to me . . . Give it back to me . . . It's mine!" she violently snarled.

'I kept running without looking back, my feet hardly touching the ground. I don't remember how long I ran before I came out of the forest. How many times I bumped my head, how many times the thorny branches made gashes on my face and arms, my clumsy falls, I don't remember. My heart was beating so fast that I thought it would explode through me and I would splatter blood all around. I slowed down a little and turned to see behind, expecting to see the grotesque face, hungry eyes; but she was not there, she was gone. That slowing down brought back the images of what I last saw her as I kicked her. It made me feel that the very last time I had seen her, when she fell back from some kind of invisible perimeter, she had only one hand. I slowed down a little more . . . that was when I felt something uncomfortable, hanging, and swaying on my own left arm. What I saw curdled all the blood in my chest, I gave an iron scream creating a brief clamour of flutters in those dark trees.

'Her missing hand was on me! The stub of her hand, from the elbow, was clutching my left arm. I was running away carrying a part of her with me. The witch's hand . . . I had brought with me, yes, the witch's hand! I looked over my shoulder, with a terror that I might see her this time again, just behind me, waiting for me to look behind. But there was only darkness, the thick darkness which drowned the forest. And I was there, in that darkness, with the stub clawing me, digging its sharp talons deep in my flesh; and the other end was dripping thick black slime. I raised my hand and saw that stub from closer and a strong putrid smell of burnt meat hit me giving an impulsive nauseating sickness in me. I threw up with the force that made me feel I would throw my guts out with that. *"Give it back . . . it's mine . . . give it back,"* she was screaming as I was running away . . . *"It's mine."* It was then I realized what she was screaming about.

'I tried peeling those ugly fingers from my arm, but it was like a locked iron claw—witch's rigor mortis probably. Every time I touched those rough grainy coarse-skinned fingers, it sent twitching into my body and reminded me of how she pinned me down with that hand, sitting on my chest. With every passing minute, her thick twisted long nails were digging deeper in my arm. I looked around and found a big rock. I lowered my left arm on the ground and with the right hand picked up the rock and brought it down with all my ferocity on her stiff stub. What followed must have echoed in her ears, and probably she would have smiled at that. A searing pain went through my entire body. A pain so white yet so dark shot through my arms and hit the roof of my skull, nearly blowing out my eyeballs off their sockets. The monstrous bellowing shriek that came out of me though was not just for the pain, it was for the realization that her arm was connected to me. Hitting it was like hitting myself.

'Why? Why was I chosen? What sins had I committed to deserve this? God was unjust. I cursed. The sight of that rotting, undead claw gave me a violent twist in my guts and made me throw up my gut fluids a few more times. I bellowed. I cursed again. As the nausea subsided, several other unpleasant sensations took its place, severe pain in arms and legs, shrill ringing in ears, and throbbing between the brows. And finally, in that moment, the only thing that was convincing was to chop off my arm.'

Anand paused and turned back from the window. He walked and sat on the patient bed facing Ghanshyam. Ghanshyam's eyes flicked a couple of times between both the arms of Anand.

'And then?' Ghanshyam asked, or probably just gestured to Anand by jerking his head up, asking him to go on.

Anand gave out a long, slow, and deliberate sigh. 'I looked around to see what I could use to hack my arm. I knew the more I thought about it, the more my knees would soften, if I have to hack it, it should be done immediately. I knew it might succumb to blood loss, but that was an acceptable loss, I was prepared for. I tore a piece of my kurta, which was already torn from my multiple falls that night, and wound it tightly just above my stinging arm so that I could cut some blood flow. I had found a jagged stone, which I planned use to pulp and break my arm. Just then, in the far dark skies, something cracked open, noiselessly, and a faint tinge of red hue appeared. It stole my attention, I forgot for a moment the rotting hand attached to me, I forgot that I was busy cutting my arm. In the few next moments, the crimson shafts of the sun started tearing the night cover. It had a freshness of hope. I dropped the stone I was clutching and raised my arm against the sun, and looked at the black talon digging into it. From the other end, it was dripping thick black liquid. That was the last time I saw it. As the night started disappearing and the sun started coming out, the witch's hand started melting, but it didn't melt and fall down, making me free of it. It started wrapping like thick molten black lava around my arm, and in a few helpless minutes, it was like a black coating of tar on my arm. And that was followed by a searing sensation, and it started seeping in my hand, as if my skin was completely permeable to it. The putrid hot molten liquid was disappearing in my body. The burning started from my wrists and quickly flowed to my shoulders and throat, chest, and then to my head. It felt my body was scorched from within; I was writhing in agony, with no control of my limbs. Hands and legs jerking in all directions, the back was incessantly and violently quivering. The sky was suddenly dark, dark red and it came down very low, just hovering above the black silhouetted trees. The clouds gathered up above me, they were red as well, and they suddenly started to whirl above me, faster and faster. And they caught so much speed, they washed off all their red colour, and that of the sky, and it was so bright as if I was looking at the sun directly, the sky, and vanished. I closed my eyes, but it wouldn't help, the light was so intense, it was frying my brain through my closed eyes. That was what I imagined death comes like, with witch's venom. If death was the way out of that pain, I had made my choice clear, it was death. Unfortunately, it didn't come. I vomited, I pissed and crapped in my pants and just before the last fragments of my conscious faded away, I saw her face in the sky and the hissing sound *"Give it back, it's mine."* I lost all my control and fell in a pool of my refuse after what seemed an unending, unbearable torture.'

Ghanshyam was listening with rapt attention, his mouth open and eyes open wide as if he was trying to find traces of that witch in Anand. It took a couple of minutes for Ghanshyam to recoil and realize that Anand had paused and had got up from the bed and walked over again to the window, peeking out from the curtains as if waiting for somebody.

'Oh, that's quite a story, I don't know what to say, and to believe it or not, I just don't know,' Ghanshyam said, shaking his head in disbelief. 'Did you just make all this up? Because I insisted on knowing a personal side of you?'

'No. You told me to tell you, so I am telling you. I didn't want to get into this in the first place.'

'You want me to believe in this ridiculous tale of yours, of some witch and her hand?'

'No, I am not asking you to believe in anything. To stay honest was my part, what to believe is yours.'

'Is this some kind of joke, Anand? If it is, it is not funny.'

Anand didn't say anything, just peered outside the window. By now the sun was already up. He saw a few people coming very close to the clinic, and after looking at the closed sign, they made surprised gesture and turned away. After the visitors had cleared away, Anand slowly walked to the corner of the bed and picked up his bag and turned towards the door.

'Where do you think you are going?' Ghanshyam asked.

'You think I am lying, I might as well go then, weaving stories.'

'Stop acting smart, what you are telling me is beyond my limits of belief. But nevertheless it is entertaining. Go on. But before that, top up my glass.'

Anand smiled faintly and so did Ghanshyam as he took the glass and made another small peg.

'I did not know at that time that it was the start of my falling into the abyss of time, that my time with peace was done, and there would be no deliverance from the tyranny of the future. The sun shone directly in my eyes, so it must've been noon. The sky was harshly illuminated, devoid of any colours. I opened my eyes to stare at four people standing above me. They had the look of curiosity and fear in their eyes. When I opened my eyes, one of them whispered something, which I could hardly hear, and all four people backed off from me. I slowly got up, my muscles were stiff and they still pained. The sky was clear, not red. I sat on my haunches, shivering, still trying to align with what I had faced, if it was a bad dream or something really that horrendous happened to me. One of the four persons whispered something to the next one and the other fellow nodded back to the rest of them and ran off. The three kept looking at me as if somebody would keep an eye on a snake to know where he is going till the charmer comes. The smell of my refuse suddenly hit me and with it brought me back to the realization of where I was. In the same instant I saw my left arm, and then immediately the other arm and then my feet and with a mighty jerk, I stood up. I raised my kurta and saw my torso. My entire body was the colour of the night. I was the living piece plucked from that night: dark, thick, and impermeable black. My clothes were torn to shreds from my run and falls, but they were enough to make out that I was not just another homeless person. I slowly got up, there were streams from my eyes, but those three people didn't see that. They were only seeing that I was an unusual person suddenly dropped in their village, a person carrying the colour of the night. They had their lathis pointed in my direction, they had a fear in their eyes, but were ready to strike me if I moved an inch towards them. I was the cursed one and should be dealt with accordingly. A cloud of dust appeared somewhere behind them, they turned back to see the clamour, I had a brief interval to run but the only place I could have run was back into the forest. Getting lynched by the mob was acceptable rather than getting into that damned forest. There was a mob approaching. The fourth person had brought along with him many people, they came prepared with torches, lathis, stones, swords, whatever they could lay hands on in that short while. I wiped my tears, it was no time to cry. I stood there and they surrounded me. One of them said with hatred, but loaded with fear, that I was the son of the witch of the forest, that I should be killed. *"Kill that son of the witch, kill, kill"* echoed the villagers.

The witch of the forest had killed many from their village and it was their turn now to kill the son of the witch. There was a storm in my heart and pain in all imaginable muscles of my body, but I was part of the royal family, I knew how to subdue the village commoners. I knew telling them my story would get me hacked before I could complete my first sentence. The only way was to instill fear in their hearts, fear was the only way to get out. I started laughing, laughing so loudly that I thought my throat would snap and my jaw would crack. But my roaring laughter did the work which I wanted to. People took a step back, and confidence filled my lungs. I said with all the menace I could muster in my words that I was indeed sent by the witch, to walk the day. She would control the nights and I, her son, would control the days. If even one drop of my blood touches the land, it would bring unimaginable calamities on them, their lands would be barren for many years to come, and misery would reign. And my mother would rip a clump of her hair and from that unleash an army of her sons. They would inflict so much destruction that they would hope for death a thousand times before they actually died. I surprised myself. How did I come up with that story with the band of pain throbbing in my head? But stories work. If they allowed me to pass from the village undisturbed and offered me a black cat as a sacrifice, I would spare their village and walk to other places for my prey. The sacrifice of the black cat was necessary, to make it feel real. I was quiet for some time, then peered into people's eyes and then gave another power-filled roar of laughter. People threw their lathis and torches and ran away.

I moved about as if I was in an abandoned, empty village. I knew many eyes were following me from windowsills and cracks in the walls and doors. I walked through the village unhindered. There were many, around twenty to twenty-five black cats killed at the end of the village, along with many incense sticks. The sight was so gruesome and I would have nearly vomited there. But I had to hold my nerves, I couldn't show my weakness. I picked up the cats and allowed their blood to fall on me, I rubbed that blood on my face and shoulders and my arms. I made nonsensical figures in the sand with cat's blood. I knew people were watching me from a distance and I had made my point. I left that place, without looking back, with a determination to never return to that wretched place ever again. I reached Raja Jaimal's palace. When I reached it, there were no guards at the door and the huge iron door was locked. After a lot of banging and calling when nobody opened the door, I understood the word about me had spread and I was not welcome anymore.

'It took me three months before I reached Baroda. Most of the places, they knew about my coming. My news bearers were faster than me. I was allowed to go anywhere, take anything. I took some clothes people kept on a drying line outside their house. Though people saw me taking their things, food, nobody dared to stop me. I saw people burning things I touched or they thought I touched, clothes, food, anything; everything that a son of a witch touched was disposable. People made religious red markings in front of their houses. I covered myself from head to toe, grew my beard, did as much as I could to conceal my colour. In those three months, I did not travel in the night. Before nights I would pull myself around a boulder or any old, broken abandoned houses. Not under the trees, you cannot see what lies hidden behind the leaves. Night-time was for weeping and laughing and talking to myself. Why? Why was I chosen by God for this punishment? I asked myself this again and again, but no reason was convincing enough. When I closed my eyes, the rotten smell of burnt flesh wafted up, followed by images of her with the dangling tongue and eyes falling off the sockets, and I woke up with a shriek. I was petrified of going through forests all alone. I circumvented even little forests, walked through many villages even though it meant walking a lot more. I also passed through a few villages where my reputation did not precede me. Every time I got a lift, I carefully checked that they did not pass through any forest or lonely areas. When I reached Baroda, the same thing happened, I was not welcomed by my family, and our gates were closed. At the outer gate my wife awaited me. The family had decided it was her fate to be with me and endure the curse. Even in those times, when the rumours spread, it became spicier. By the time the rumours reached my family, I was a son of the witch, and at my birth time, she had killed their real son and fed me with his blood. That's why I looked like them. But now she had claimed me. On my way home I had been drinking people's blood. If I didn't find people, I would do it with animals or corpses from any graveyard that I crossed! When my wife saw me, she quickly took her eyes off me and lowered her head, looking at her feet. As if by locking her eyes with me, I would hypnotize and bewitch her. When I went near her, she cried in the most pitiful voice repeating not to kill her, not to suck her blood out, not to peel her skin with my nails and eat her. I don't remember all the things she said after that. She made a monster out of me. I realized that there was no point in taking her with me. I walked away, without giving her a second look. I walked away from everybody I knew, far, far from everything that was familiar to me. Walked as days turned into night and nights gave birth to new days. I discovered walking at night was not dangerous. There were times when I doubted myself, if indeed I was a bad omen.

'Ahem.' Ghanshyam cleared his throat. 'Where did you go, and what about you being so old? And you are not the colour of the night, you are much fairer than me, so what happened?'

'A lifetime,' Anand replied.

'Sorry?' Ghanshyam asked, confused.

'You asked me what happened then. A lifetime happened. I don't remember now all the places I travelled, how many parts of India I saw. I lost track of how many temples and religious places I visited, all the while covering myself, hoping and praying for a miracle.'

Ghanshyam was now helping himself to a third peg of whisky. He was enjoying this story though his head still hurt.

'The years rolled on. I kept on travelling, searching for a cure. Witnessed kingdoms colliding, newer kings emerging, rising of forts, temples, mosques from dust into palatial buildings. Some battles became history, some just made people go to dust for the lure of power, a few became memory, a few didn't even register with anybody. I was also enslaved for few years by a Mogul king, knowing whose name is not necessary, but I found every opportunity to run away from battles. Killing somebody was something I could never do after what had happened with me. I escaped from his army and ran towards the southern direction. I kept running for a long time. Long locks of black matted hair, covered in orange from head to toe, I kept on moving. Many people thought I was a religious person. Though I hardly spoke to anybody, I read a lot, made sure that I kept on moving. After wandering for many years, I found a small abandoned temple and settled myself there. I stopped hiding my body, eventually. People there gave me the name Kaaliranga, as a devotee of the goddess Kali. I occasionally gave religious sermons I learnt during my wanderings to people in the temple, so that they thought that I was indeed a god-man and they would allow me to stay there. After ten to fifteen years rolled by, I understood I was not ageing. People around me thought that it was because of some secret yoga I was doing.'

Ghanshyam smiled at his last sentence. 'Is that the reason you keep on changing your place? So that people don't find you age?'

'Kind of.'

'I don't believe, but go on with your story.'

'I left that place of southern India and again started my long wanderings. As long as I could eat to survive, I had no dependencies. I was free of any attachments, but there was no happiness, no satisfaction, just an empty hollow inside me. On the way, I worked as a mason, as an assistant to a philosopher, a servant for a businessman, a teacher in a remote village, I don't even remember all that I did. I learnt many things, and the more things I learnt, the smaller I felt with the vastness of everything. I am certainly no genius, but I had something that most people don't. I had time, ample amounts of it. What I didn't have was satisfaction. I was free of attachments, there were no responsibilities, I never awaited anything, nothing surprised me, but nothing made me happy. There was emptiness inside me, a deep hollow.'

'Did you never see that witch again?' Ghanshyam asked.

'No, not yet. Mogul kings were expanding their territories. I saw strange people with colourless skin and even stranger clothing make their way across India. It was quite late into the British Raj that I realized that we were ruled by these people. In fact I have married many times, loved many people but more important than anything else, I learnt the way of detaching with them. It took me a while to confirm that I did not pass my witch's curse into my generations. I didn't. They were all normal. Nobody should see their children die, but I saw most of my kids grow old and die. It was painful for me to leave my families in a gap of eight to ten years, but I could not stay with them, not when I knew that I would be younger to them in few years. Many times I faked my death, when it was difficult for me to leave.'

'That would be selfish. Knowing that you will be giving your families less than a decade, still going ahead with that?'

'Many marriages and families die within those years. People die. I sincerely loved people when I was with them, and gracefully left when it was time to leave. And just for you to know, I did not keep on marrying every now, and then most of my marriages have a gap of fifty to sixty years.'

'When was the last time you were married?'

'Not necessary to discuss.'

'Right. But I see you here as this, as you are now. What happened to your unusual colour?'

'My wanderings led me to the Himalayas. On those snowy peaks, in that harsh, dry weather, I felt like I was leaving my internal turmoil behind. I had heard about great sages who dwell in those mountains, but I never saw anyone for the next three years. In those three years, I had learnt how to survive in that weather. What people say, what does not kill you makes you stronger, worked with me. One day as I was roaming on those mountains, like any other day, I saw a small hermitage. There were couple of ascetics, with faces so peaceful that they were infectious. I stayed with them. For the first few months they did not acknowledge my presence. But my perseverance got me attention. We hardly communicated using words. But I learnt a lot of things from them, including meditation and yoga. They gave me some herbs which made my hunger vanish and still nourished me for long. I was there for a year but I did not yet feel like sharing my story with them. I was much better than what I was before going there. But still now peaceful, something which I was unable to identify bothered me. Then just like that, one fine morning, I left that place and I started walking down the mountain. I travelled many days and realized I was lost, which didn't really bother me. The knowledge of what to eat and how to survive better in those conditions I had learnt in the past year. One of those days as I was walking, I heard a soft whisper, as if somebody spoke two inches away from my ear. I turned sideways sharply but there was nobody, I looked behind but there was nobody. I looked ahead and I saw at about hundred two hundred metres somebody standing in thin white dhoti, the waist up was naked. I narrowed my eyes to see again, in an instant that person was about half the distance now and in the next instant he was in front of me. He was a person who looked around twenty-five, with a radiant glow on his face, so radiant that I was unable to look in his eyes. He had black hair let loose on his back. He had a thin frame and exceptionally long limbs. And he was beautiful. He was looking into me, not as if he was reading my eyes, but something within. He then talked to me for the next hour, without parting his lips, in the same manner as if whispering with a distance of few inches from my ear. He knew everything about me, my name, my experience of the witch and of my family. He even knew what my family was doing at that moment. I was having no desire to know about them, the only desire was to know about myself. He said I took much long time to reach there, but he was happy that I finally reached there. I understood he was also like me, ageless, but for different and better reasons as compared to me, who was because of a witch's venom. He knew I was troubled. He said he had a solution for me. He said he knew the solution to my problems, he had a miracle to bring satisfaction to me. Serve, he asked me to serve people. That was the reason things happened to me, because I am destined to serve and help people, cure ailments. There are enough people to preach about God and religion. I should have only one focus, and that is to serve and cure people.'

Anand took a long pause, his eyes set somewhere beyond, gave out a silent sigh, and then closed his eyes as if they would reveal something more than he wished to. Ghanshyam stayed quiet.

'He then touched my left wrist and as soon as he did it, I could feel his slender fingers were strong, they caught my wrists strongly. He looked into my eyes and gave a slight hint of a smile. A shudder went through my body, but no pain. He then opened his closed fist. There was a black moth in it and it flew away as soon as he opened his fist completely. Now he smiled some more and I have not seen anything so beautiful, so pure, so transparent as his face yet. I saw my hand and then the other hand and the rest of my body, the colour of the shadow had gone, I was back to myself. I asked him if my mortal curse was over and I would live a normal mortal life. He said I had the power of the undead and he had just taken out the venom from it, I still held the power. I should use it for serving people.'

'So you are suggesting you are kind of eternal, immortal, unending?' Ghanshyam asked.

Anand held his faraway look for few seconds and then turned to Ghanshyam. 'No. I am not. I asked him the same. He said I will die, eventually. But I will have an exceptionally long haul. But before my time comes, he will find me again and meet me, till then I must spend it wisely.'

'What if you don't?'

'I didn't ask that, he didn't say that.'

'Have you ever met him again?'

'No, not yet.'

'There were no limits to my happiness. Suddenly I felt fulfilled. He disappeared before I could ask him anything more.'

'Do you know who he was?'

'I can make guesses, but I don't want to go there.'

'What happened then?'

'I learnt the science of medicine and the art of healing. I worked with many doctors, I studied at medical institutes, the top ones of those times. Money was not much of a problem then, if you had a desire to learn, you could always manage. I just needed to work for a few years or so and I would save enough. I got an opportunity once to treat an English lady, they took me with them to London. I stayed with them for a few years and then travelled Europe. But this time I was not wandering, I was learning medical science from many places and practicing it along the way. But when I came to India, I saw that many people wanted to be associated with me, they wanted me in their social circles. That was the last thing I wanted. So I had to fake my death. I became a nurse. A nurse serves people much more than the doctor, but people hardly ever remember a nurse. Nobody cares to ask a nurse's name and that was perfect for me. I started going around villages, serving people, but didn't stay at any place long enough.'

'Do you know the secret of your living so long?'

'Apart from the witch?' Saying this, Anand gave a small audible laugh. 'My cells regenerate perfectly without any flaws during the duplication process. We grow older because over time, the capacity to regenerate cells for internal and external organs weakens. My cells are exact and perfect copies.'

'That is very convenient. Tell me something of medical science, what makes you have perfect cell regeneration?'

This time Anand started laughing, a mocking one. 'There have been billions and billions of dollars of research going into this theory of the fountain of youth, a dramatic slowing down of the process of ageing or preventing it altogether. And you want me to tell you casually standing here in a few words, why I have perfect cell regeneration?'

'That is a primary book science.'

'Indeed it is. The not so primary needs hours of sessions and the honest confession is after all these years of research, I don't have a perfect answer.'

'This is a joke, tell me it is. Whatever you have said has no proof, it is just a story.'

'Yes, there is no proof.'

'If you are really so old, tell me something that only a person from that age would be knowing.'

'You are the one who is joking now. If I would say something, you would say I have read about it, if I say something which is not written, you hardly have anything to verify. So, why?'

Ghanshyam understood that he was right; apart from written texts which he could also have had an access to, there was nothing really to cross-question that story.

'Memories do stretch, right? The creative mind weaves stories and repeats itself in the mind till it actually changes the memories of the past.'

'Maybe, yes. I am not forcing you to believe me.'

Anand opened the curtains and a flood of light hit his face. Ghanshyam looked at Anand's silhouette in that bright light, and for a few moments, he looked as if indeed he was somebody divine. Ghanshyam sipped his whisky, lost in the story somewhere. Both were silent. There was no voice in the room except for the whirling sound of the yellowish old and cracked ceiling fan.

'So you are not Anand? You are Ulhas?'

'Yes, one of my earliest given names was Ulhas. Right now I am Anand.'

'Whatever you are saying has no proof, you could be lying. Anybody with some research can say what you have said. You could go if you want to. Why this drama, why this story?'

Anand walked to Ghanshyam, felt his wound, and said, 'You must be feeling better.'

'Yes. But that is now beside the point. Why did you come here? What research can you do in this place?'

No response.

'Why do you trust me, why did you tell me all this? How do you know that I will not squeal on you?'

'You want to try telling my story to people? Whom will you tell, these villagers? What will you say? That Anand is much older than what you think, or that he had a close encounter with a witch? Or that the person who was here with you so long and worked in my clinic was a hoax?'

Both were silent for a few minutes. Ghanshyam knew whatever he would tell about Anand to the villagers, if it was anything negative, people would not believe in him. People loved Anand. So did he, and at that moment, that feeling irritated him.

'Why this village, why me? You could have selected anything else, maybe the Amazon jungle, you could have been freer to do what you want.'

Anand kept quiet, looking outside the window. His watery eyes were shining in that light.

'Why here, Anand?' Ghanshyam asked softly.

'A promise,' Anand replied without looking at Ghanshyam.

'What the fuck, another story?'

Anand kept on looking through the window, through everything that was beyond the window.

'You know what, now that I hear you, I feel like I spent few years with a very intelligent freak, you can go, I don't want to know anything more from you, you have a fertile imagination and this is enough. Please go,' said Ghanshyam, who looked shaken; the combination was more than he could deal with, the story, his concussion, and alcohol.

Anand moved back, walked up to Ghanshyam, and without saying anything, hugged him. Ghanshyam did not react with the same warmth. While turning back, Anand whispered in a nearly inaudible voice, 'God bless you' and walked out. Ghanshyam's eyes followed Anand, who as usual walked briskly. Soon his fading image had vanished from Ghanshyam's sight. Ghanshyam was still lost in the story.

Ghanshyam had wanted to ask something of Anand since the start of the story, but he had missed the train of thought in the wild story and now he sat recalling what it was that he wanted to ask Anand. What was it that had disturbed him? Then suddenly he remembered what he wanted to ask.

'Wait,' Ghanshyam shouted. He got up from his chair and walked to the door; there was no sign of Anand. He ran out, till the end of the open street, but Anand had gone away.

Ghanshyam rushed back to his home, leaving the dispensary open. His home was hardly thirty metres away. He rushed into his bedroom. He opened his iron cupboard and threw out all his clothes. Behind his clothes, there was an old-looking tin box. With shivering hands, Ghanshyam took out that box and opened it. He shook the box upside down, emptying it of what looked like a child's collection, a school badge, and a few coloured cards. At the bottom there were a few black and white photos. He took out all those photos and started looking at them frantically. He stopped at one of them, which was his mother's wedding photo, the only one his mother had, a photo taken by the village engineer against his mother's and particularly his father's wishes. The photo his mother kept very close to her heart.

Ghanshyam's face was white as chalk. Images of his mother floated before his eyes. He remembered the image of his old mother when she was being cursed and driven out of the village by the so-called moral guard of the village. The allegation against his mother was that she was a promiscuous woman even though she was old and a widow, often found keeping company with a younger man. When she was being accused and pelted with insults that scarred her image as a woman, she did not defend herself or protest, as if protecting the identity of the young boy was very important. She had told Ghanshyam that she was innocent and he would one day realize this. Ghanshyam hated her for that and called her names, for bringing shame to him. Because though he didn't tell anybody, he himself had seen her going in secrecy and meeting a young man, half her age. He had heard their voices from the closed doors of their bedroom. The village head had made a decision to exile her. She kept on begging the village folks to let her live with her son. But neither the villagers nor Ghanshyam had shown any sympathy to her. Ghanshyam was raised by an elderly childless couple who had enough money to have an extra member in the family. Ghanshyam missed his mother and never got any real love in his life after that. Ghanshyam's perspective towards women had changed after that; he never had faith in women.

Ghanshyam moved his fingers over the black-and-white photo. Tears rolled down his cheeks.

'You called me *Dighu . . . Dighu*,' the doctor was mumbling.

The next day, the villagers found the body of their beloved doctor, who looked like he had died of a heart attack. All around him were some torn old photographs, and his assistant, another beloved friend of the village, Anand, seemed nowhere to be found.

The Utterly Average Life of Ashok

A little fact about me:
I visit people only when invited. And so does my twin brother.
I am committed to the job I do.

Do I like my job? Liking or disliking is something that I am not allowed. I am not allowed to make preferences. That is against the job policies. I have to be fair and fair I am, though you will find me quoted throughout the history as unfair, including most mythological stories, a bane, a curse. But I am beautiful and seductive, rather, very seductive. I am dark, as well. They call me glum, melancholic, morbid, and the like. Never good. Goodness has no connection with me. I move with my dark cloud and latch on to people who call me with their choices. I am supposed to be a teacher, a strict one when the call comes.

There are times in my job, while being fair, I've gone too far. By the time I leave, I leave in my wake streams of tears, punctured hearts, destroyed relations, and shattered lives. Not always. And not that I enjoy doing that. I deliver dispassionately. Bitch, as you might call me, but that is what I do and I do it with complete sincerity.

The choices people make latch me or my brother with them. My stay with people is decided on what they choose and their subsequent choices. Because of the nature of my work, people usually associate my arrival with a prefix: 'unfortunately'. They do not realize that they sent an invitation to me. Yes, it is difficult to connect the dots many times, but I am true to my word, I come and go on what people choose to do with the choices they have. Sometime back, I had been coined another name and I kind of like it, it suits me. It is Erie. Miss Erie, but over the last few hundred years, Miss Erie has come to be called Misery.

That is a good enough introduction of me. About my twin brother, he does the opposite of what I do. They prefix him, yes, you can guess, with 'fortunately'; he is Opportunity.

We can never accurately guess the consequences of the choices we make. A seemingly innocent, unaware decision we make changes the entire course of the remaining life. Call it cause and effect; call it a butterfly effect, or whatever you choose to. Names to the phenomenon don't really matter; what matters is the impact of those choices. Some are short, hardly noticeable, some tend to cascade and some linger on and on over lifetimes, or worse, over generations, transcending the lives of the makers of the choice. Bitch, isn't it? Every time you make a choice, you either invite me or my twin.

The interesting part is that the destination is always fixed, and the time you spend on the route as well. The destination is death, the routes to reach death are different, but the time you'd spend on the route to death is fixed. So with whom you would spend more time on the route, with me or my twin, is what we keep looking forward to. On the route, what I see, hardly anybody else notices. That every time a choice is made and the split is made on the route, there are few exit route choices available on the new route to take back to the original route, but either people are too egoistic to change or turn a blind eye to it, or simply don't notice it or they just find the new route seductive.

About me, once in a few decades I get distracted, somebody steals my attention. It breaks my heart to latch on to somebody who is full of life, whose heart soars like helium balloons, whose eyes twinkle with innocence and unawareness that they have called me in their lives. And once invited, I cannot refuse. That's what my job entails. Also, my job forbids me from developing any kind of liking for anybody; not that my liking makes me latch on to them, but my boss thinks it might cloud my judgment.

This is about Ashok, the kind of person you would see every day on the streets, with a perfect camouflage of crowd. I leave to your guess what he did to invite me into his life, if it was one or many choices that he made that made me latch on to him for so long.

_-**_-**_-

The air hostess in smart blue-and-yellow uniform stood near the narrow exit of the airplane, her face plastered with a coat of foundation, plastic black eyelashes perfectly curved and her bright red lips mouthing 'Thank you, sir' without actually making any sound. As Sid passed her and moved towards the exit, he wondered how those girls could maintain those looks after these long flights! As he slowly walked the ramp, his mind kept showing him, in slow motion, those glossy puffy red lips saying, 'Thank you, sir' and then the mind camera moved up and down to show those girls spruce, dainty, and all decked out. Sid turned back to see her face once more, and bumped into a person just ahead of him. Crushing his nose hitting just below the neck of that person reminded him what a person in economy class flying for ten hours straight smells like. After a couple of 'Excuse me', Sid realized he missed seeing that air hostess. But that little crash switched off the mind movie for Sid, and he woke up to the fact that he was outside the plane and now in India. In the next two steps, the hot and humid Mumbai air wafting the smell of people, carpets, machines, and something he could not place the name, but it identified with Mumbai, made him forget everything about that air hostess and jolted him to the real world.

Sid had come to India nearly after two years. Though he had spent all his life in Mumbai, he had nearly forgotten how he would feel after he saw his city after a gap of two years. As he walked towards the passport control, he saw airport authorities in their white uniform talking on their walkie-talkies, and it seemed to him they looked suspiciously at him. He felt they were whispering about him to the authorities. Probably they caught him eyeing the air hostess, he thought. He nervously adjusted the straps of his laptop bag, set his gaze on the dirty bluish-brown carpet of the ramp, and hurried his pace.

He could feel the trickle of sweat under his arms. Even if you are not a criminal, for a first-time returning Indian to India, those looks of the officers around are a bit overwhelming. I have seen innocent people fumbling with their answers at customs and spending a horrible time and hard-core criminals going out as saints.

It was the first time he was coming as a NRI to India. Two years back he had left for U.S. to do masters in computer science at Southwest Minnesota University, not one of their top 100–200 universities. He would have got a better education in India, and he knew that. Going to the US was not for education; rather, leaving India was the primary objective. The reason he gave his father was that all his friends were going abroad for further education, and in a few years, they would be making lots of money and he would be stuck as a middle-class person commuting in Mumbai local trains carrying a steel tiffin box and an office bag, being one amongst the countless heads, having nothing better than what he already had. All emotional pressures, he could muster on his gullible and docile father. He felt his being average at everything was because he was stuck in a very average setting. The building he stayed in, the area around their residence, his school, his friends and his father as well. The entire environment stank of being average. He thought that only way to get out of the average rut, he needed to break out, break out totally, put himself in a new surrounding, new place which was far away from the averageness of the life he lived. He kept on grumbling in his graduation years to his single parent, to his hapless father, about how the entire place he stayed was pulling him down.

If you are thinking, why am I talking about Sid instead of Ashok, whose story I said I would be telling, then stop wondering, I am Misery, I don't have the usual way to tell stories; in fact I am not used to telling stories in the first place. Coming back to Sid, he spent his childhood in a very modest Mumbai setting. And 'modest' is a mild way to put it. A disturbed schooling because of shuttling between his mother's side grandparents' and his own house. He was in his tenth grade when his mother died; something changed in him after that, something forever. He was never the same after that. The usually emotionally suppressed Sid had become short-tempered and agitated, especially with his father. He knew his mother's cancer had nothing to do with his father. But his father never kept his family together; maybe he was a loving husband, but he could have taken better care of his mother in her final days. They were not the typical happy middle-class family as he remembered. The diagnosis of his mother's cancer, at the start of his tenth grade, had snapped him. His academics started rolling down, and during his mother's final days, both his father and mother spent a lot of time with doctors and at hospitals. They did not have enough money to put him in the tuitions for his tenth grade, which was kind of necessary considering the level of teaching they did in his school. What started as a roll down with the announcement of his mother's cancer was an avalanche by the time she died. Every time he saw the sorry hapless state of his father, it reminded him of his mother, and instead of feeling sympathy for his lonely father, he felt anger. He tried a couple of times to control his emotions, but it only came out stronger. He was frustrated that his father was trying to fill in for his mother, trying to fix his morning milk and breakfast, which tasted horrible; attempting dinner was even worse. Most of the times, he used to skip having lunch and dinner at his home, though for lunch they had it delivered from a lady who stayed a few blocks away and charged them nominally and gave a clean lunch. But there was no relation to taste whatsoever. When Sid used to be home for dinner, it used to be a silent affair. His father used to eat in silence, hardly protesting his son's constant channel hopping on the TV as he sat for his dinner. After dinner, Sid used to put his plate in the kitchen sink and retire to his own room and slam the door closed. His father did the dishes silently, without any complaints. Though there were times when Sid used to do the dishes as well, the times he saw his father looked really tired after his day-long work, when he hardly had any strength left to get up and go to his bed, Sid used to pick up his father's plate and do the dishes but after that, without waiting for any kind of acknowledgement, he used to go to his room and slam the door. Sid knew and so did his father that it was not that Sid hated him, it was just that he felt irritable in his father's presence, the way his father used to be calm when he misbehaved or spoke disrespectfully used to unnerve him. So the learning Sid had when he was graduating was that he should stop speaking to his father other than what was necessary. It took his father's full gratuity and lot of provident funds to put him through some agent to US for his masters.

Sid used to call his father once a month after reaching Minnesota. Since the last six months, after he had got the internship at the university and started receiving his stipend, his calling frequency had increased; he used to call him nearly once a week. Slowly in the last few months, the length of the conversation was increasing. What didn't happen face to face started happening over the phone, generally asking about his father's health and reporting how he was doing academically. In one of the phone calls, he had confessed to his father that he had started drinking alcohol but drank rarely and very little and that he knew his limits and also told him that he was very far from drugs. And that he had not married, that the weather was very stormy on some of those dark evenings. Or that there was a reading vacation in his university. Or that he had attempted playing American football. He gave lengthy answers to his father's short questions, the kind of questions which during his days in Mumbai he either never bothered to answer or answered with a curt grunt. Sid could listen to his father's voice being choked with emotions on the other end. Last month when he told his father he was coming to India for a month or so, there were a few minutes of silence before his father said how glad he was and how desperately he would be waiting for him. Sid was doing now well academically. He had made a few projects which were appreciated by his professors, but somehow that year because of recession, there were hardly any companies visiting the campus. He did not succeed in securing a job in the six months of internship. His visa was going to expire and he needed to secure a job and then reapply for the US visa.

Ashok Pradhan, father of Sid or Siddharth, stood leaning on the arrival barricade at the airport, with his shoulders hunched, looking through his thick glasses, beyond the crowds, trying to spot his son from as far as possible. In the last two years, Ashok looked wearier, more broken, and more pitiable. His eye bags were darker and more pronounced; the permanent mole on his left cheek now had two or three strands of silvery hair that sprung out like a fountain. He kept on bobbing his head around, trying to spot Sid. The person next to him with a plaque of some Mr Jiteendra Khosla gestured to Ashok saying, 'Relax, nobody has come out yet, the flight has just landed.' Ashok nodded to him, but continued his leaning and arching of his head. Suddenly the phone in his trousers gave a small quick ring of SMS. The most basic model phone, just enough for voice and text, it was a luxury according to Ashok. He smiled reading the SMS, and read it as if it was a long text. It was just one word, 'landed', from Sid. Ashok did not have the facility to SMS or call an ISD number from his mobile. He wished to reply, 'Welcome, son. God bless you. Waiting for you', so he said that in his mind. He clenched his phone for a few seconds before pocketing it.

About four decades back, Ashok was not at all like Sid. Ashok, in the prime of his youth, was more of a flamboyant, handsome person. And he knew he was one of those handsome people, who could charm girls around him. Decked out in the latest fashion clothing, especially those bell-bottom pants with heavy printed shirts, a similar printed scarf tucked in, thick black horn-rimmed glasses and sporting a pencil-cut moustache, he used to go around Bombay, as the city was known then, on his Royal Enfield bike. Pushpa used to wait at the bus stop, holding a few books close to her chest, not waiting for the bus, but for Ashok. The bus stop was their pickup point. Ashok used to stop a few metres ahead of the bus stop as if showing he saw her by chance, and she used to move out of the line and join him on his bike, also expressing a fake surprise. Though nobody around them was surprised any more, it was a routine thing. At the bus stop, there was this person who invariably looked at his watch just before Ashok came to pick up Pushpa, and after he saw him coming, he used to smile, reassuring himself. Ashok used to drive her to their favourite coffee house and both used to order a cup of filter coffee. After that they went on his bike to the next bus stop, where they used to wait for the next bus, and part ways for the next day. This went on till the day Ashok received a job offer from the new textile mill. Since he was a graduate, he did not join as the regular workers in the mill, he was the engineer of the plant, with a good pay. Words like pride, growth, prosperity, success, family, and the like boomed in his ears. He was a very happy man. That afternoon, he and Pushpa had French omelettes with the filter coffee followed by two scoops of vanilla ice cream. They were happy, like young happy couples are supposed to be. There was a lot of resistance for marriage from Pushpa's father, considering that she had found her own match and deprived her parents of the 'right' to find a groom for her. In those times, love marriages were only happening in movies, and the girls who found their own match were looked down upon. Pushpa's father did not speak to her for a few weeks. But Ashok's new job, his status, Pushpa's mother's continuous insistence for their daughter's happiness, and Pushpa's typical Bollywood style of flooding pillows with tears, not eating, and silent tantrums made him finally drop his wall. He allowed Pushpa to go on with her life. Very filmy, very Bollywood, very clichéd. Pushpa's father, though, never liked Ashok.

Marriage, happy life, good job—everything was set for Ashok, an enormous ocean of possibilities ahead of him. The first year went as if it was their extended courtship period. There was no change with the social obligation called marriage; life was still carefree and filled with youthful romance. What was better was it was coupled with a handsome salary from the job. Things just couldn't have been better. They used to stay in a chawl, which is like an array of one bedroom, a kitchen joined with hall, a kind of apartment, in a three- to four-storied building. Most of the apartments had a common toilet and bathing place. This was a usual place in those times in Bombay, where people from the modest-income group stayed, or the budding class who had not yet saved enough to move to a better place. Ashok and Pushpa were from the latter category. It made me smile whenever the old lady living under the staircase of their building commented on Pushpa, which she hardly missed: 'The way both of you lovebirds look, somebody will cast an evil spell on you. Put lots of kohl in your eyes, darling, to ward off those evil eyes.'

Somewhere in the second year, on one of their trips to Pushpa's home for dinner, her mother took her in their bedroom and asked worriedly, 'Pushpa, is everything okay between both of you? Or you just write letters to make us happy?'

'Mother, I think all my teenage life, you made me fast on Mondays with a wish that I could get a husband like Lord Shiva. I don't have any doubts that my prayers have been answered much more than my expectations,' Pushpa replied, holding her mother's palms as if sincerely reassuring her.

Her mother saw the twinkle in her eyes, her face full of satisfaction, the red vermillion powder between the partings of her braids proudly sported.

'I am sure of that, your husband must be taking good care of you,' her mother said, caressing Pushpa's face. 'But then tell me, why no kids?' her mother continued, coming now to the point she wanted to ask.

'Mother, how do I know? I know we have a good life and that is what I wished for and I am happy. He loves me; I don't know anything beyond it.'

'Did you consult the doctor?'

'No! Both of us did not feel like that. It is hardly a year!'

'It is one year and four months, enough for a healthy husband to impregnate a healthy wife!'

'You are being ridiculous! I don't think I want to talk about this!' Pushpa shouted at her mother.

'Pushpa, you are staying here tonight and coming to a doctor with me tomorrow,' her mother declared. Giving options was not her style.

The doctor's visit told them that she did not have anything wrong, and maybe in some time, she would get a child. This statement from the doctor led Pushpa's mother and her father to conclude that there was a problem with Ashok. But to ask Ashok about it did not seem right, and both of them suddenly felt sorry and extremely sad for their daughter. Pushpa was very angry at them for their remarks about Ashok having a problem or being impotent, and left their home very angry, telling them she was happy without them and their cruel words. She never asked Ashok to get a check-up. Ashok did not have a similar problem with his parents. His parents died when he was in his senior high school, of tuberculosis, both of them nearly at the separation of a few months. He had completed his education staying at his uncle's place.

Sometime in the early days of their third year, it was one of those nights when there was an electricity cut in their chawl. The flickering oil lamp lighted in front of the huge photo of Ganesha was the only source of light in their home. Just able to see each other's faces from a distance less than two three inches, they did not mind that. Ashok looked tired after a busy day at the factory, so this soft, light conversation after dinner was relaxing for him.

'You look very tired today. Bad day at the factory, again the worker unions are creating a problem?' Pushpa asked a predictable question but every word felt good to Ashok. As Ashok leaned on the back wall, Pushpa could see the contours of his face changing because of the smile he gave. Ashok remained silent for a few minutes as if winding down after the day. Pushpa was quiet as well.

Ashok gave a small sigh and leaned forward; he took Pushpa's hands and cupped them with his own and said, 'I think you are missing kids. I can see it in your eyes, when you look at other kids, when we go to our friends' places, when you feel that your friends want to ask about it but are not asking . . . right, dear?'

'No! What are you saying? You are complete for me, I never miss anybody, I love you and I can die like this, looking at your face, please don't ask me such questions, please,' Pushpa pleaded. Her eyes were already moist.

'I love you,' Ashok said and kissed Pushpa's forehead and pulled her head onto his chest, hugging her tight. He could feel his vest getting wet from Pushpa's tears. Holding her like that, he said, 'I know you have had your check-up and you don't have any problem.'

Pushpa pulled herself out of his grip and looked at Ashok, his eyes also moist now.

'Your father told me last month when we met at your cousin's wedding, that you had gone with your mother for the check-up and that you are all right and I am the one with a problem.'

'I hate them!' Pushpa started sobbing.

Ashok moved closer to her and wiped her tears, which felt warm to his fingertips, and kissed her gently on her eyes, soaking his lips with the salty water that flowed now without stop. He kissed both her eyes and gently lifted her face and kissed her trembling lips. The way life offers sweet surprises, would they have savoured more of those delicate, romantic moments had they known that the next few minutes would be their lifelong cherished memory? Would the behaviour be natural, had they known the fact that all their lives, this moment of ecstasy would always live? For the first time, they made love not on their usual bed but between the kitchen and bedroom doorway, where they sat. The sweat drops shimmered in the flickering light of the lamp on the already moist shoulder of Pushpa before it rolled down on her arm, while both lost each other in the blissful ecstasy. What they held in their arms was their world, and everything else, her parents, his worker union, the neighbours, everything had ceased to exist. It was the deepest peace they experienced, as their bodies shuddered in each other.

That year was 1982, the year that was one of the blackest years of Bombay, especially for the textile mill workers. The Great Bombay Textile Strike was called and there was a huge strength of thousands of workers on the streets, bringing a screeching halt of the famous Bombay mills. The mill workers were threatening the managers for getting higher pay and bonuses. Young and cheerful Ashok was suddenly getting letters on his table about threats from workers. Ashok found himself caught in between the workers and the real managers. He was a post just above the workers, not to be part of their union and junior enough not to be a real manager. He had absolutely no power to assist the workers. The experienced and senior managers used Ashok to talk and negotiate with the workers. Looking at young Ashok, the workers also had a bit of sympathy for him, so though they threatened him, they never really harmed him. He remained negotiator from both the sides. Most days he spent arguing debating with either of the parties. By the time he reached home, it was midnight, he used to be fatigued, tired, and heavily stressed. On one of these days when he threw himself on his bed and closed his eyes, he felt the warm touch of Pushpa on his chest.

'Pushpa, I am too tired today, even to talk.' Ashok could barely manage to speak.

Pushpa moved closer to him, very near to him at his ear.

'Pushpa, let me sleep, I am in no mood today,' Ashok said with his voice up and irritated. He felt hot air breathed in his ear as Pushpa came closer and whispered, 'I missed my period for two months now.'

Ashok turned like a spring, wide-eyed to look at her smiling and acting coy. She then arched her neck and kissed Ashok. Ashok reciprocated more passionately.

In a couple of months, the bulge started showing, and both were on top of their world. Though the strikes were still going on and the salaries were not being paid and they were near broke, they had no limits to their happiness; it was a perfect world for them. Ashok, anyway, for most of the time did not need to go to the office. He took utmost care of Pushpa, with all the new learnt tenderness. Talking to the womb each night was their sport. Pushpa did not talk about her pregnancy to her parents till they heard from neighbours about the growing size of Pushpa. They came to live with them. It took around a week for Pushpa to start talking normally to her parents after they apologized near a hundred times to her. Time rolled on; money was becoming a real issue. Ashok had sold off nearly everything he could to have decent care for Pushpa. Others were not giving jobs to managers from the mills, considering that the worker would destroy the sheltering company. It was a very tense and difficult times in Bombay. All four of them were supported from whatever money Pushpa's father could manage. But just before retiring for the day, on their beds, their practice of talking in coochy-coo language to Pushpa's now inflated belly brought in all the peace that couple needed. Pushpa had entered into the ninth month and the doctor said that it would be any time they would need to do the delivery. In the last week when the doctor examined Pushpa, she said that it would be very dangerous for Pushpa to have a normal delivery. For a typical Indian middle-class family in those times, not to have a normal delivery meant a lot of tension and anxiety. Also the operation would cost a lot of money and Ashok was already in debt with many people. People had stopped loaning any money to people working in the mills. This time around, Ashok had started crumbling; he had no source of income left. He finally decided that he should engage in hard-core manual labour and possibly drive an autorickshaw to get some money.

It was any time due for Pushpa when a boy came knocking at Ashok's door, passing on a message from his bosses that he was immediately needed at the factory. They had finally decided to settle some amount with the workers, and if Ashok could negotiate the deal, he would be handsomely rewarded. He felt like a bolt hit his stomach. He did not want to leave Pushpa, but money was very much needed. He turned back to look at Pushpa's tense expression.

'I will be back very soon; this should not take much time. If I have done so well when they were not paying, I should be their hero now. I would get a lot of blessings, don't worry, relax. And you know better, we need the blessings. I will be back sooner than you'll miss me,' Ashok said to Pushpa.

'Is it necessary? Can't somebody else go?' Pushpa said, holding Ashok's hand.

'No, I don't want anybody else to go, I have done a lot and we need the money, Pushpa. Let me go, I will be back soon as I said.'

'Take care of yourself and come back soon,' Pushpa replied.

The way we don't realize that the next moments are the most cherished, the same is with the moments we want to forget. Till reality actually hits, even just few seconds before, we are not aware of how things can turn. It was a fateful day for Ashok. The kind of compromise the bosses were talking was just eyewash and Ashok knew the workers would not agree to that. The bosses, as usual, were adamant and pushed Ashok to talk with them. Ashok, against all his will, with his mind completely preoccupied with Pushpa, walked with two security guards to the group of the workers. The union leader along with a few other workers came forward. Both the parties were tense. Ashok had made up his mind that if they didn't agree to the settlement, he would not negotiate, and go back to the bosses, saying that they were rejecting the offer.

'So, baby boy, tell us what your papa is saying,' the union leader said to Ashok, ridiculing him in his usual style.

There was a new person in the group with the union leader, who looked very restless and as if provoking Ashok to say or do something which they did not like. Ashok started reading the legal language which had that they would not be compensated for the months of strike and the new salary from next month was just a bit more than their old salaries, far below what their demand was. At this, the new fellow in the group gestured Ashok to stop reading.

'Go and tell your papa this,' he said and snatched the paper from Ashok's hand and tore it violently, spitting on it, and then crushing it under his feet. Ashok turned back and started walking coolly to the office, when the new fellow called him again.

'Listen, baby boy, come here, tell him this as well.' And he removed his slipper and slapped Ashok very hard with his slipper. Ashok was thrown off balance and fell down. The union leader and the security people tried pulling the new worker away from Ashok, who was still kicking him in his ribs. In this melee, the security fellow pushed both the union leader and the other fellow. This was taken as insult by the workers, and what resulted of the melee was that Ashok and the two security guards landed in hospital critically injured.

Ashok not only missed witnessing his son coming into this world, he could not even see him for next one month, as he stayed in a far-off government hospital, recuperating from the injuries. After around two months, Pushpa came with their kid and her parents. Ashok was in bandages; he was just able to see the baby but not hold him. Pushpa and Ashok spent a few tears as she gingerly brought her forehead near Ashok's shoulder and they argued about whom the kid looked like. It was there they decided to call him Siddharth. It took a full five months for Ashok to completely recover and walk independently. Till then Pushpa's parents stayed with them. The conversation between Ashok and his in-laws was restricted only on need basis. Once in a while, at the dinner table, Pushpa's father would exaggerate about how painful the delivery was for Pushpa and that they had to manage everything; had Ashok got a better job, it would have meant good for their family. Pushpa gestured with her eyes to Ashok to stay silent and ignore them, but he would get up from the dinner table and walk out of the small apartment. Nobody exchanged any words after that. By this time, most of the textile mills had shifted out of Bombay, including the one in which Ashok worked.

Even after completely recovering, Ashok had lost much more after the factory incident, including his confidence—the joblessness of all those months ate his self-confidence completely. He was unsure of everything, more aloof, and wore a sad look most of the time. He had taken a job in the refrigerator repair company. The pay was just average; he knew he must work many overtime hours to repay the debt he had incurred. Pushpa's parents had gone back to their home. Ashok used to take a local train early morning and returned around eight thirty in the evening. By the time he came back, Siddharth was usually sleeping, and Pushpa would be waiting for him, to have dinner together. At dinner they used to have long stretches of silence. There was no use in asking Ashok how his day was; he used to get irritated at that.

'What do you think my day was like? It is not easy like you sitting at home with a kid,' Ashok used to yell at her. Pushpa remained silent for most of his outburst, and as she lowered her eyes, a drop fell on her plate. Their financial condition was just enough to manage food and nominal household expenditure. Ashok fell into the usual trap of stressed husband coming home late and tired. He eventually started coming home drunk, though he was never a wife-beater, he did start yelling and cursing loudly at Pushpa for no reason.

Three years passed and nothing much changed; Pushpa used to have more and longer visits to her parents house. In three years, Ashok and Pushpa aged around ten years. While Ashok overworked to have a better life for his family, Pushpa stayed torn between her husband and Siddharth, trying to make the ends meet. Ashok then changed his job for a better one for which he had to travel daily two hours one way in a local train to reach his work. But since the pay was good, they were okay that both Pushpa and Ashok would hardly meet or talk with each other. After around five to six years, their financial condition saw some relief; years of hard work started to return something good. The downside was, Siddharth never really became close to Ashok. For him Ashok was just like a stranger coming into their home and sleeping in Mother's bedroom; at times this person yelled loudly at his mother for very simple things. Ashok missed seeing all the moments in the growing-up years of Siddharth, which generally parents claim to be the most beautiful moments.

I quietly witnessed the years slip by as the family turned into just people staying under one roof. It was when Siddharth was in his tenth grade, Pushpa complained of stomach ache to Ashok. But he was too busy or too tired to take any note of that. His only advice, when she complained, was to try some antacid or a glass of soda. She meekly turned away without telling him that she had been trying that for a week but the pain was getting worse each day.

Teenager Siddharth was interpreting whatever he saw in his own way, with his own sense of judgment. He was seeing his mother cringe with pain even after drinking glass after glass of some cheap soda. His father came late in the night, completely drained of energy, with bloodshot eyes, coming home just to crash on the bed and then stayed deaf to any complaints. His mother held the side of her stomach tight and cried in her pillow. It was an agonizing week for everybody when Pushpa had a series of vomiting. The local doctor's drugs were not able to control the dehydration and eventually Pushpa was admitted to the city hospital. After around fifteen days of being in hospital, her reports came and it was declared as the last stage of stomach cancer. Ashok was completely shattered at the news. That night, Ashok sat beside Pushpa's hospital bed, holding her, who was barely conscious, weeping all night. In two days when Pushpa's parents came, they took Pushpa and Siddharth with them, and Ashok was not allowed to meet her. Ashok had to continue with his job and Siddharth had to come back home since it was his tenth grade. Siddharth had gone from bad to worse in his academics. Ashok had lost all his heart in his work and had taken to heavy drinking. Pushpa cried her heart out at her parents to allow her to return to her own home and give the dignity to die happily with her husband and child around. Pushpa lived a month after that, which they spent mostly with doctors or in hospital.

It took Ashok around a month of grieving after Pushpa's death to start acting normal, but I know he is still acting; he never came out of that grief, he still considers himself guilty. Siddharth failed in his tenth grade. All his friends had moved ahead looking for junior college, and he had to repeat his exams for his tenth grade. He blamed his father's negligence for his mother's death as well as his failure at academics and so did his grandparents.

I saw each moment, how Ashok was reduced from being a person to just a responsibility. At the age when people start taking their lives easy, he worked double the time, earning as much money he could for Sid. Sid on the other hand never really bothered. His hatred had mellowed, but he was indifferent to Ashok. He hardly stayed at home, nor did Ashok. One evening Siddharth came back home and threw tantrums for going to United States as if it was as easy as going from Mumbai to Bangalore. Ashok knew Sid did not have any kind of scholarship, and to send him to the US was not a one-time affair. He knew he would need a recurring supply of money. Ashok emptied all his gratuity, provident fund and finally sold his small Mumbai apartment they lived in. He started giving rent for his stay in his own house. He did not tell Siddharth about all this, and Siddharth as usual did not bother about where the money came from.

It was after more than two years today that I saw Sid and Ashok sit for dinner together, just the two of them in their old apartment.

Ashok had set the table, while Sid had freshened up. The cutlery set looked very new, the kind of gesture that told Sid that it was bought for him. The condition of the kitchen looked as if there was hardly any food being cooked there. In fact, looking at Ashok also, it felt as if at all he ate home-cooked food. But that evening, Ashok had lot of things made for Sid. Just when they were about to start their dinner, the electricity went off. Ashok kind of knew this; he had the candle and matchbox ready near the sugar and tea tins. He turned a steel vessel upside down and lit the candle on it, placing the vessel in the centre of their small dining table. In that dim light, in the light and dark shades, Sid suddenly felt that his father looked old, very old, much older even than some of his professors there in the US who were much elder than his father by age.

'Baba,' Sid said softly.

'Till when are you going to be in India?' Ashok asked his question with his mouthful, not noticing Sid was starting a conversation.

'If everything works well, then two weeks.'

Ashok stopped eating for a few seconds and gave a long laboured exasperated sigh. 'I hope everything works out well for you.'

'Baba, don't you want me to stay more?'

'What I really want is what is good for you. If you think you can stay only two weeks, it must be important for you to reach back in time. I am an old man now, what I want is not important. You have a future to secure, make sure that you get the best. I think I will reheat the dal.' Saying this, Ashok picked up the lentil soup bowl and jerked himself up and moved towards the kitchen and fumbled to reheat the dal.

Sid knew the dal was perfect; he had seen in the dim light his father's eyes moistening as he got up. Sid wanted to get up and put his hand on his father's shoulder and tell him to sit and that he didn't really need to take care of the dal. Something else needed to be taken care of. But he did not get up. He sat there, choking his emotions, just as his father was doing. He wondered for a moment how easy it was for him to get angry at his father before he had left for the US. But now, he felt relieved when his father interrupted him when he was trying to say that he was sorry and wanted to ask how his father managed the two years. He felt at that moment that probably his father knew what he was going to ask and so he intentionally interrupted. Sid sat motionless on the chair as his father stood near the gas stove heating the dal. I stood there listening to their minds, their unspoken words, the sound of their hidden emotions. Ashok returned with the scalding hot dal and put it on the old newspaper that was on the dining table.

'You must be tired, sleep immediately after this dinner, we will catch up tomorrow morning of what we missed for two years.'

'Yes,' Sid replied and forgot to take the hot dal before he finished his dinner.

Sid had come back to renew his visa, from a student visa to H1B visa. Two weeks was very optimistic. The next morning he had contacted an agent he had been given as a reference by a few of his friends from Mumbai staying with him in the US. The agent had said, in best case, it would be three weeks. Sid was not unhappy. He felt a kind of a relief. In fact, though he did not want to settle in India, not then, till he could recover his money spent for education at least, now he somehow wished that the visa process took time and he got some time in India.

Ashok had got up early and had kept breakfast ready for Sid. He had left for his job at eight in the morning and did not return till late evening. When he came back, Sid was working on his laptop he had brought with him from the US. As Ashok walked in and smiled, feeling pride that his son was working on a laptop, Sid could see his entire body was dead tired, a frail body carrying a tired spirit.

'Sid, I hope you are not very hungry and can wait till I will cook something for both of us.'

Sid looked up at his father, who had just arrived as tired as he could just imagine and wondered what he should be feeling, to feel guilty or hate himself for what he was doing this to his father or feel love towards his father. But what he actually felt was sadness, some kind of pain in his chest. I could see the darkness around his heart, hear the sobs of his heart. 'No need, Baba, I have ordered pizzas for us tonight.'

'Oh, I forgot, you must not like our taste so much now.'

Sid did not say that he did not like pizzas any more; it was for him that he had ordered them.

It was the second night in row with no electricity, and both of them sat in a hot, humid room, fanning themselves with old torn magazine. The flame of the dim candle stayed steady in that windless room, and I felt everything around them was watching them just like I did, both the father and son, especially the father devouring the 'veggie delight' pizza.

'Hmm . . . this is nice, I never knew pizzas are so good,' Ashok said with the corner of pizza still a bit out of his mouth, spitting crumbs of crust out of this mouth as he spoke. 'Do you eat this lot there?' Ashok continued with his mouthful.

'Yes, this food is quick, less messy, and cheap. It is the basic student food in the US. Sometimes we eat Chinese.'

'I don't like Maggi, I don't understand how can somebody eat something like that.' Ashok was quick to respond.

'Maggi is not Chinese food, Baba,' Sid said, laughing.

'Whatever, I don't like that.'

I was happy to see both of them laughing together, though I am not supposed to give in to the feeling, regardless of it being happy or sad. I wished to leave them both like that, framed in that moment. But leaving or staying with somebody is not my choice—and wishing is forbidden for us. And I knew I am not done here, not yet, not completely. The funny thing is after I latch on to somebody, even I don't know all the effects—the choices can be many.

If Pushpa could see from somewhere, she would be feeling peaceful to see that finally the father-son duo was getting along with each other. Ashok had started coming home earlier, looking forward to each evening, hoping for the electricity to go off; it was much nicer in the dark. Sid did not have any friends left there, so more or less, he had evenings free. He had taken an Internet dongle by now, and one of those evenings, he showed Ashok his university, his place of work, his hostel, his friends, and a few other locations around. Both of them had a good laugh looking at the pictures. One of those white girls along with Sid in his university, he saw her in a lot of photos, throwing her arms around Sid, and in those moments of laughter, Ashok asked Sid in a serious tone if he loved her. Sid looked at his father in disbelief for a moment and then laughed even more loudly. 'No! She is not even my girlfriend! It is just the way it is there in the US.'

'Nice,' Ashok said, winking at Sid. Sid smiled, knowing that his father was imagining him being the bad boy of the US.

Sid suddenly got up and asked Ashok, 'Baba, you know what, I did not tell you yet, but I have brought with me a nice bourbon whisky, why don't we have it together?'

Ashok looked at him for a few seconds before turning his face towards the dark corner of the room. He slowly got up and walked till the kitchen platform and stood there. Sid followed and gently squeezed Ashok's shoulder.

'It is okay, Baba, I don't drink so much, it was just as a small celebration between us.'

'It is not that, son, it is just that I have given up drinking long before.'

Sid could see in that dim light, his father's eyes welled up. 'Since Mama's death, right?'

Ashok nodded his head a couple of times before wiping the corners of his eyes and then left Sid standing there and moved to the bedroom to sleep. That night, I could see both of them were not sleeping. It must have been around 3 a.m. when Ashok felt dryness in his throat and got up for a glass of water. I knew it was action time for me. Ashok tripped on something in the dark and fell, the corner of the wall hitting his temple, and he landed pretty badly on his right elbow and knee, resulting in a severe concussion, dislocated elbow, and ruptured ligaments. But this time though I swung into action, I hoped it was more for paving the road for my twin. In the hospital sessions those followed, Sid tended to Ashok, forgetting everything else in the world.

Ashok had to be in the bandages for six weeks. He was upset that he was not able to go to work and his pay would be cut.

'Baba, you don't need to work any more. I will be doing well enough for both of us. I have applied for a job and I have it.'

'God bless you, dear, but as I recall, it is time for you to go back. It is near to three weeks since you have come. It is so silly of me to get lost in myself; I did not ask you your visa status. When you will be leaving?' Ashok asked this without any wish to know the answers. He had never forgotten regarding the visa, he had not forgotten it was already three weeks, he wished it was possible for Sid to forget about it.

'Baba, I said you don't need to work any more. You have done much more than what you were supposed to do.'

'No, I haven't. Not when it was required.'

'Baba, I am staying here till you get better. And I have brought papers for your application for your US visa. The chances are slim to none for you to get the visa. But I have made an attempt and leave the rest of it to luck.'

It makes me smile when I hear somebody saying 'leaving something to luck'.

'Son, it's a typical movie punchline, but it's true, the last three weeks I have spent with you are enough for me to die happily. I see that you are doing well in everything. I have had my life; seeing you like this today, I feel it was worth it. The US is not for me, I would like to die here—die here peacefully, where I feel your mother's presence. Go live your life, your dream, don't pull a baggage.'

'Baba, you are right, it is a movie punchline. Not mine, yours. Please drop this. This is not fair, you cannot play great always and I get killed by the guilt . . . just . . . just come with me.' Sid said this and broke into tears.

'I am sorry, Baba, for my behaviour until now, I really am. I am guilty of making your life so full of hardships and sadness. You are suffering right from my birth. I know that. I really know that and even if I wish, I cannot turn back the clock.'

Ashok tried to say something but stopped; he extended his hand with a wish to stroke his son's head and make him calm, but Sid stood out of his arm's reach. And Sid didn't move closer from where he was standing.

Sid opened his mouth wide and as if sucking in a mouthful of oxygen before he continued, 'Baba, you know, it is not that I have suddenly realized that I need you. I am still selfish. It was not an overnight revelation because I stumbled across Mama's diary or some letters she had stored for me, like what they show in movies. In fact, I never had any movie life, I had a perfectly average life, and even the tragedies in my life were average. The tragedies were not big enough to make a story or hero out of me, they were just enough to keep tormenting me slowly. I realized because in those months in the US there, I felt alone, Baba, I don't have anybody to call my own. I felt alone, Baba, you understand? Very alone. And I hate that feeling. While I see my friends' parents calling them, sending them pictures of girls, forcing them to get married, seeing my friends get irritated at them for this or getting on their nerves with lectures on what they should not adopt from Western culture and that they should do this or not do that . . .'

He paused for a few seconds, held Ashok's left palm. 'I don't get a chance to get irritated any more, Baba. And I want to. I have not settled in my life yet. I still need the advice of my father; I want him to scold me when I do wrong things. I want him to bore me to death with his lectures on bad things about Western culture, I want him to force me to get married and to rebel and say no to him, I don't want a father who is dying in India to send me money or just filling in responsibility. I want to laugh with him; I want to drink whisky with him. I miss you, Baba. And when you give me such a one-liner, I hate it. After Mother died and even before that, you have missed being my father. I need a father, Baba, I need love, not sacrifice. Any more sacrifice will kill me, will kill me with guilt. I wish to be normal, happy person. Help me to be one.'

I sat there with rapt attention listening to that conversation. And as I said, sometimes I enter lives of people to make way for my brother; I think this is what I did this time. I could see both of them weeping, embracing each other for a long time. The emotional flood probably washed out many of my traces.

Sometimes, I too break rules. I get passionate. I kept on watching these two people as my brother worked with them. I could see Sid holding Ashok's shivering palm as the flight to New York took off from Mumbai.

Werepotato

Based on a true story

He said his name was Alok, though nobody bothered, not any more. And he knew it.

He sat there immovable, as dirty as he could be, as stinking as he could be, and as obnoxious as he could be. With all that, he was perfectly invisible amongst other similar things around, there on a white saucer with blue border and dirty brown patches. Damp, his skin peeling off in many places, he looked ugly with green shoots all over.

Alok was a werepotato.

All day he stayed in the saucer and stank. After midnight, he became a man and stayed like that before the first rays of sun hit the horizon. Throughout the day he was in his potato form. Sheila used to pick him up in the morning from wherever he was and put him somewhere in the house, far enough to avoid his revolting reek. Most of the time, she didn't have to search much. He was under her blanket or with one of her friends in that miserable brothel. She had got used to him, his loathsome personality, his stink, his being suddenly violent at night, his carnal urges, his being with her friends, nearly everything about him—the only one who never paid her for her services. There were cases when some of her rogue clients didn't pay, but consistently exploiting her and not paying was only Alok. And by now though she was used to him, every sight of him made the bile rise in her the pit of her stomach.

Alok was not always like this, nor was Sheila a prostitute. Both were young and showed signs of potential to do something bigger than the usual. Sheila was his girlfriend from his senior high school days. Those were promising days. Dreams, aims, new businesses, a glimmer in the eyes, money, power, or whatever that entices the young minds. But they missed the point that life is not a typical teacher, in the way it teaches and the tests it gives—that many times life has a nasty sense of humour.

Alok floundered. And gave up, crumbled. The mortar used in his making was probably weak. Like many others, he found solace in being forgetful, alcohol being a handy friend. Life went spirally down. The usual happened—debts, loans, goons, blood, weeping, alcohol, more alcohol, and fights with Sheila. It is not exactly known which event exactly condemned Alok to become a werepotato, but he did become one. Sheila did not understand where she lost her Alok, the Alok whom she once loved.

With night, Alok came back full of lust and consumed her. After he went limp, he used to roll over and snore, no answers to any unasked questions. Sheila realized she was reduced to being just a reminder to Alok of his masculinity. Humping was the only thing that Alok broke any sweat on and rejoiced with satiation on the self-conformance about being a male. This went on for a long time. Every night Alok used to come suddenly to her as if sex-deprived, did his thing, and went to sleep, all this while he stank of cheap alcohol and bad breath. Nearly all nights, Sheila threw up after he went to sleep. She used to weep herself to bed. There were many nights when he came back and accused her for his state, beat her till she bled, and fell unconscious. But she did not leave him and she didn't know why. The best years of her life she lost with this werepotato. She aged faster than her age.

Circumstances, the desire to survive, and greater than all that, for a revenge on Alok, she resorted to prostitution. She knew Alok well; while being the potato, he could see, feel, and at times weep, which kept it damp and stinking. Her having sex with a multitude of people in front of him gave her the pleasure of vengeance. At night he used to come to her more sloshed than before, angrier, and force himself into her. He used to beat her and curse her. But with each slap, she laughed, mocking him in his state. Her friends who were in a similar business as her knew about him. At times, when Sheila used to be with a customer, he used to walk to one of her friends' rooms. His alcohol was paid with Sheila's money, so he didn't disturb her when she was with a customer. In that inebriated state, he was sane enough to understand this.

Lately, Sheila had one of her clients as a repeat afternoon customer. He said to her he loved her and was ready to marry and would go to all the way to be a good husband. Alok mutely witnessed this, sitting in that white saucer with blue border and dirty brown patches. On those nights, there was a barrage of expletives and Sheila was gifted with more bruises and concussions. The screams, curses, and beatings reached the next level.

One of those mornings, Sheila got up with a swollen lip and a bleeding forehead. Her new boyfriend helped her to calm herself. He promised to move in with her. That morning, she washed the potato clean, peeled it with a sharp peeler. She took one of the biggest cleavers and chopped the potato in equal cubes. She dunked those cubes in hot oil and seasoned them with hot chilli paste. She had that served to herself and her boyfriend. Both of them relished the breakfast though the smell was a bit on the harsher side. After the breakfast, she smiled to herself without an ounce of guilt. After all these years of association, Alok was eaten up. After the breakfast, they made love.

The bruise-less nights, the new-found freedom were like a new life. Sheila felt happy. She felt she should have eaten her special breakfast earlier. She decided to give up the flesh-selling business and start anew.

They decided to move out and relocate to some new place. They started planning on their dreams.

And on one of these days when she came back from her shopping, she did not find her boyfriend anywhere. Her heart sank, and tears welled up in her eyes; she realized she had been fooled by a glib liar.

When she went to her bedroom to change, she saw in the centre of her bed, a dirty stinking potato.

The White Lotus

It was a hot summer day in Pune. Buses swarmed at Swargate, the main bus depot. Inside the buses, a mob of people was packed and pushed against each other, with hardly any space to move. The insides of the buses stank of sweat and outside of smoke. And it did not really matter to the people on either side of the buses; it was an everyday smell for them. There were people everywhere spreading in all possible directions with insect-like briskness in a cacophony of agitated horns. But the magic of the place was about the order in the chaos. An aerial shot of the place looked like an enchanted place where people and the overstuffed vehicles moved as if drawn into perfect lines, as if following some kind of magnetic field. From above, it would seem the entire colossal collection of people and machines was designed to happen the way it was happening. It was as if the city was a living organism, and people and machines were some internal part of it, in which the chaotic condition did not affect the unaware organism. The things were just in everyday perfectness.

Nikhil got down from the bus and adjusted to the blinding light. He had been travelling for nearly twenty-three hours without any good sleep. The moment he got down and looked around, he knew this was the land where he would be spending his life. He knew his life had finally taken a start, a start he was waiting for.

Nikhil's life had a sudden turnaround. Till just about few days back, all the days were exactly the same for him; from dawn to dusk it was the same routine, which was *doing nothing*. He was subject to constant taunts, ridicule, and criticism from his parents and other elders in the village for being of no use. And they were not far from the actual situation. His father had insisted that he study till tenth grade. And he did that, just that, studied till tenth grade, and his father later regretted that decision. His being a tenth-grade passer had given him an excuse for his lethargy. Nikhil would not toil in the farms like other boys of his age as he claimed it was not the work of the educated; he claimed that he was waiting for his opportunity to come.

His father knew their financial condition was dwindling and the patch of farmland they had would be taken away since they were not able to repay the debt on the loan, while his mother's main concern was neither farm nor financial condition: it was that nobody of good, respected family would see Nikhil as a suitable groom and she might have to get old without having a daughter-in-law. Nikhil's father was sad and angry every time he saw his son doing nothing and what irritated him more was that amidst all these conditions, Nikhil strangely carried about himself a feeling of contentment. Though technically, he was not really lazy, he was more like a charming affable person around ready to help anybody and he was always available. But he would not do a regular job; he was not ready to labour on the fields.

Nikhil's feeling of peace came from his belief in the prophecy of a travelling fortune teller. Though he was told about his fortune in front of his parents and many other people, he was the only one who remembered it. He had faith in it, rather a blind one.

It was about two years back, in their village Dhanora, a saintly person (he looked like one) had come. People called him Baba Rudranand. He had settled himself under a big fig tree. Dressed in a long orange robe, long white beard, with beads of *rudraksha* wrapped around him from waist to chest, he carried around him an air of awe and fear, more than mysticism. Baba Rudranand had received a warm welcome in their village, and people went in throngs to offer him fruits and sweetmeats; some also offered petty cash, all of which Baba politely distributed to people. He did not eat or drink anything, which made him even more saintly in people's eyes. Nikhil's parents had coaxed Nikhil to come with them to visit the saint. They had to wait for nearly three hours before their turn came to meet Baba Rudranand. As per

Nikhil, it was all futile, but his mother's desire and the unflinching conviction that this meeting was going to do them good was so strong that he quietly endured the wait in the scorching sun. By the time their turn came, Nikhil was all sweaty and sleepy. All three of them prostrated themselves in front of the imposing personality of Baba Rudranand. Before Nikhil's parents could ask anything from their now revered Baba, particularly Nikhil's mother who was worried about her son's future in general and marriage particularly, Baba lifted Nikhil's face from his chin up and stared at him, contemplating on the lines of his forehead. Baba then closed his eyes, mumbled something, and brought his other hand on Nikhil's head and held it there, as if he was meditating on his skull. Nikhil's sleep and weariness were overtaken by his anxiety at the baba's strange behaviour. In fact suddenly the bored talks hushed and everybody around them fell silent. After what felt like a long time, Baba opened his eyes and looking at Nikhil, he said, 'A very good fortune awaits you, be ready when it comes. You are not meant to stay in this village.' Those were the only words he spoke to their family. Though they made Nikhil's parents happy, they wanted to hear more, more specifics. They were disappointed that whatever was said was so general that it was of hardly any importance. Nikhil's mother wanted to ask about Nikhil's bride, but she had to come home disappointed.

It was only Nikhil who was perfectly happy with the message. From then on, he started living in a dream state; he was convinced that he would not be staying in that village and a huge fortune awaited him someplace else. He just did not know yet where that someplace was. But all that was two summers back and nobody remembered the saint or what he said, except Nikhil.

Three days back, Nikhil's uncle had come from Pune to visit his father. Nikhil's uncle, Govindrao Shinde, was a wealthy man who owned acres of sugarcane farms in their village and many farmers to till those. He used to send the canes to many sugar factories in Maharashtra especially around the areas of Pune. Govindrao had visited his father to offer some money as loan after he came to know about their condition. Govindrao was his father's distant younger brother, and taking the money from him was stabbing Nikhil's father's self-respect. Nikhil's father's eyes were moist. He looked at his son and grumbled, 'See what it has come to when I have an able young man in the house.' Nikhil shamefully lowered his eyes, looked at his mother who was also silently crying. Nikhil walked out of the room, dabbing his eyes with the unwashed, greasy, pink piece of cloth that hung on his shoulder. It was not very usual of Nikhil's parents to take money till last few months, but then suddenly the yield coming from their farm had dropped, a few harsh seasons, and their condition had gone from bad to worse. Govindrao was the one to help them. But Govindrao was notorious; he recovered his money when people failed to return on time. Also, his interest was higher than other lenders. Nikhil's parents felt they had no option. There was, for a few minutes, an awkward silence after Nikhil walked out and both his parents sat quiet, their eyes travelling from each other to Govindrao to Nikhil, who had just walked out. Govindrao understood the situation from the sullen silence and took a cue. He cleared his throat loudly though there was hardly any problem there. He called Nikhil in his big thick voice. Nikhil came in and stood at the door, his face red with embarrassment. Govindrao gave out a 'humph' kind of grunt and gestured with raised eyebrows and a tilt of his neck to come and sit beside him. Nikhil felt his uncle Govindrao enjoyed this situation of theirs. Govindrao fished out a small dirty yellowish tobacco bag from a vest pocket. He rubbed the tobacco with white lime paste on his palm, taking all the time in the world. The rest of the three watched in silence the treatment of the tobacco on his palm as if it was of any big significance. Finally after the tobacco quid ended up behind Govindrao's thick lower lip, he looked at Nikhil, and gave out another sarcastic grunt as if making a mockery of Nikhil.

'Niphhill, listen,' he said and spat there across his shoulder a mouthful of red liquid, throwing few strands of tobacco around his own chin. Wiping his mouth with his left hand, he continued, 'I have good news for you. A job for you.'

Listening to this, there was an immediate fear in Nikhil's parents' eyes. They looked at each other; they felt that he would put Nikhil as one of his henchmen who collected money from non-payers. Since Nikhil was strong and swarthy, he was fit well for that role. Even though they were in bad financial condition, they did not want their son to be a goon. Govindrao ignored the emotions of his spectators. He was looking only at Nikhil, who was also focused on what he was being told. 'Nikhil, don't worry, the job is not here, not in this village, it is in Pune.'

As soon as Nikhil heard of Pune, his eyes widened and ears were all attentive. He knew he wanted to go out, he believed it would happen and finally this was it. He was already thanking in his mind his uncle and his god even before he got the job or understood anything about it. His mind was telling him that finally the prophecy would be true.

His uncle continued, 'Today, while coming from Pune, I met my old friend Vasantrao Deshmukh. He said his friend in Pune was looking for somebody to help him with running his shop, do bookkeeping and help him with general chores. Since it was a matter of money of an old man, he was looking for somebody who is honest and has a good heart. Your name did not strike me then, but now looking at you and see how useless you are, I think you will be a good choice for that job.'

It was a relief for Nikhil's parents but they were not very sure of Govindrao. Nikhil's father had travelled only once outside their village to a temple in a place called Jejuri, which was about fifty kilometres from Pune and he was nearly lost in the throngs of crowd there. That was his father's closest experience of Pune. He was worried his son too would get lost there. His son had no idea of how to survive outside the village and would probably be tromped on out there. He asked Govindrao, 'Govind *bhau*, will Nikhil be safe there?'

Nikhil's mother, who was sitting on the small platform of the door between the kitchen and their only room, stood up to join the conversation and said in a deeply choked voice, 'He is our only son, if anything happens to him, we will be left with no one. He might look big, but he is still just a boy. And you also know that he still has to get married.'

Govindrao looked at them and said in a stern voice, 'Eknathdada!' Not many people called Nikhil's father with his name; he was mostly called Appa by people. 'Eknathdada, this is the only chance for this rotten donkey to do something. You should be the first one to kick strong and hard on his backside if he does not agree to go! Look at him, he is bigger than most of the people around but is dumber and lazier than my buffalo. Push off this idiot, at least he will make an attempt and earn something good for you and himself. Do you want to see him rot his youth sitting here, doing nothing?' Then looking at Nikhil's mother, he said, 'Maybe he will also get proposal for marriage.'

Nikhil was already jumping in his mind at the prospect of going to Pune. Though he loved his parents, he wanted to get away from the village. He had been reciting every morning the line from Baba Rudranand that he was supposed to move out of that village. He also wanted to get away from the constant criticism, sarcasms, and failures. He was completely convinced Pune would be his land of karma.

A decision was made. The day he was supposed to leave, he was given a few details about how to reach Vasantrao Deshmukh. His mother gave him the best cloth bag that she had preserved on top of an old wooden cupboard where it wouldn't be accessible to most of the people. It was the same bag she had brought from her father's house when she was married. She tied a black thread around his neck and a dot of black kohl on the backside of his ear, a common practice of warding off any evils that might come upon her son. She put a bright red vermillion mark on his forehead, mumbling blessings. He touched his parents' feet and was on his way to dreams. The journey that started with a long walk, a bullock cart had a few buses to be changed till he reached Pune. Govindrao had guided him well; he was in an elevated mental state, so the apprehensions of changing so many buses and going to an unknown place, which was scary as per his father, was short-lived. The landing on the land of Pune, his dream place, was not like what he had imagined: that he would slowly step on the ground, feel it with closed eyes, then touch the soil with his fingers and apply it on his forehead as a mark of respect. He was pushed out of the bus by people behind him, and at the same time, there were many others trying to get in. The rickshaw drivers mobbed the passengers who had just alighted from the bus to take them for their last-mile drop. They fought amongst themselves for the prized passengers who wanted to go the farthest or the one who looked most gullible. But nobody flocked around Nikhil; looking at his state, the rickshaw drivers knew he was a person worth ignoring, which in a way was better for Nikhil. It gave him some time to look around the place after he was almost thrown off the bus. He had never imagined that there could be a place like the place he was standing. He was at Swargate, the main bus depot of Pune where every minute there were at least six to eight buses loading and unloading with throngs of people. The city had a distinctive smell of perspiration mixed with black exhaust from buses, and a tinge of overripened fruits. Probably there was a fruit seller nearby, he thought. There were lots of people walking all over the place, trying to reach somewhere in great urgency. Everybody wore nearly the same expression, which looked like it was a combination of hurriedness, anger, frustration, and readying to fight. Pune was far from what he had imagined. He understood why his father had never ventured there. Nevertheless his hopes were high.

He was on his search for a person called Vasantrao. When Govindrao had given him the address of Vasantrao, he had also inserted a few notes of tens to reach the address after he got down in the city. He was hungry, rather very hungry, but did not wish to use the money. The fruity smell a few minutes back had ignited the hunger in his guts. The food packed by his mother was already gone in his journey that ran through the last twenty-three hours.

He was desperate for some kind of help around. Finally a rickshaw driver, probably the unfortunate one who didn't manage to get any fat customer from the bus approached him, asking him where he wished to go. Nikhil was still in a state of overwhelmedness, intimidated by people around him. His slow, slouched walk, his lost expression gave him away. It was easy to spot a newcomer. He didn't say anything to the rickshaw driver; he pulled out the scrap of paper given to him by Govindrao very gingerly and showed it to him. The rickshaw driver scrunched his eyes, trying to decipher the bad handwriting of Govindrao. 'The place is far, it will be sixty rupees.' Sixty rupees! Nikhil could have an entire week's lunch with that much money! His entire journey from his home to Pune he had come to thirty-nine rupees and now just for going within the city, he was being asked for sixty rupees, and he knew he didn't have that much left in his pocket. But he knew without help, he would be lost. Tired and hungry as he was, the thought of taking another bus was unimaginable. He stood holding the bar of the rickshaw, and then gave a sad little pout, his eyes notched up their expression of how miserable the condition he was in, rousing as much sympathy he could. 'I don't have enough money; I only have forty-one rupees.' The rickshaw driver fell for those eyes; he gave a few local slang terms and said it was Nikhil's lucky day since he was already going in that direction. He could take him there for forty rupees, but to the exact destination he would have to walk something like a kilometre or so. Nikhil readily agreed and all his body thanked the rickshaw driver. He forgot forty rupees was all that he had left. For now, the comfort of sitting in that rickshaw and moving at that speed towards his destination was a pleasure. If you have enough money, you can have any pleasure of life, he thought. If he had the full sixty, he would have been dropped royally at Vasantrao's residence. But with this luxury of a few minutes, he was ready to walk another kilometre or so.

The rickshaw ride, he didn't forget for a long time. First time in Pune and sitting in a rickshaw in the first few minutes is certainly a daring act; it challenges the adrenalin control of your body. The rickshaw interior was a colour riot; the seat cover was glossy fluorescent green, the plastic flowers on both sides of the front bar covered with dust were miserable rose fakes, a red plastic cover on the rickshaw meter and both the inner seating walls had two film actors in extreme garish colours. The rickshaw tore through the traffic and Nikhil gripped the front bar with all his strength, and for most of the time, he kept his eyes closed. On the narrow, pothole-infested roads, packed with bikers, hawkers, and pedestrians all at the same time, the rickshaw zoomed through them as if they were in some city race. The engine sounded like a concrete mixer, and the brakes were so tight that at a few instances Nikhil thought he would be catapulted out of the front window. The driver smiled to himself once or twice when he saw the pale face of Nikhil in his rear-view mirror.

The rickshaw dropped him in what looked like one of the busiest areas of Pune. Nikhil gave him forty rupees, and the next instant, the rickshaw was already lost in the traffic. The last rupee that Nikhil was left with, he held for a few minutes.

There was a soft tap on his leg from behind. He saw two little kids begging. The elder one looked like she was eight years and she carried another boy on her, who looked to be around two years. Both of them with tattered clothes, weeping eyes stood before him with palms outstretched. Nikhil looked at them, pursed his lips, gave a sigh, and dropped one rupee coin in the girl's palm and walked away. The beggar kids stood there looking disappointed and unsatisfied, as if what were they going to do with just one rupee? If somebody has to give something, give something respectable, they thought.

Asking directions every ten or twenty steps, Nikhil walked for forty minutes on an empty stomach and finally stopped in front of an old building, which looked it could crumble any time. This is where Vasantrao's address brought him. Nikhil stood in front of the building, a little sad. Is this the place he was supposed to reach? Was this what the fortune teller had in mind? Did he leave the peace of the blissful village for this overly crowded, unpleasant, unfriendly place? He looked at the two-floor building, which looked like it needed paint at least ten years back, the dilapidated overhanging balcony, and the small room on the lower level which led to a narrow wooden staircase taking you somewhere up in the darkness. On either side, the building was flanked by similar-looking equally narrow and worse-looking buildings. That entire street was lined with many tiny shops. There were few shops in a gap of one-metre space between the buildings or pillars; people sat there with sewing machines and their hands and legs following a rhythm of the machine. There were people sitting on the road, selling some sparkly coloured sweets buzzing with flies. Many of those shops had small handwritten boards hanging. It was strange that people had to hang boards like that. PLEASE TENDER EXACT CHANGE, IF NOT, YOU WILL BE CHARGED 5 RS. EXTRA. PLEASE BE PATIENT. THE SHOP REMAINS CLOSE FROM 1:30 TO 4:30 PM—DO NOT BANG THE SHUTTER OF THE SHOP. DON'T ASK PRICES IF YOU DON'T INTENT TO BUY.

Nikhil wanted to do a final check before getting into that building. He asked the person in the shop on the left of the building if he knew Vasantrao. 'Up.' It was a quick and curt reply without looking towards Nikhil. Nikhil didn't understand what he said, and if it was said to him. Nikhil again asked the same question, slower this time, being as polite as he could be. This time the shop fellow looked at him; the rudeness in his eyes told Nikhil that he was wasting their time and he should have understood the first answer itself. Nikhil didn't ask any further question and hurriedly walked up the squeaky staircase, which had no banister, just a thick rope tied on the right side to function as banister. The staircase led him to a closed door, hardly visible in that darkness; though it was still afternoon. He knocked with the small stubby black chain that hung on the door once and waited. There was no answer for few minutes. On knocking the second time, there was loud shout from inside "Are you planning to break the door and rob the house? Can't you wait?'

A thin, baldish person, probably in his early seventies opened the door. He was wearing white pyjamas, had no shirt or vest, his chest smooth except for a few thin, twisted white hairs around his nipples and just above the pyjamas. This smooth chest was diagonally divided by a bunch of white threads, his religious symbol. A pale yellow round mark was on his forehead, and he held two incense sticks in his right hand. The way he looked through that pair of thick glasses at Nikhil, it was evident that he was not happy to be disturbed.

He looked at Nikhil's bag on his shoulders and said, 'We are not interested in buying soaps, pickles, or any such things. Nor do I have any change. Don't disturb people at this time, you should have read the board below. Now go.' The doors were closed before Nikhil could react. Nikhil wondered about the board he missed reading. He looked at his bag and thought if he really looked like a person who sold kitchen items. Because, though it was a rude remark, he was happy that he was not looking a poor naïve villager. He knocked again, gently this time. This time, Nikhil started speaking before the door was fully opened. 'I am looking for Shri Vasantrao Deshmukh. I have been sent by Govindrao from Dhanora.'

Vasantrao's frown mellowed; his brows, which he had knitted at the sight of Nikhil knocking again, came back to their original position and he opened the door, making way for Nikhil to come in. Inside the house, Nikhil realized it was very different from outside. The house was spic and span. Everything looked perfectly organized. It was a small room, not lighted enough and a bit overstuffed, but it was neat. There were racks of books placed one over the other, arranged according to their height and thickness. Most of them looked to be religious books in local language. There was a medium-sized TV set in front of the sofa, behind which, on the wall, there was a photo frame of Ganesha the elephant god, adorned with gold jewels. In the corner of the attached kitchen was a place made where a desk stood with multiple gods, and an oil lamp which was still burning, showing that the worship either just ended or was going on.

Nikhil's observation trance was broken by Vasantrao's announcement: 'My wife has gone to her parents' house and my kids don't stay with me. There is not much I can offer you to eat.' Vasantrao didn't feel the need to ask questions to Nikhil about how he felt or what he wanted. He was offered a glass of water, and Vasantrao walked out in his any-time-crumbling balcony and shouted for a boy on the road telling him to send up a cup of tea and vada pav, the Indian burger. The idea of vada pav and tea tantalized all his senses.

Vasantrao was quiet while Nikhil devoured the vada pav. After Nikhil looked a bit satiated, he told him that he could take rest for an hour and then they would go to his friend's place which will take about an hour by bus. It seemed to Nikhil, Vasantrao didn't like wasting any time. But the thought of travelling by bus again made Nikhil feel exhausted and beaten.

The bus journey this time was not as bad as Nikhil had imagined. It looked like they were going out of the town. They passed on their way the Pune army cantonment area. This area of the city was like a different world. The army cantonment had nicely trimmed hedges, lush green lawns, huge buildings, and models of fighter planes. The entire time, Nikhil kept looking out of the window like a five-year-old boy travelling with his father on a picnic. The bus took them out of the city area beyond the cantonment. It was a sign of relief for Nikhil, since the area looked more similar to his village. From the place they got down from bus, they walked for about ten minutes before they stopped in front of a huge house. Old, but huge. It looked pale, almost as if draped in a shroud of mourning. There were wild creepers all over the façade, which looked like it was begging for maintenance. The front had four pillars supporting the extended balcony, forming a kind of porch over the front gate. There were two rusted bicycles on the extreme right of the house, with all tires flat. The balcony was in solid wood, ornate with old Peshwari architecture. Nikhil and Vasantrao walked to the entrance and Vasantrao gently tapped the iron chain on the floral, spit-stained wooden door. On the left of the door, there was a nameplate, which was the only thing that looked shiny. It said 'G. P. Bhagwat', and below that, in small letters, it was 'B. Sc., M. Sc. Physics (Hons.)'. Vasantrao filled in the details for Nikhil: Ganesh Prashantrao Bhagwat. It took a few minutes before they heard some rustling from inside. The door was opened by a frail, slim and gentle looking man who looked in his late eighties. He wore white clean pyjamas and a sleeveless white vest, and was nearly bald except few clumps of thin white hair near the ears. Bifocals hung low on the bridge of his nose through which he peered at his guests. He was the first person Nikhil met after coming to Pune who smiled at him. The friendly smile on Ganesh's face lingered for a few seconds which was like a welcome message for Nikhil. It is usual in this part of the country that people call each other dada, especially when one of the persons is a bit elder. If the age difference is of a generation, then the elder one is called kaka, which actually is a way to address an uncle.

'Dada, he is the boy you were asking for,' said Vasantrao as he gestured to move in the house. Ganesh nodded and moved aside, holding the door to allow the guests in. Nikhil followed Vasantrao into the house. It was a big room with minimalistic things. The windowpanes were dark with a thick coat of dust hardly allowing sun in the room. There was a centre table and two-piece sofas, on the two sides of the centre table. Ganesh signalled them to sit on the sofas and he himself went in the kitchen, saying that he would bring some water for them. It took some time for him to be back with water; in the meanwhile, Nikhil's eyes were scanning the house. The corridor which was straight from the door they entered led to another room and continued to a door on the backside of the house. Both the front and back door were in a straight line. The back door was open and he could see the backyard. From what he could see through the open door, was an overgrown lawn and in the middle was a big cylindrical pot, which looked to be made from marble, yellow with age held a cactus-like plant. Instead of a stem, the leaves were grown from leaves. Though Nikhil was good at identifying plants, it took him few minutes of craning his neck and narrowing of eyes to recognize the plant. It was not a common plant, but he had seen it in his village with few wealthy people. The plant was called brahma kamal, which literally meant 'lotus of the supreme god' and also a night-lotus. It was not the original brahma kamal, which is supposedly found only in the Himalayas and gives flowers every twelve years, but this one in Ganesh's house gives flowers once every year. The flowers bloom on this plant late in the night after ten and wither away by morning. According to the popular belief, if you see it in its full bloom, then your wishes come true. It was an auspicious flower, and when it blooms, people worship it, though Nikhil himself had never seen this flower. His train of thought was broken when Ganesh returned with glasses of water.

Ganesh gestured Vasantrao to speak.

'Dada will pay you eight hundred rupees monthly and you have to stay here with him, look after all his needs, run the shop, in the evening serve him dinner, keep an eye on the maids who work here, and run all kinds of errands for him.'

Nikhil was not listening to anything that Vasantrao said. After hearing 'eight hundred rupees', his mind was shut off; for that much money, Nikhil was ready to do anything. He didn't need to be told any details. This was the amount his father managed to collect after a couple of months of toiling in the sun.

The kitchen was on the right side of the hall where they sat. Ganesh explained what to find where in the kitchen and then asked Nikhil to make tea for all of them. Nikhil had hardly ever made tea in his own home, other than few exceptional cases when his mother was not well. Suddenly the thought of his mother made him homesick. The thought that he was really far from his house, his parents would be toiling hard in the fields, going lower than what was needed for basic living so that they could pay Govindrao's loan, while he would be sitting in the comfort of a house miles away. He cursed himself that he never understood the sacrifices they made, he never understood or tried the language of his mother's eyes. His eyes welled up as he gazed beyond the walls of the kitchen. The tea would have boiled over and created a mess on his first task, had he not seen it just in the nick of time. He breathed thanks to his mom that the first-impression problem was averted.

He served the tea and they reciprocated him with their smile. Good beginning, he thought and again thanked his mother. Vasantrao told him he could get two leaves each month when he could go home and give money to his parents. Both Ganesh and Vasantrao then engaged in some small talk for a few minutes before Vasantrao left. Nikhil was intently observing this elderly gentleman with whom he was going to work, the way he spoke softly in hushed whispers.

After Vasantrao left, there was a silence of a few minutes. Ganesh gestured Nikhil to switch on the fan, showing him the switchboard on the wall next to the door. Nikhil had missed observing the overhead fan, which was nearly brownish black with the dust deposits. It seemed the so-called maids never really cleaned the house, except the everyday-usage things; there were coats of dust and lint everywhere. The fan started with a clear rhythm of tak-tak-tak, and then as it caught on the intended speed, it wobbled in all directions and looked like it would fall down any time. But it didn't bother Ganesh; in fact he looked relaxed with that gust of wind on his face. It was apparent that along with the breeze the sound was also relaxing for him.

Nikhil squatted on the mat in the centre of the room, with his back resting on the side of the sofa and made himself comfortable. Ganesh sat opposite to him on the sofa, leaning towards Nikhil. 'How old are you?' Ganesh started with small talk.

'Twenty-five.'

'Have you gone to study anything?'

'Yes, till tenth grade.'

'Are you married?'

'No.'

'Why not?'

Nikhil didn't speak. He kept looking at his toes.

'Good that you are not, you will not be asking for many leaves.' Ganesh gave a mild laugh at his own joke. 'What all can you do?'

A montage of sarcastic moments flashed in his mind, the ones he had been hearing for about two years now. 'Good-for-nothing', 'lazy donkey', and many other cuss words swarmed his mind. He had started from his village with lot of self-confidence but the first few hours in Pune had shaken most out of him. But he realized he didn't have a choice; he could not betray his parents, he could not go back, he could not prove the villagers right that he was actually a good-for-nothing piece. He had to do something for himself and his parents. He brushed away all his negative thoughts and aroused a new-found willpower and said, in a low but confident voice, 'Kaka, whatever you tell me to do.'

'Can you do *whatever* is the question,' Saying this, Ganesh got up, rubbing his palms on his pyjamas without bothering to hear Nikhil's answer. He walked to the adjacent room. Nikhil could hear the sound of somebody fiddling with utensils from the other room. After about ten to fifteen minutes of fiddling sounds, he heard the sound of a bell, the typical bell which is used for worshipping in Pune. Looking at the sunlight from the backyard, he could realize it was nearly dusk. From where he was sitting, he could see only the door of the room which was parallel to his position. He was not able to see anything inside the room.

It started getting darker. But Nikhil didn't get up from where he was sitting. He could see the flicker of light moving along with the sound of the bell, as a reflection on the door. He guessed it was the oil lamp which kaka must have lighted for the evening worship. After the bells stopped, Ganesh did not come out. As the darkness around grew, he could see the light of the oil lamp clearly from his position. Looking at the long quivering shadow of Ganesh on the opposite wall in the light of the oil lamp, Nikhil could guess that kaka was chanting on a rosary of beads. After nearly forty-five minutes, Ganesh appeared at the door of the other room and stood there watching Nikhil sitting in the same position he had left him. The half-lighted figure of Ganesh looked eerie. He spoke from where he stood. 'You know, I have been expecting you.'

This startled Nikhil a bit. It took a few moments to locate Ganesh's mouth; it seemed like a dark figure talking to him.

'We will not have electricity for the next two hours. It is usual here, from six thirty to eight thirty, there is an electricity cut. Then from five to ten in the morning and in the afternoon from one thirty to four. Every day.'

Nikhil had not noticed that the fan had stopped and there was no tak-tak-tak sound. He was lost in looking in the flickering shadow of Ganesh and missed noticing anything else. Only when Ganesh had walked to the door, he realized he was sitting in complete darkness other than the light of the oil lamp from the other room.

'The maid has cooked the food this afternoon and it's kept on the kitchen platform. She comes only once in the afternoon and cooks for both the times. Today we don't have enough for both of us, but we will share, you will not sleep all hungry.' While he spoke, he picked up a candle from the room where he was worshipping and lighted it.

'Take this candle, go to the kitchen, heat the food on the stove, and bring for both of us. There are three chapatis and some rice and dal. I am not very hungry, I will just eat rice and dal, you can have all the chapatis.'

While going to the kitchen, he peeked in the adjacent room and saw that the entire room was empty but for a huge ornate miniature wooden temple in the centre of the room. There was a mat made out of what looked like cheetah skin and there was an oil lamp with five wicks. There was sufficient light from that lamp. There were two incense sticks at the corner of the temple, and the fluid, smooth smoke from those sticks was highlighted in the oil lamp, giving a kind of supernatural look to that temple. Inside were many gods in silver. There were also a few photo frames inside the temple. Above the temple there was a big painting framed in heavy silver cast; it was of a woman's bust. An exquisite beauty, even in that oil lamp light he could see her dressed in a deep-green saree, her neck nearly covered with gold ornaments, a big nose ring with few pearls. The place where her thick black hair parted was dark-red vermilion, the sign of married women. A big round red mark on her forehead, kohl-lined perfect almond shaped eyes. It seemed the lady was almost real there. The frame had a garland of brown flowers running across, which indicated she was no more. There was something about the picture; he couldn't quite figure out what, but he felt something strange in him, looking at the picture. The hair at the nape of his neck stirred as he stood there looking at the lady in the green saree.

They had a quiet dinner. Nikhil liked the affable and gentle nature of Ganesh; he liked the food as well. The stay here would be okay, thought Nikhil, and the piece of his brain which agitated with apprehensions about Pune settled at the dinner.

Nikhil slept in the hall on a thin carpet. And Ganesh slept in the room with temple. He had carried his carpet and blanket into that room. Nikhil was extremely tired. After the bus journeys, he looked forward to getting some good sleep. Having a good rest would make his next day better, he knew that, but when he actually lay down, he was not sure if he would be able to sleep peacefully in those new surroundings. As he closed his eyes, everything he experienced in those two days swam before his eyes; his mind just wouldn't shut off. He again felt homesick. He missed his mother.

It must have been a few hours before Nikhil woke up. He felt he was hearing somebody speaking. He didn't fully get up but arched his neck back and forth in all directions to see who was speaking. The sound was not coming from the adjacent room. Was there anybody other than Ganesh in the house? He tried identifying the voice; the voice was very low like a whisper. It was distinctly Ganesh's voice, and it was coming from the direction of the backyard. Nikhil tried to understand the words but could not. He could not hear the voice of the other person Ganesh was talking to. The hushed tones echoing softly in that darkness seemed creepy. Who was Ganesh talking to? Was he a sleepwalker? Signs of senile dementia? Whatever it was, he was uneasy and scared. He lay down slowly, changed his position, and tried to sleep. But his mind was hardly able to shut off from the hushed whispers.

He had hardly got a few hours of sleep when he woke up with the sound of bells from the next room. It was around five thirty in the morning. He propped himself up and waited for a call from his master. It took around forty minutes and a few spurts of dozing in that sitting position for Nikhil before Ganesh came out. Ganesh had with two incense sticks in one of his hands, and with the other hand, slowly and smoothly he was directing the smoke in different directions of the room. While he did all this, he was chanting some Sanskrit slokas which Nikhil did not understand. Nikhil watched Ganesh as he went around the room and kitchen, and then he stood before the wooden staircase and directed the smoke to go up, which it was anyway going.

After that ritual, Ganesh came out of the temple room and sat before Nikhil. 'Nikhil, now that you start here, I want you to obey the rules of the house. If you don't comply, I will not give you any warning: you will have to go or face even worse punishment. Do you understand me?'

'Yes.' Though he did not understand what was the worse punishment he could be subjected to, but he dared not ask.

'First, you will wake up every day at five thirty in the morning. Take a bath with the water from the well in the backyard. I will be worshipping at that time; you will not disturb me. Make tea for us before six, with as little noise as possible. I don't like being disturbed during my worship.

'Second, the plant that you see in the backyard, you will not go near it. Never. Not under any circumstances, not for watering or any other thing.

'For the floor above, there is nothing up there, the maid comes at eight every morning to clean the house, I cannot follow her, so you will go up with her and ensure she does not touch anything other than cleaning the floor, I don't really care if other things are not dusted. Recently somebody touched things they were not supposed to and I did not like it and that is why you are here.

'You will go to the shop, which I will show you today and run it for me. Lunchtime is from one thirty to four thirty, in that time you may come for lunch and have a short nap. Close the shop at six thirty. Come back here and give me the day's money. You will enter the money in account books. Today is the seventh, so you will get money every seventh of the month, starting next month.

'The next room's door I never close, but nobody is supposed to enter. If somebody does, I will know.

'Come, I will show you the kitchen, the backyard, and the shop.'

While walking to the kitchen, Nikhil once again saw the room with the temple and imposing photo. Even this time around in the morning, the lady from the painting almost spoke to him. He wanted to ask who she was but thought it would be prudent to keep quiet. The backyard door opened to a small patch of land which had light grass, and in the middle of the land, there stood the plant of brahma kamal. There was no fence to mark the end of the end of Ganesh's property, but beyond what looked like a grass patch were big dense trees. The next-door neighbours were around three hundred metres away on the right side. The other side there was a small temple. On the left was a narrow well; a copper bucket hung there tied with a rope. A small copper jug was next to the bucket, and a thin cake of dark pink soap was stuck on another thin green-coloured one.

'For toilets, you can carry water in that and go at least fifty metres beyond these trees. The toilet here is only for me.' The container he showed for carrying water was an old plastic can of some unrecognizable paint. It was open and had a metal wire tied on the rim acting as a handle.

'Now take a bath, wash your clothes clean, and then make tea. Do not touch anything in the kitchen without having a bath.

'And the most important rule: keep a check on your curiosity, do not get into where you should not.'

Nikhil thought about the conversation he had heard last night. 'Yes,' he replied.

'Good, get clean, and I am waiting for my tea. Do it before the maid comes, after that we go to my shop.'

Nikhil guessed Ganesh might have worked for some government bureau, the kind of people who breathe in and out rules written in tiny fonts in a tattered book. Only they know where to find the book and which rule to impose; they lick their fingers, turn a few pages in their book of dos-and-don'ts rules and throw a rule on you which you had no idea about. Those people even wear the kind of thick glasses Ganesh was wearing.

He shivered bitterly as he took the bath in that cold water from the well, all the while thinking of what suddenly happened in the last three days, from the easy-going life in a village, he was now taking a bath in cold water drawn from a well at somebody else's house, with somebody who was imposing a set of rules more than his school headmaster had told him in his entire schooling life.

It was nearly eight when the maid arrived. The maid was swarthy, short, and looked like a fat matryoshka doll. She had a small bun of oily hair at the back of her head, a big red dot on her forehead, nearly round eyes, and buck teeth. She wore a bright red saree tied in the way typical women from villages do: one of the corners of the saree is tightly tucked behind, giving both the legs freedom of movement. She gave a warm smile to Ganesh when she walked in the house. She picked up the broom and a thin plastic board to collect the dirt and started walking around the hall. She was popularly called Lalu-maushi, Ganesh had told Nikhil.

'Today you start from the top floor,' Ganesh told her.

'Why, kaka? Let me do the usual.'

'Do as you are told, start from the floor up.'

'Huhn,' Lalu-maushi gave an irritated grunt and walked up the stairs.

'Go behind her and see that she keeps only to her business and you as well, or else I will know.'

Nikhil followed her up, wondering, 'If the old man knows everything, what am I doing here?'

The floor upstairs was one vast room. As soon as he got on the top floor, he again felt the hair on his nape stir, and a slight shiver. He looked behind to see if Ganesh followed, but there was no one— then why did he feel that he was being followed? There was a big, sad-looking, lonely double bed in the centre of the room, which faced the balcony seen from the front façade of the house. On the far end of the room were a few metal boxes. On top of them were many books in Marathi, English, Hindi, and Sanskrit. They were full of dust. Many books were on physics, a few were of philosophy, and a few seemed to be religious. Behind the bed, on the wall was a black-and-white photo, a big one, hanging a little oblique, in a cheap golden frame. Ganesh was in a black suit and a polka-dot tie, hair gelled and neatly combed, giving a wave over the forehead. He had thick black horn-rimmed spectacles. He looked a handsome young man. Beside him was the lady from the room below. She looked equally good in this black-and-white photo. Including the photo, the dirty fan that hung overhead, all the books, and nearly all the corners of the room were cobweb festooned.

'I don't like coming to this room,' Lalu-maushi said, startling Nikhil. 'And who are you?' she asked without any acknowledgement from Nikhil about her dislikes.

'I am going to stay with kaka, my name is Nikhil.'

'Oh, very well! Exploit poor people like us! Kaka is bringing more people but will not increase my pay by a single cent! I have to sweep and mop and clean, even make his food and now for two people, but still the old man will not give me more money. Where is he going to take everything?'

Nikhil didn't bother to respond to that.

There were a few books at the bedside, most of them in Marathi. *Beyond Life and Death*, *The Ever-Seeking Soul*, *In the Realm of the Undead* were some of the titles he could read without touching or moving anything there. There was a notebook and a pen besides the notebooks but Nikhil dare not touch any of those. He was watching as Lalu-maushi swept, hardly touching the broom to the floor. She completed her sweeping the room in about five to six minutes and then mopped with a dirty tattered brown cloth in the next five minutes. As they walked down the stairs, Nikhil followed her. It happened again. He felt there was somebody behind him, somebody following him. He turned sharply. There was nothing. His heart jumped a beat and he felt a twitch in his limbs. He felt in him there was something, something that followed him up there and now was behind him.

Later Ganesh took Nikhil to his small shop, crammed from floor to ceiling with hundreds of petty items, leaving just enough space for one person to sit. It had everything that a person could possibly need if he was staying around that place: multicoloured soaps, flour, quick food, brightly coloured candies, incense sticks, local cigarettes, cheap drinks, stove pins, yellow-white cotton bales, and many other household stuff packed in that dingy space.

Ganesh took two hours explaining to Nikhil how the shop was run. More rules, more guidelines. Nikhil was attentive like a schoolboy who wanted to prove the bullies of the class that they could never touch him in academics.

The day was exhausting for Nikhil, mentally and physically. Too much focus on too many things. Sleep deprived. He was already asleep before Ganesh finished his ritual in the next room. It must have been a few hours of sleep, and again the faint murmur in the middle of the night started as the night before. It was completely dark. The fan overhead rattled incessantly like a background noise, tak-tak-tak, it went on. But that didn't disturb him; what disturbed him were the eerie hushed whispers coming from the direction of the corridor. The cold gust of air meant the back door was open. He forced the side of his palm into his mouth and bit himself hard, to stop him from making even the smallest of whimpers. The last thing he wanted was to attract the attention of Ganesh or anybody Ganesh was talking to. He suddenly felt thirsty, his throat contracted, and he felt a hard throbbing in his chest. He wanted to get up and drink water. But he knew he wouldn't. He wanted to get up and see with whom was Ganesh speaking, but he left that for some other night. He wouldn't take a chance, not tonight. The instinct of self-preservation told him not to get involved in that, not now, just stay put. After all, Ganesh was an old man, they tend to become senile at some point in time, maybe he was just talking to himself; maybe he had this problem of sleepwalking. Nikhil tried reasoning his impotency to get up and see what the whispering was all about. The fact was, whatever it was, the old man was freaking him out. He lay awake, dismayed at what kind of place he landed in. Why this place of all the places in Pune? Should he just walk out the next morning and go back to his old life? That would bring a lot of shame to him and he wouldn't be able to face his parents. Why, why here? Maybe he should talk to Ganesh the next morning. Yes, that was what he should do. He lay awake, with his eyes wide open, looking at the fan overhead, realizing it was still doing its bit, tak-tak-tak. Gradually, without him realizing, he fell asleep, to be woken up in a few hours, by the morning bells from the next room and the strong smell of incense sticks.

He followed the morning regime: bath, tea, and Lalu-maushi. Just before going to the shop, Nikhil gathered some courage and broached the topic of his hearing at night, acting as casual as he could. He didn't want to show that Ganesh's night avatar was freaking him out. But his chalk-pale face betrayed him. It was clear that he was trembling with anxiety. He stammered as he said, 'Ka-k-kaka, I heard somebody speaking last night . . .'

Ganesh looked at him and his genial expression changed to a frown. He was silent, clearly uneasy. And then he looked away from Nikhil, pursing his lips tight and the frown going a degree north, accentuating all the wrinkles on his face.

'I . . . didn't mean to . . . kaka . . .' Nikhil started justifying.

Ganesh got up sharply, more sharply than his body usually allowed, walked till the door of the temple room, and stood there. Then turning back, he said, 'Get ready, we should not be late to reach the shop. And remember what I told you when we met, don't get into places where you should not. Nothing bothers you as long as you don't bother it. Do what you are told to do and you will be happy.'

'Yes, kaka.'

'Don't bother *it*? What was *it*? Nikhil kept on thinking while they walked to the shop. At the shop though, in a few hours he forgot about it and got busy tending to the customers.

As long as the light lasted, everything was okay, everything was comfortable. But as the dusk settled and gave way to darkness, Nikhil started getting edgy. At the dinner, hardly anybody spoke. Ganesh tried having eye contact with Nikhil a couple of times, but Nikhil deliberately avoided. The anticipation of sleeping again in that big hall, waking up in the middle of the night, the hushed whispers softly bouncing in the darkness, was getting on his nervous. Ganesh finished the dinner and quietly got up, washed his hands, and retired to his temple room.

That night nothing happened; probably Nikhil was too tired to wake up with some whispers. He was smiling when he got up at five thirty the next morning. Finally he got the sleep he was looking for. The day went better than the last two.

A few days passed. Some nights he woke up and heard those whispers, some nights he didn't. He convinced himself that Ganesh probably talked in his sleep and there was nothing really so scary about it, though he still felt different vibes whenever he went on the floor above. He felt somebody was watching him in that house, always. Probably what Ganesh had said, 'I will know if you do something you should not', had an element of truth in it. But slowly Nikhil was becoming adjusted to all those things. Weeks passed and so did months.

Nikhil worked sincerely for Ganesh. No complaints, no extra demands, never poking his nose in matters which did not concern him. The house looked neat and clean. Both Ganesh and Nikhil got food on time. The shop ran well. The regular customers at the shop had got used to seeing Nikhil and they were getting comfortable with him. There were days when Lalu-maushi chattered incessantly and there were days when she would be completely silent. In both cases, Nikhil hardly acknowledged her. She used to say, 'Our Ganesh sahib does not have a right frame of mind. People around say that he has gone crazy after his wife's death. He can die any day. God only knows what will happen to this house. Do you know anything about this?'

Through all these months, the nightly murmurs continued. Some nights Nikhil would get up feeling disturbed; on a few nights, he would sleep through. It was not a concern any more, but curious, yes. Though Nikhil never asked Ganesh again about it nor showed any signs that he actually wanted to understand what he spoke about. There were a few nights when the voice was a little more audible than the rest of the nights. And he realized it was not like a person speaking in sleep, it was more like a conversation. It had its little ha has and oohs. He knew people hallucinate, especially after some tragic event in life. What Lalu-maushi said about Ganesh being crazy must have been linked to his hallucinating. Maybe Ganesh talked with his deceased wife, hallucinating her. He had got used to the time that Ganesh would walk out of his room, pass the corridor, and open the backyard door. He would stay out for around thirty minutes or so and then come in. Nikhil had by now timed everything without getting up from his place.

Nikhil's job in Pune had changed his image in Dhanora. His parents had been also happy. His pay from Ganesh was helping his parents back home. Changes happened quickly. Nikhil was married to a daughter of his father's friend. Nikhil had taken only two days of extra leave from Ganesh for his marriage; it was not that Ganesh would have denied him a few more days off, but he did not want to stay now in the village. Leaving his newly-wed bride with his parents, Nikhil had returned to Pune. Every time he went back to his village, he would take a saree or something from Pune for his wife.

It was the time of late August. That night it rained heavily, which was not new to Pune; mid-August to mid–September, heavy showers in the night were usual. Nikhil heard Ganesh walking out. Nikhil folded his legs and pressed the end of the blanket under his feet, adjusting his body to the cosy parts on his mattress. He wondered what drove that old man to get up in middle of the night and walk in the rains. It was a torture, insanity! What was he subjecting himself to? He felt a wave of pity for that frail old man. He nearly ripped off his blanket to get up and walk up to Ganesh and stop him. But he didn't. The thought just stayed as a desire; he didn't know how Ganesh would react. It was okay till now, leaving him to what he was doing; probably it would stay that way.

That night he didn't hear any whispers, only the pelting rain. The smell of the drinking earth was sharp that night. But there was that night another smell: sweet, scented, distinctively different. Twenty, thirty minutes passed and he heard Ganesh's steps coming back. He didn't hear the bolting of the door yet. There was a mighty sound of a thunderclap and a gust of wind accompanied by a loud sound of the back door banging on the wall, followed by the sound of a fall and a shrill cry. Nikhil was awake; he bolted immediately to Ganesh.

He saw Ganesh sprawled on the floor, near the door. He probably was not able to control the force with which the door flung open or he slipped. He was lying face up, legs folded clumsily, hands spread on both sides, completely drenched. He was forming a pool of water around him. Nikhil switched on the light, just to realize that it was a little before the electricity-shedding hour started. He sat down and slowly, carefully supported his head from behind with one hand, and with other, he helped Ganesh to sit against the wall. In that darkness, he felt the dark liquid with the tips of his fingers, but he was unable to decide if it was his blood mixed with water or it was just his soaked head. Nikhil steadied Ganesh and walked into the temple room to get the candle. In the temple room, there was light in a corner of the room near the temple, beneath the imposing frame, from the oil lamp. In the pale light, Nikhil locked his eyes with the lady in the frame. He saw the frame nearly daily while passing from the corridor, but right now it looked different; he didn't know what, but it was different. Nikhil picked up the candle, still looking at those piercing eyes, and just to light the candle, he momentarily took his eyes off and he felt the stirring at his nape and a faint sound as if somebody gave a soft sigh behind his ear. Suddenly overhead the thunder gave a deafening roar startling Nikhil. Nikhil quickly came out of the room to Ganesh, but just before he came out, he thought he realized what was different of the picture of the lady in the frame. She was probably smiling more than usual.

Ganesh was sitting as he had left him, head tilted on side, water still dripping from his head over his brows, nose tip, and chin. Without his glasses, he looked different with those bulging eyes and thick blackish brown bags under each one. Near the door, Nikhil saw Ganesh's glasses, with one of the lenses cracked diagonally. He picked it up and gave it to Ganesh. Then with one hand under Ganesh's armpit, Nikhil gently made Ganesh stand. Carrying the candle in his other, he slowly walked towards the hall; he knew he would have to cross the temple room. He didn't wish to go back in that room, not that night. But he knew Ganesh would want to go back there, to his sanctum sanctorum.

He turned back to see that he forgot to bolt the back door, and he paused a minute, looking over his shoulder at the open door. Just then a blinding flash leapt out of the black clouds, followed by a sharp peal of thunder crackling above the house. And in that momentary flash, Nikhil saw the brahma kamal, with a ghostly white full-bloomed lotus-like flower, swaying in that rain and wind. A gust of wind wafted its sweet smell and took off the light from the candle. His nerves jerked and his limbs twitched violently with a strong shudder that travelled from his head to toe. Ganesh looked at Nikhil and now took the support of the other hand as the candle was extinguished anyway.

As they came across the door of the temple room, Ganesh gestured Nikhil to take him there. Ganesh sensed Nikhil's reluctance and moved a step ahead and took support of the door frame and walked in by himself and sat down against the wall facing the frame of the lady, staring intently at it. Nikhil sat beside him, and with both hands, he examined Ganesh's head to see if there was any injury. There was no blood, though he had a large swelling on the back side. But Ganesh didn't look in any pain. He looked lost though. In the next few minutes, Nikhil wiped Ganesh and changed his clothes with dry ones. Ganesh meekly subjected himself to the extra care without saying anything. Nikhil then made hot tea without milk and with a few strong herbs and spices and brought it for him. Ganesh's expressions thanked him. Both of them sat silently in that room. Ganesh was sipping his tea, gazing at the frame on the opposite wall. Nikhil all the while avoided looking at it.

'I knew you would come, that you would help me . . .' Ganesh said, looking at Nikhil, smiling and kept his hand, now warm after holding the cup of tea on Nikhil's knee, and lightly squeezed as if reassuring his gratitude. Nikhil pursed his lips and nodded. 'And I didn't mean now,' Ganesh continued.

'Fortunately, it looks like your fall was cushioned. You are hurt but not very bad.' Nikhil changed the subject; the gratitude mood was getting a little embarrassing for him.

Just then the electricity was back and Nikhil had left the switch on. He saw Ganesh's face clearly in that yellow tungsten light. The face had a subtle smirk and peaceful eyes. His hands were shivering, as he held the cup of the tea and took small sips.

'What are you smiling at?' Nikhil could not resist asking.

'It is time, Nikhil. It is time as she said. I did not know what way it would come, but it has come.'

Nikhil understood what Ganesh was speaking about. 'It will come when it has to, for now take it easy on yourself and catch a good sleep.'

Ganesh liked the kind of understanding Nikhil showed. 'Yes, right, Nikhil, things happen when they are supposed to happen. I have discovered my wait is over. My so-called soul has made a decision to cross the line. Whatever I do, or think, or anybody else does, it is not going to change that. Exactly like she told me.'

'You want me to ask you who she is, right?'

Ganesh looked askance at Nikhil and smiled.

'How about we do it tomorrow morning at breakfast? I would like to know who she is,' Nikhil said and got up, gesturing Ganesh to his small makeshift bed in that room.

Ganesh stretched his hand from the position he was sitting in and held Nikhil's hand and looked expectantly at him. 'I may not get another chance, sit here.'

Nikhil gave a light sigh and sat beside him.

Ganesh smiled, 'I am at the stage where I don't care what you think of me, delusional, lunatic, or whatever. In fact I never really cared about what people thought of me. All our lives we keep on thinking we are bodies made of cells which obey the laws of physics, then we learn it may be more of mind or a combination of chemical reactions on the carbon tissues conceiving thoughts. It is only at the time of death or being very close to it, we find out who we really are.' Ganesh paused as if allowing Nikhil to understand that he had made a profound statement. He gulped down the remaining tea and set aside the cup.

'She is Kamala, my wife,' he said, pointing to her photo. 'See how beautiful she is . . .' His entire face smiled as he said that. Nikhil made himself comfortable in the corner beside Ganesh, waiting for the story. He observed Ganesh, the old frail man with boyishly gleaming eyes in those cracked spectacles, white thin strands of hair growing here and there on the otherwise bald scalp, staring at something he loved. There was a lot of beauty in those moments and Nikhil felt a compelling wave of love rise in his chest for this old man.

'I talk to her.'

'I guess I know about that.'

'You guess you know?'

'Yeah, I hear your voice every night. I didn't know you talked to her—I just felt you spoke in your sleep.'

Ganesh smiled mildly scoffing at him. 'You don't know anything, Nikhil.'

'Tell me then,' he replied, with the curiosity of a kid to hear a story.

'I can talk to her whenever I want, but I choose this time. Middle of the night, the time is very personal. Under the blanket of silence, it's just me and her. I knew you would not sneak up on me. I had that confidence in you. After the day's work, I go to her and talk about the day, just as we used to when she was still living. It is only few hours later now, I allow the world around me to sleep.

'She knows everything about you,' he said, looking at Nikhil and Nikhil smiled back at him.

'Nikhil, sixty years back when the society was not very accepting, they said I made a mistake. The mistake of falling in love. I fell madly, crazily in love with a girl in our neighbourhood. And with a few theatrics, I won her heart. How enchanting were those days . . .' His voice tapered and choked and stayed silent for few minutes. He slowly closed his flooded eyes, draining out the tears he didn't bother to wipe. Nikhil went in the kitchen and brought him a glass of water. He took a sip, took a long breath, gave the sad sigh of a helpless man, and got back to his story.

'Nikhil, in this senility, I forget every little thing, but not what happened so many years back. How I held her soft velvety hands, her eyes capturing the sunlight, and her giggles like the sweet jingling sounds of tiny bells. She used to curl her dangling tendril on her finger before tucking it behind her ear. She used to turn red, real red, Nikhil, the red of roses when she blushed, or even when she sneezed. We used to meet further away from our houses, behind an old school so that nobody would know about our secret love. Those were the days, the days of pure bliss; I should have died with those as my final moments . . .'

'Kaka, you were so romantic!'

'Ha ha, yes. But as it happens in movies, we were caught by her uncle. I was twenty-something and she must have been around sixteen. Either side of the parents was not ready for us to tie the knot. So we did what young lovers do.' He wanted Nikhil to ask what and Nikhil obliged.

'What did you do, kaka?'

'We ran off!' Nikhil was seeing how happy Ganesh was as he recounted his story.

'We came to Pune, got married. Life was simple and full of love. Getting a job in school was easy, so the food and water were taken care of, a temporary shack was used till we saved enough money and got this house made.'

'Nobody from your families hunted you down?'

'No, it was not really that movie-ish. They didn't care to find us out after we ran off, nor did we contact them and they are not important for our story.

'I made decent money then. This house was our dream home. It was far from the city, but with our savings, this was the place we could actually make a house for ourselves. Each little thing in this house has our love, our hopes, and our dreams that we wove together.'

Another stream of tears ran down Ganesh's face. He lifted his glasses and squeezed his eyes with his fingers.

'We used to spend most of our time in the room above. It was a glorious and luxurious room by our standards. She decorated each little thing thoughtfully there. In the evenings, after I came back from school, I used to read her books and at times even teach her physics. Time was on our side, Nikhil, and when you have time with you, nothing ever goes wrong. Everything that we did together, we loved it: whether it was her cooking experiment or the walls in this house we painted or songs those we sang together. The best thing was we never realized how short life was for us together, it was a blessing because we never worried about being separated.'

Ganesh took the support of the wall and gingerly stood up, popping his knees. He walked to her painting and moved his fingers tenderly over her face as if touching her. 'Nothing matters when I am with her. My soul's sole purpose is very clear, it is to love her. In life or beyond . . .'

Nikhil noted the usage of present tense but he did not question it, nor did he probe Ganesh on his remark about life and beyond.

Ganesh turned around and looked at Nikhil. His expression juggled between being sad and nostalgic. 'She left this mortal world during her first pregnancy. I had made up my mind that there was no meaning to life without her, the purpose of my life was done and it will be forsaken in absence of her at my side. After the midwives who were tending to my wife left to inform a few elders and friends about Kamala's death, I was alone for some time in the house. I brought out a knife to slash my wrists. I was about to commit the sin when I heard her voice, soft and gentle as always. I thought that my mind was playing tricks on me, but the state of illusion, the state of madness in which I would have her was far more acceptable than anything else. Even if it meant I was conjuring her with my imagination, I was okay as long as I could see her, speak to her, and the best would be if I could touch her. I saw her standing in front of me, in her deep green saree, which you see in this painting. She looked sad. I saw her body covered with a white sheet having bloodstains. She also looked towards herself with a look as if trying to say she failed in her responsibility. I fell on my knees and started begging to take me with her. The world was not liveable without her.

'"It is not time for you yet to be on this side."

'"There cannot be any time without you here."

'"You are not the only one alone. If you leave your side now, maybe we will not meet, and it might turn out to be bad for us. Please don't break the law of the universe. I will wait for you, for whatever time it takes. I will be there with you whenever you need me."

'Before I could ask her anything, people from the neighbourhood started pouring in. Kamala's image diffused in the background. People were hugging me and consoling me, without giving a thought if I appreciated that. My brain was smoky, unable to grasp the reality. What had happened? Did I actually see her, or indeed was it my imagination? A few women came in, held me by my arm, and gestured me to go outside the room till they cleaned Kamala's body. I don't think anybody cared to understand what was going on in my mind. Suddenly there were so many people around me when I wanted to be alone. People I don't recall talking to ever were mourning for Kamala in my house. The cremation was as if their responsibility, people started making arrangements, and before I knew, I was back at home with her ashes.'

Ganesh paused as a professional raconteur allowing Nikhil to visualize his story.

'It was utterly lonely without her, Nikhil, I missed her. The house which was alive with us, which breathed in fresh love every morning had died with her. Everything around me, the tables, the chairs, the kitchen utensils, including the walls, seemed to miss her, mourn her. I sat with the urn of her ashes on the steps of the backyard. Hoping, I would go into that delusional state and start speaking to her. I was desperate for that state of madness. She loved our home, and this would be the best place to spread her ashes, better than the Ganges. This is where I want her to be. I opened the urn and dug my fist in that partially coarse and somewhat smooth ash and spread it in the backyard. It was against the tradition, but that was the least thing I cared about.'

'For the next thirteen days, there were people coming to our home. A few elders even slept here. There were many devotional songs being sung. Nobody asked me for permission, it was a given that those were rituals and should be done. I didn't like any of those, but I didn't deny anyone what they were doing. I had found my space in that crowd for myself in my own home. I just wanted to talk to her again, and nothing else mattered. I was not even in a complete state of mourning and that puzzled people. In fact, it irritated a few. They wanted to see me bellowing my lungs out, they wanted the pleasure of consoling me. They didn't like the curious and stolid expression I wore instead of bereavement. Some people had started talking about whom I would be marrying next!'

He smiled as he said the last sentence. Nikhil was patient with the story, no questions asked, just nodding of the head, and eyes that encouraged Ganesh to continue, to tell more about him and Kamala.

'For me the changes were so much in so little time that all of it felt like watching a movie—a fugue state of some kind, a feeling that I am not part of what is happening, though sadly, the reality was that I was the only part that was left of the story. Thankfully after those thirteen days, nobody came. The ritual was done; people were back to their lives. I was alone this time, all alone. I started going to school. I used to get this uneasy feeling that when I was away, the house was empty, standing still, silent, walls staring at each other. If I was late, the house would be dark, completely dark with nobody waiting.

'I wanted to contact her. I had decided, was ready to go for whatever it took. I consulted a few pundits who were supposedly reputed in this arena of contacting the departed. And it was a disappointment. Tried reading few books on this subject, but again it turned out to be a disappointment. I had nearly lost all my hopes. On one of those nights, I was sitting on the doorstep of the backyard, lost in my thoughts when something disturbed me. I realized it was a smell, mild in the beginning and then it grew stronger. It was not just some smell, it was intoxicatingly good. I looked around and saw a beautiful white flower had bloomed in middle of the backyard. It was as if it emitted light, a calm moonlight. Lotus-like, with papery thin fragile petals with a pale yellowish-pinkish core. Something so divine, so tender, that it made me forget all my weariness of life for few moments. I came to know much later that it is called brahma kamal or the white lotus and that it flowers very rarely. The plant must have grown in the days I was lamenting, though I don't recall seeing it before that moment. I had a strong feeling that somehow it was linked to Kamala, her ashes I had spread in the garden and the white flower was her symbolic presence near me.

'I went near the flower and touched it. I asked aloud if she was around. No reply. I again asked the same question. Silence. Not even the wind whispered. Third time, I had tears in my eyes and asked her to reply if she was around. I was so convinced that she was there and was not replying to me. This time there was a faint sound of some distant rustle, in a few seconds, those which followed were louder. And then I heard the sound which I was dying to listen to. It was her voice! Though it was at the beginning as if coming from afar with a bit of electrical resonance, it was clear and in a few seconds it was as if she was standing just beside me. She said if I believed she was there, she would be there. And I believed, every muscle fibre in my heart believed that she was there.'

Something stirred in Nikhil; he didn't like the place the conversation was going. The innocent senile romantic story was now bordering on horror. The old man was converting his autobiography into a spooky story. Nikhil looked around. Was there was some rustling in the far corner of the room? Kamala's huge photo, imposing in that room, looked creepy; her eyes were staring at both of them as if listening to the conversation. And Ganesh's eyes looked absent, lifeless, lost; it was only the body recounting a story, the soul was somewhere else, probably in some other time.

'You know what, get some sleep, and let us talk tomorrow morning,' Nikhil said. But Ganesh didn't hear or acted not to listen. He continued his story.

'I believed she was there, rather I knew she was there. I don't know what the life of this plant is, but I can see that this one is living since many years, since that time. Of course, I take good care of it. Since that time, I have never travelled out of Pune so that I don't miss taking care of it. Talking to her every night brought the peace that I was looking for. I left teaching in school, I opened a little shop which you look after now, since gradually my attachment to all these material things started fading out. I realized that death is not what we perceive it is.

I was able to connect to Kamala any time I wished at the speed of my thoughts. I never stopped loving her because of a change in the form of her existence. The experience of talking to her was like a meditation for me, it was taking me to higher spiritual levels, my desires and needs started dropping. I knew that I had to hang on in this body till the right time comes, so only what was needed by to live was continued by me.'

Nikhil looked at him in disbelief. What went on behind those slightly bulging, puffy eyes? The man sitting next to him had spent nearly an entire life for love, without a real physical companion! Was this love or insanity? He suddenly felt small, the feeling that happens in the deep recesses of the chest; he would probably never experience, never the way this frail old man experienced each day. The rationality of the story was not important any more, maybe Ganesh was conjuring up everything in his mind, the deep setback of his wife dying had driven him nuts, but to live a lifetime like this old man, you had to be deeply, madly in love with somebody.

'Does she . . . she, I mean . . . does she talk back, reply to you like we are talking right now? Or it is more like only you talking to her?' Nikhil asked, immediately feeling stupid for asking it.

'You mean to ask me if she gave me any proof or I just imagined and kept on talking alone to a plant? You think that I am an idiot, suffering from hallucinations, an effect of deep psychological trauma?'

'No . . . I am not judging you . . . and I don't understand psychological trauma . . . they are not words in my dictionary. I just ask because . . . I just felt like asking. You don't have to answer it.'

Ganesh smiled without looking at Nikhil.

'Look at this, I was a physics teacher, I did not believe in afterlife, souls, or ghosts. And this is the precise problem, the way we the living have made assumptions about death and afterlife, its association with ghosts, judgment days, and most of all, the way we understand fear. Some concepts, Nikhil, are experiential, and I cannot explain to you anything beyond. I don't know what the exact truth is, but I know what I feel. My body feels her presence, her aura, her being there listening to me and many times answering the questions I asked with the language which many times did not have voice or words. Nikhil, I am a man of science. But at some point in life, you realize that many truths you were taught, the knowledge you gained by reading or listening are just a bunch of words to shroud your brain from exploring the real things. We walk on this narrow strip of so-called convenient truth, maintaining balance all our lives with a fear that falling off would hurl us into a deep expanse of irrationality, an illogical and unscientific chasm. We live and die in this pretence, and worse, we propagate it to our next generation. Whereas truth is all around us, engulfing us from all sides but, Nikhil, we just turn blind eyes to it, because somebody taught us that it is illogical, unscientific. Just have to stop following what is taught to you and start believing in what you feel. The truth will find you, Nikhil, it will find you.'

For a few minutes after, both of them sat in silence. Ganesh had slouched back against the wall and Nikhil sat beside him. Ganesh was staring beyond the photo of Kamala, and Nikhil was looking at Ganesh.

'What are you gaping at?' Ganesh asked.

'I did not understand everything, but that is okay since I have to experience to know it!' Nikhil joked.

Ganesh didn't find that joke funny; his expression didn't change. He was still gazing beyond the photo.

'Every night I go to sleep thinking it will be my last night in this place, in this form, in this prison. But life was not so kind. Every morning I get up to pick up strands of my life and live another day without her. It has been a long painful struggle, and I have endured it like a brave warrior, but not anymore, thankfully.'

'You are wonderful, kaka, but may I ask, why do you say no struggle anymore? I know how tormenting it is for you but we don't control our lives,' Nikhil said and brought both his palms on Ganesh's knees, gently squeezing them and trying to look in his eyes.

This time, Ganesh gave a slight smile, looked in Nikhil's eyes, and they were not really so sad. He brought his hand to Nikhil's shoulder and held him there for a few minutes.

'She said, today we meet.'

'Kaka, what does that mean?'

'That my job is done, my wait is over, and it is time.'

Though his voice was getting weaker, bliss was spreading on his face as if finally the dark clouds were uncovering the moonlit sky.

'She told me this, and it will be true. She said I spent my life well. Nikhil, she said I spent my life well!' Ganesh was becoming excited like a kid whom his mom promised to take him to his favourite circus.

'Listen carefully, Nikhil, after I'm not around, I want you to check my drawers on the floor above. I have something for you.'

'Kaka, you are okay, it is not so bad. I know you may not like to hear this, but for this injury you will survive.'

Ganesh smiled and said, 'Nikhil, the time has come, and I know it, I can feel it nearing. How exactly will I go, I don't know, but I *will* go. I also know that the best thing to do is to leave this ageing machine peacefully.'

It was about early morning by then. Both sat silent for long. Nikhil wondered if finally Ganesh fell asleep. But just when he was about to hold him by the shoulder and slowly lower him onto his mattress, Ganesh woke up.

'Nikhil, to have you in our lives was nothing but happiness. I bless you, my child, bless you. You will have a good life ahead and will receive a lot of love . . .' Ganesh said in a groggy voice just before going back to his sleep.

Nikhil noted the words Ganesh chose for his blessing: 'To have you in our life' and not his life.

Next day, the local doctor declared Ganesh dead of a heavy internal haemorrhage.

Nikhil did the last rites for Ganesh as per Hindu tradition, as a son would do since there was nobody else. It was late evening by the time he came back to the house. The house somehow knew that its master would not come anymore. First time the house must've have felt so empty. Nikhil's hand was shaking as he opened the house. The door opened into a dark and lonely room. He didn't feel like going in. He stood there on the threshold of the door for a long time, till his shadow merged with the darkness of the room. He gave a long mournful sigh and walked in. He stood there in middle of the room with the main door closing behind and enveloping him in the darkness. He thought about the frail frame of Ganesh in his thin white top and pyjamas, his wrinkled face and his absent eyes behind those thick glasses. The realization that he would never see him again made his eyes wet. He slowly walked to the backyard and sat on the steps for a few minutes looking at the brahma kamal. He spread Ganesh's ashes in the backyard, more around the brahma kamal. He knew this was what Ganesh would have liked to be done.

The electricity would be cut off any moment and he wanted to check the drawer Ganesh had told him about and leave this house forever. He climbed the rickety stairs to the floor above and looked around. It wore the same expression as rooms below, lonely, dark, and mourning. He found the drawer he was looking for and rummaged through it. He found some old photos of Ganesh and Kamala; both of them looked vintage. Both their last remains were part of the backyard now, he thought. There was a light green envelope in the drawer which held just his name in capital letters. The envelope contained a will: 'Will of Ganesh Prashantrao Bhagwat'. He had transferred all his property, including the shop, in Nikhil's name. It was done on a legal stamp paper with signatures of lawyers and witnesses. The witnesses were surprisingly Mrs and Mr Vasantrao Deshmukh. Nikhil was wondering when Ganesh would have done all this since there were few times when Nikhil had taken leave. As Nikhil read further, he noted something and his brows shot up and his eyes were wide as saucers. He read and reread what he saw; the paper slipped from his hands and he stood there motionless for a few moments.

The date on the will was two years before Nikhil had met Ganesh!

After the initial shock, he told himself that maybe the year in the date was a misprint. But he knew that the chance of getting a date incorrect in a will was highly unlikely. Nikhil folded the paper back in the envelope and came down in that empty house, the house which he thought gave a palpable feeling of missing its master. He walked to the temple room. He stood in the doorway, gazing at the portrait of Kamala, imagining how Ganesh and Kamala must have been united. If at all what Ganesh said was true, they must be happy and watching him standing there. This thought gave him a shudder. He could feel goosebumps all over his hands. He was lost in his thoughts, thinking about life after death. Were they really united? Were they somewhere young again? Ganesh out of his ageing body, back with Kamala? He didn't realize he was starring at the portrait for those few minutes and it had slowly gone out of focus. And suddenly he felt as if Ganesh and Kamala in the picture smiled at him. Nikhil was completely shaken out of a trance and took a few steps back and hit his back on the wall of the corridor.

The skin on his body crawled, and he felt that spending even one night there would be impossible. He had never done that before. What if there was indeed the presence of Kamala or Ganesh there? They might not mean any harm to him, but the idea of living with ghosts was not welcome. He wanted to run away, but while he was still struggling with that fear, suddenly there was a loud noise and the back door opened and banged on the wall with a gust. It was raining outside, the same as last night. Nikhil was pushing himself against the wall, moving slowly towards the backyard to bolt the door. There was a faint smell of the wet earth. And in the next few seconds, the earthy raw smell mixed with a fresh, delicate, and light fragrance. There was crackling lightning which illuminated the backyard and the brahma kamal, and from the corner of his eye, he saw a light translucent image in that rain, an image of a lady in deep green saree! Nikhil gave out a deafening, mortal cry from deep within his guts. He lost his balance and leapt away from the backyard, towards the temple room. But as soon as we looked to his right, the temple side, an even bigger iron cry tore through him. The image of the lady was at the door of the temple room. Kamala was standing in front of him, in her poster-green saree and all the jewels, looking exactly same as she looked in the photo. On the left was the backyard with brahma kamal and on the right was the temple room where she stood. Nikhil, with all his might, threw himself towards the drawing room to run away from the house, but he just fell flat with his head near the doorstep of the temple room.

'Please don't . . . please go away, I have not done any harm to you or kaka, please . . . please . . .' And Nikhil had already broken into tears.

The voice, when it came to him, had rich deep earthy resonance, and it seemed to echo in that empty house. Each word lingered for a while even after he heard the next word.

'Do not fear me. I mean no harm.'

'No! P-p-plleeease go away . . . I have no connection with you . . . only kaka had and he is not here anymore . . . please go away . . . I beg you.'

'I am sent by your kaka, if you don't listen to me, he will not be at peace. I am sure you owe this to him . . .'

'I don't talk to ghosts . . . and I don't know about kaka, but talking to you will leave me dead, without peace, so for the sake of kaka, please go away . . .'

Nikhil was contemplating if he should make another attempt to bolt towards the door. And he did that, he got up with a jerk and made a lunge towards the outer room. But he saw her in front of the door and he again gave a heart-rending cry. There was no place he could run to; there was no escape. Why did he come back, he thought. He fell a few steps back and sat on his knees facing her, crying, gesturing her to leave him alone. He was gasping for breath between his sobs, and his chest muscles exploded under the galloping heart. She stood there calm and composed, smiling at him every time he made eye contact with her, which spooked him even further. She seemed to be made of smoke, translucent, and Nikhil realized she was not standing on the floor at all, she was floating above it. And then he saw she had no feet below the saree. He closed his eyes and tried to think if she had hands, was she shaking them or were they still? He didn't remember seeing her hands. Was this just a dream? Would this all go away and would he find himself waking up wet with his sweat? Where would he find himself? Was the whole story with kaka all part of a dream or he would find himself in the room above? His lungs were still parched and he was breathing through a series of gasps. He slowly opened his eyes, wishing that there was no Kamala.

But Kamala was right there, in her green saree, her jewels, her hands by her side, standing next to him.

Again that rich deep wet voice spoke. 'I am appearing like this because you wished to see me like this.'

'I don't wish to see you at all, why would I wish to see you in any way?'

'Because that is what you have imagined me as. Had you imagine me in yellow saree, I would be here in yellow saree. If you imagine me with a hideous face, that is what I will appear like.'

'Is there a way for me not to see you at all?'

'Yes . . . if you collect yourself, and listen to me.'

'Why are you troubling me? Why not leave me alone?'

The voice now had an edge of anger. 'Nikhil . . . I have not troubled anyone ever, not in life nor after. And I don't like to be called a ghost, even if as per your understanding I might be one. I have something to tell you, your kaka wanted me to tell you . . .'

Nikhil understood he didn't have options. He looked at her through his tearful eyes. A minute passed; both were looking at each other. Nobody said anything. His heartbeats gradually slowed and gasps turned to breathing.

'I knew you would come,' she said.

Nikhil didn't reply, just stared at her.

She smiled; it felt like her translucency was reducing and she was taking more definite form, or maybe Nikhil felt like that because now he was actually looking at her.

'Come here and we will talk.' The voice was back to the rich earthy tone. There was again the sweet smell of the flower in the air. They both walked to the backyard.

'Sit down.'

Nikhil obliged and sat down on the doorstep of the house, still pale as bone, looking at her, bewildered. The faint light from the temple behind him shone on her face and the brahma kamal. He realized she was indeed very beautiful. She stood near the brahma kamal, hands lightly clasped in front, her forehead decorated with saturated red colour of the vermilion. Her neck was decorated with beautiful gold jewellery and tiny shiny, silvery dots in her deep-green saree glittered. Her smile was comforting, and it stayed on the edges of her lips. Unlike ghosts he had heard about, she almost looked a goddess, enchanting.

After a few moments of silence, which Nikhil felt were a lifetime, his heartbeat and breathing normalized. His brain felt relaxed from the clutches of fear. It started working logically. He knew the only way to get rid of her company was to listen to her, to listen to what she wanted to say about a message from kaka.

'You've met kaka?' he asked.

'Yes. And I am happy that you asked me this as a first question. Usually people are concerned about what death is like, am I just a soul, is there heaven and hell, where did I go after my death—the curiosity about the afterlife! How funny it is to be worried about the afterlife while still in life!'

Nikhil didn't encourage any of those questions. He wanted to get the message from kaka and get everything over with. 'Is he good?'

'Yes.'

'How long will you be staying like this, both of you?'

'The time, as you understand it, does not apply in this form. The important part is that it really does not matter.'

Nikhil didn't believe himself that he was actually having a conversation with a ghost. If he told about his experience to his wife or parents, would they ever believe him? Probably they would; they believed in anything. The best thing though would be to keep this entire episode a secret. He immediately corrected himself that it would be true only if he saw the other side of the night, else it would anyway stay a secret.

'Ghosts are a concept made by people who have not died.' She spoke as if she read Nikhil's thoughts. This terrified Nikhil even further and he started sweating in that cold monsoon breeze.

'Don't be afraid, Nikhil, we are not meeting for the first time, we have been meeting for a very long time.'

'Huh? I have never seen you, just heard from kaka about you.'

'You have not met me in this form, but you have met me in many other forms, the first time you were very young, you don't even remember. The time you would remember me is when you met me in the form of Baba Rudranand, or the rickshaw driver at Swargate or at times a few customers at the shop or your own Vasantrao.'

'What do you mean, these people were all you?' exclaimed Nikhil.

'No, they were they—but not in their control when you met them. I controlled them.'

'I don't understand.'

'Nikhil, many things challenge the basic understanding you perceive through your physical senses. And unfortunately you are bound by those, so I may not be able to explain to you everything. There are a few people in the world who allow us a portal into their bodies. Not everybody, only very few people—that too they don't know they have portals. Using their portals, we can control not only their physical bodies but also their emotions, their thinking, and their senses. And we leave the body after our work is done. There are, though, some parasites who feed on the bodies for much longer.'

'So you are a ghost who possessed some people to connect to me?'

'I don't like the way you put it, but if this is how you would like to understand, yes.'

Nikhil looked away from her into the trees beyond the backyard. Everything around them was silent, absolutely silent, not even the usual crickets were making any sound. She had confessed she was a ghost and that too who could possess people.

'Do I have a portal? Will you possess me as well?'

'No and no.'

'Will you kill me?' Nikhil asked as innocently as this question could be asked. And he didn't understand why he asked that.

'No, not tonight and not by me.' She gave an audible laugh as she said that. 'You have a long life, Nikhil, don't worry.'

'You are scaring me,' Nikhil said, keeping his eyes from his own knees in that sitting position to her knees. He was not able to look in her eyes.

'Why? I told you I will not harm you. You see me this way, in this dress, because this is how you imagine me, your kaka did not see me like this, and somebody else we will see me in a completely different form. I don't have a form and I don't need one. You have built my image from the picture that you have in your mind.'

'I assume you were waiting all this while for kaka, now that you have met him, why do you do all this, why not just take the next birth and continue,' Nikhil quizzed.

'Ha ha,' she laughed and said, 'You speak about births as if you know about all this. Birth and death are concepts created by fierce imagination of living people. At least in the way most of the people understand it. There is no beginning with the birth and no end with the death, it is a continuous circle and sometimes we are caught between stages. I am in an intermediate stage between death and birth. And I have chosen this.'

'Are you going to escape this with stage with kaka? Is kaka also in this stage? Can I speak to him as well?'

'Many questions and none of them are important for you to know.'

'Right, so tell me what you came to tell me about. And start with why me? Why take all the trouble to reach me in my village and bring me from there to here? Why use me as your puppet?'

'I vowed to be on your kaka's side, always. And my promise should have been only till my death. But something made me linger on.'

'What something?'

'You.'

'What rubbish!'

She didn't reply to him immediately, just stared at him calmly. 'Your kaka said I died in my pregnancy. He didn't say anything about the son, did he?'

Nikhil sprang up from where he was sitting and shouted, 'That is ridiculous and you are crossing limits now! You don't mean to say that I . . .'

She stood there smiling. 'Yes, I mean to say exactly that.'

'Impossible, I know who my mother is . . . I am not an adopted son . . . and if at all I was your son, I should have been much older by now . . .'

'When I gave birth, the baby was alive. I held him in my arms for few seconds before both of us left the world. I could not exit along with my baby, suddenly leaving your kaka all alone. I was ignorant, there was nothing that I could do about it. But the love pulled me back. I wanted to give him his son. Even for a small time, I wanted to connect him with his son. That was my only desire. There was nothing in the world more important to me than getting my loving husband connected with his son.'

Nikhil stood there a few feet away from her, speechless in disbelief about what she was saying.

'Nikhil, between that time and now, you have taken a couple of births. I have been following your so-called soul. Don't get into how I could do that, just believe that I could. Every time I found out that I could not bring you to my husband, I got you killed, yes, I got you killed. There was no mercy; the only goal was to make you meet my husband. In this birth, things fell into place perfectly, but my husband unfortunately was already very old. I could not give him the pleasure of a son at the age where he would have really enjoyed a company of his son.'

'Did kaka know all this?'

'Yes. We made a will to transfer all this property to you, after I knew that you could be brought over here.'

'I suppose, if for some reason, I would have not reached here, you would have got me killed as well, correct?'

'Yes, but the fear was my husband was getting older and that had made me desperate, I would have killed many others for it—which I avoided so many years, but thankfully I didn't have to kill anybody for you. Keeping you away from education and work, and your father from money was enough for you to be here.'

Nikhil felt like leaping on her and choking her, but he knew better than to do it. He stood there dismayed. Before he knew it, he was crying, staring at her with contempt.

'Nikhil, don't hate me for this life that you have, I didn't do anything bad to you. Your father had a very brief moment of misery, just enough that was needed to bring you here. And since you have come here, I have taken care that he gets what he needs. Now you have this entire house and everything in it. Sell it off, for all I care! I am sure this piece of land in the coming years will fetch a lot of money. And for you hating me or loving me, it does not make any difference. Not anymore.'

'Why tell me all this? I could have peacefully left this house and gone back to my village. Why this house and the story? You have robbed me of my happiness and you claim to be my mother?'

'Time will make you forget everything. Nothing lasts forever. You will forget and start enjoying. Don't worry about me visiting you—not in this form, for sure.'

'But why tell me at all?'

'Because, I believe that now that my husband is with me, my confession is the way for my release.'

'That is selfish, isn't it?'

'I don't know about that, but you decide what you want to, son. Bless you . . .'

And she diffused in the darkness. Nikhil looked around but she was not around. The trees beyond the hedge swayed in the breeze. The wind had started whispering and there were faint sounds of crickets from the dark corners. It was silent but not like what he had experienced few minutes back. This silence was breathing. He felt strange, a bit groggy as if he just woke up from a deep slumber. But things around him were crisp. His skin felt the night and the soft chillness of the air around.

Years passed. As Nikhil was told, there came a time when the boom in information technology made his land price higher than he had ever imagined. Pune was not the Pune he had migrated to. When real estate agents approached Nikhil with huge offers, Nikhil did not sell the land, at least as yet. He just looked at them, gave a blank smile, and politely rejected the offers.

When his wife and son moved to the city of Pune, they felt life was perfect, except one complaint his wife had. She felt very weird about Nikhil's habit of speaking at midnight to himself in the backyard as if speaking to the silly plant.

Millions of spiritual creatures walk the earth
Unseen, both when we wake, and when we sleep
—John Milton, *Paradise Lost*

Dark Business

Finally I killed myself.

It was a very difficult decision. I had given it a lot of thought and finally was convinced that this was the only way out. My body lies at the bottom of the pit they dug for road repairs. The mud below me was soaked with the gush of blood and splatter. The bullet had pierced the lungs and the heart and made a large exit wound in the back as it came out. The heart had stopped but the mind went on for longer. The eyes stayed open in a state of shock. First the lungs and then the mouth were filled with blood. The process of dying was much longer than I had known or imagined. The body tries to hold on tightly, those few last desperate moments, to the life as it leaves the mortal body.

I am not sure of the effect of this on my wife and children. Most likely they will be sad, especially my eldest son, or at least that is what I would like to believe. Probably they will get used to my absence and then things will get better. That is how it is supposed to be. People get used to the conditions. I suppose they pine for some time and then reality takes over. Life is kinder than we think of it, it makes people forget. My family will also let go, if not forget completely though.

I have seen so many dead people in my life, but none of my previous experience comes close to what I felt at that moment, lying there in that dirt pit motionless. I had been taught what has a beginning has an end; for my body, the end had started. I wished that I felt happy, because that is what I wanted, that is why I killed myself. But nothing like this happened. My body lay there soundless in deathly tranquility, something that was never experienced before, oh yes, pun intended. The body I loved and cared for so much was now in the pit, waiting to be found by the police and get cut open on post-mortem table with the innards thrown all around. That did not matter though.

I don't remember my exact age; maybe it started when I was just over seven years. It might have happened before but I don't remember it. I was not sure of what was happening to me then. I thought it was an extension of my dreams. As per my mom, I always had lucid dreams, though till then I was not afraid of those dreams. I still vividly remember that night which I could say was a start to everything that happened with me or rather *to* me, which decided the course of my life. What might have happened a few days back or even yesterday, whom I might have said something to, just this morning, keeps on getting washed away, but what happened that night when I was hardly seven still lingers on me. I keep wondering why it happens that a lifetime with many days and many nights is decided on a singular insignificant-looking event. When it happened, I had no idea the rest of my life would be picking up a direction from there.

Even back in those days as a seven-year-old kid, I was given a separate room. And that was because my father made a good amount of money to afford a big house. My room was the one at the top of our house, the one which overlooked the huge eucalyptus trees of our backyard. The room had a single bed (oversized for a boy of my size then, facing the huge window), two racks of books, and a writing table, with chair for my size. I liked my room; it gave me the freedom, the lazy afternoon with my comics, and most important, it gave me the isolation I liked. Not that I had many friends anyway.

I don't remember anything special that happened that night. If it had, then I would have remembered, so most likely it was a usual night. I went to bed thinking of the dreams I would be getting. And many times as an adult I thought, why would somebody sleep thinking of what kind of dreams one would get? So maybe I might be getting similar dreams before as well, but my memory didn't scribe those. I guess it must have been a couple of hours of sleep, when all of sudden I felt that my entire body became rigid. I knew I had started to dream but it still was an uncomfortable feeling. I wanted to get rid of that feeling. I tried flexing my body and started to move, but nothing happened. I tried moving my arms, but nothing moved, not even a slight twitch. My legs, I tried a heavy jerk—no, nothing. Eyes! I was not able to control my eyelids. I was wailing inside my body, shouting, screaming for help. If my mom had come in that moment to check on me, she would have seen me sleeping snug, calmly in my bed. She would have come, smiled, kissed me, and gone back without knowing that I was in the sealed in the coffin of my body. Then, I hardly knew anything about death (and I still don't know much about it). I was convinced that I was dead. That is what death looked like, getting locked forever in your body. Forever, or after people find that you are dead, they lower you in a wooden coffin and let the body rot in a deep hole. Little did I know that it was just the start to all the horrors that I would be going through for the rest of my life.

All of a sudden I felt a sensation on my toe, as if there was a worm nibbling there. And it crawled slowly up my leg. The worst part, though, was that it did not crawl on the skin; it moved under it, as if it penetrated in my leg through the hole it made in the toe. And then another one, a few centimetres away, and then another one of the next leg, and then few more around my hands, and before I could realize what was happening, I had tingling sensations all over my body. Maybe they were not worms, just that bloody sensation, but as they intensified, I felt I could move my fingers and the toes and I opened my eyes with a hope that I could see things around me, hope that I was not dead after all. As soon as I confirmed myself that it was silly of me to get so scared, that it was just another nightmare (I didn't know then that bad dreams were called nightmares), I sat upright with a spring in my back. I was relieved to get rid of that horrifying paralytic feeling.

I got out of my bed. The air was chilling. It sent shivers in my body. I felt light, very light. I walked to the window facing my bed. My eyes were adjusted to the darkness outside. It was windy and raining hard. The eerie silence of my room accentuated the lashing sound of the raindrops on the windowpane. I stood there motionless and silent for a few minutes, unfocused eyes staring at indifferent space beyond, listening to the pitter-patter of the rain and the hushed whispers the wind made as it moved across the trees in my backyard. In those minutes, in that darkness, I lost myself in following the pattern of the water droplets on the windowpane with my finger as they flowed down and joined each other, making a fast-moving line.

I turned back, and in that soft light of my bedside night lamp, I saw the time on the wall clock. It was three. As they say, the darkest hour of the day. I was not feeling sleepy, not after that experience of being locked in the body followed by that damn tingling sensation. Picking up a comic book might help me, I thought. As I walked back to my bedside drawer to pick up the comic book, what I saw left a permanent scar in my memory, the scar that reminds me how it all started. My brain twisted into a tight knot and my mouth turned into sawdust and I don't know how many somersaults my heart took and if it seized up for a few minutes. I froze for a few seconds and then gave a sharp, shrill iron cry. But the lips contained them inside my body, not even a whimper came out of me. I was completely mute. There was somebody sleeping on my bed, and in those frozen moments in that dim yellow light, I saw his face. That somebody was me! It was too much for my seven-year-old brain to understand.

I stood there blanched, chalk pale, watching myself sleep in the grip of mortal terror when I heard somebody speak. The voice was neither very near nor far, as if from the adjacent room. And that voice was not of my parents. Those were whispers—husky, scary whispers, murmurs. I could hardly understand the words but could understand that the voices were coming towards me. I wanted to go to sleep again or make my body get up. I tried to sleep over my body but it did not help. I tried picking up the book from my side table and hitting my head, but I was not able to pick it up. I was not able to touch anything! My hand was going *through* those objects, as if those were made of light smoke. I closed my eyes, thinking that when I opened them again, I would be getting up from my bed and all this would be an extended dream. Nothing like that happened. The voices were coming closer. I tried shaking my body but my body was no different from any other object in that room. The voices were closer and louder now.

And then, I saw them. Two old ladies, with wrinkled cheeks and dark skin bags hanging below the chin, on their necks, deep in their conversation, walked into my room through the walls! Yes! Through the walls. I was not sure if my voice could be heard by these ladies, so I clenched my teeth tight, not allowing any sound to come out. They were busy in their own conversation and they didn't notice me or probably didn't heed any importance to my presence and they passed out through the windows where I was standing few minutes back. I stood there devoured by raw fear and I still wonder how I didn't die that night of a heart attack. Maybe I was fated to go through many more worse things in my life. How I wish that it should have been the worst night ever of my life and I should have died then, but I didn't. I didn't die then, unfortunately. After few minutes or hours, I don't know, I had lost track of the time, I felt I took a deep breath followed by quick short breaths and I woke up with a big shout. I got out of my bed and looked around me; this time, there was no body in the bed. I had it with me. I touched myself all over and felt relieved when my hands felt the touch sensation; the heaviness of my body reminded me I was still alive. I had woken up drenched in my sweat, and probably not just sweat; my pyjamas clinging to my thighs told me that. The room was warm and humid and not cold as I experienced moments back. I gave one more iron scream but only silence replied. This is one of the disadvantages of living in a big house and sleeping in an isolated room on the top floor. Though I don't remember why I gave up after this scream. Why didn't I persist with my screams? Maybe I had a doubt that I would invite them again, if I made myself more audible. Of course I did not sleep that night again. And I didn't have enough courage to walk alone down to my parents' room. I cried mutely, burying my head between my knees, sitting beside the cot, resting my back on the bedside drawer. Those ladies covered with gruesome gray wrinkles, and ash-grey faces—were they real or was all this just an imagination, just a bad, bad dream? I knew it in me though. It was not a dream; it was real, very real. And I also knew in that moment that it probably would not be my last experience of that kind.

Next morning, I looked pathetically remorseful. My mom held me with both her hands covering my head in her bosom for nearly thirty minutes, rocking softly back and forth, kissing my head frequently, and comforted me, saying that it was just a nightmare and I should try and forget it. She felt guilty of not waking up, not being with me when I called her. I don't remember everything she said in her soothing voice, but I do know it felt good. For some time, I did doubt myself, and felt everything I went through last night was actually a dream. I remember me praying to God to make my sleep dreamless, though I am not sure if I was audible at all last night. She assured me that I could sleep in their bedroom till I stopped getting those nightmares.

That night and a couple of nights after that were without any of those experiences. And I started believing, telling myself that it was just one of those experiences and everything would be okay. On the fourth night while sleeping with my parents, my body went rigid again. I fought against it with all my strength but remained stiff as a log. In a few minutes, the tingling sensation followed and I felt as if I was lifted out of my body—exactly the same sequence, just like the last time. I knew the tingling sensation would relieve me from the paralysis and it would be followed by that creepy feeling of leaving my body. My terror scale had already notched several points up on the anticipation of whom I would see today. Those ladies, would they spot me hiding? What do these people do with kids, eat them? I tried waking my mom, but I think I was late. I was already floating above my body. This time I checked myself lying there on my bed with my parents around me. I knew if I shouted, nobody would hear it, but I still gave it a try. There was no change in the silence. The room remained cold, frightening, and eerily silent.

And then it started—like the previous night, there were voices again—started as muffled whispers and in a few seconds became louder. I was frightened more by the sounds than by their silence, but I knew I didn't have any choice. This time there were many voices mixed and overlapping. I continued sitting near the bed and cried silently.

There was an excited shout from the left side; before I could realize what just happened or who shouted, two boys nearly my age came running in through the walls. They were playing some kind of game: the smaller of the two was trying to catch the other one. Both of them ran away through the other side of the wall without noticing me. From the right again, those two ladies talking to each other passed from the room, this time followed by a young couple lovingly embracing each other. In the next few minutes, I felt as if I was sitting in some park and people were passing in and out as if there were no walls and my house did not exist. I sat there weightless, watching these activities, telling myself this was all just a dream, just a dream.

It was then when I saw her for the first time. Even now, her face is clear before my eyes. Chiselled in stone and buried deep in my heart, the memory of her face is as if I saw her yesterday. The shrivelled old lady with a tattered, dirty whitish-brown bandage on her left eye, dark-grey wrinkled skin, loose bags of skin hanging from her arms, smiling, stood in the corner of the room. She was directly looking at me! She had after all spotted me! With her arms outstretched, she mumbled something which I realized a few moments later. 'Come to mamma, baby . . . my baby, come to mamma,' she was saying. Everything about her was scary, including her broken yellow front teeth. She was smiling but there was a definite desperate unhappiness on her face. She started moving towards me . . . oh God, oh God . . . I was going to die a bad, bad death that night—that's what crossed my mind. But sadly, I didn't. I survived her.

'Come, son, come and don't be afraid. Mamma will take care of you,' she said and started taking a few hurried steps.

I still wonder how come I did not die of a heart attack after seeing that. I closed my eyes and curled my fingers to make a tight fist. For those few seconds, I thought that I might be prepared to punch her, or push her hard if she touched me. And for those few moments, though short-lived, I felt that there was a way to get out, a way to fight back.

Tring . . . trrring—all of a sudden there was a deafening noise in the room. I opened my eyes, and the room was as the room was supposed to be. The old scary lady was not there, nor any others of her kind. I woke up shouting loudly and so did my startled father. It was the alarm clock that triggered that noise. My dad nearly knocked out that alarm clock in an effort to silence it. My mom also sprang up bewildered, shocked by my iron scream. She pulled me towards her as an impulse. She held me tight to her bosom and just let me be there; she didn't say anything. She was crooning to me in her soft hushed words: I didn't need to fear, it was just a silly alarm clock that my dad had set on a wrong time by mistake and all that. A few minutes after that, I kept quiet as Mom shouted at my dad for not being careful about setting the clock right.

Only I knew that he could not have set the clock on a better time than that, though he denied the mistake. He maintained it was set to normal waking hours and it was not supposed to go off in the middle of the night. It was showing 3:05 a.m. at that moment. I knew very well it was the alarm clock that saved me that night. If it was a mistake or not, whatever it was, for me it was a divine intervention! I was in a state of shock, with all the colour drying out of my cheeks, my eyes still unsure of what I saw. My mom laid me down on the bed, as my dad switched on the full light. She moved her fingers slowly through my hair, kissing my forehead once in a while. My dad stood there for some time and then probably my mom gestured him to sleep in another room. I didn't say anything to them that night. Though just before I slept, I told my mom that I didn't want to dream. *I don't want to dream . . .*

By the time I came for my breakfast, my dad had already left for the office. Mom noticed that I still wore the chalk-pale expression from the previous night's incident. Till then, she thought it was the alarm clock that scared me. It took me a while, but I told her what made me shriek, how the alarm clock actually saved me. I gave her all the details of what happened, how I had lost my body and how helpless I felt. As I told my story to her, I could see colour vanishing from her face. I held her tight as I narrated the scenes and she held the chair tightly. By the time I finished, she was convinced I was not dreaming. She sensed something wrong happening to me. She grabbed my shoulders and pulled me close to her and kissed my head multiple times, saying nothing would happen to me, nothing at all. Of course she had no idea what she should do about it, but there was determination in her concerned eyes to help me. I still saw those flickering eyes, concerned, sad, and yet resolute, ready for waging a war with whosoever was troubling her son.

We didn't have cell phones then, and my father was on field duty. She had to deal with a few hours all by herself. She paced the kitchen frantically, whispering prayers, and saying aloud a few times, nothing would happen to her baby. As the confusion receded, she discovered even worse. What if those things that I saw killed me in sleep? What if those things entered my body? The fear and confusion were lifted, giving rise to pure panic. She lighted an incense stick in front of our family deity. The family deity was supposedly the protector of our family for generations. Her huge photo hung in our kitchen, garlanded with orange flowers. She then called her sister; she depended on her for the problems she could not solve by herself. And honestly, I don't recall a single instance where my aunt provided any good solution to any of those problems. This time was no different.

My aunt's solution to my condition was to put ten iron nails, a few spices like turmeric, chilli powder, and a raw lemon (pierce the lemon with one of the nails) under my bed. At a gap of three to four nights, I experienced the same. Thankfully the lady with the bandaged eye did not come. Mom and Aunt both were surprised that Aunt's solution didn't work! Mom asked her confidants in the neighbourhood. They were no less quirky. On their advice, I was taken to a certain temple every Monday. I had to offer milk mixed with honey to the (supposedly) holy man there. He would then take that with few currency notes and apply bright-red vermilion on my forehead and neck. I knew none of these would help me but somehow it was helping Mom to relax and keep the hope, and that was enough reason for me to try out her experiments. Four to five decades back, psychiatrists were not famous, so that was not an option. The eventual declaration was coming that I was possessed. I was asked a lot of questions about what I did in the last few weeks, by Mom's so-called confidants from around the neighbourhood.

Because of not sleeping at night, my performance in sports and academics was dipping. I stopped playing with my friends and restricted myself to my room. My life was going from bad to worse. Both my parents looked to be aged in just few days. One of those afternoons, against my father's wishes, Mom called an exorcist on recommendation of one of her confidants. I was made to sit before him naked. Tears were running down my cheeks as he lit some kind of fire and threw some powders in it, making it bigger, brighter, and wilder. I don't know how much more I would've had to undergo with that weird exorcist, had my dad not returned just in time. My dad hated the pseudo god-men of this kind, self-proclaimed and especially when they were suggested by Mom's friends. When he saw the ritual going on in our house, his eyes flickered from me to Mom and then on the exorcist. I could see his vein throbbing on his temple, and his Adam's apple bobbing up and down. He threw his office briefcase, toppling the chinaware on the side table and came with a fury I had never seen before, and kicked hard on the iron vessel containing the fire, throwing all the burning wood all around the house. In the same smooth motion, he ripped the god-man from his seat and pushed him towards the door. My mom shouted and tried to intervene, but she also received an equally hard push flinging her like a rag doll to the other side of the room. The exorcist was flabbergasted and so was everyone in the room. There was a barrage of expletives and curses from both the sides. Mom sat horrified in a corner, pleading to my dad not to behave like that with god-man, that his curse would worsen their son's situation. The neighbours cleared out within the first few seconds of action from Dad and that was a relief. Sitting naked in front of them was the most embarrassing situation for me till date. Dad and Mom didn't speak to each other for a couple of days, and for these days, I was free of those nightmares as well. I started feeling that the ritual, even though half done, had worked out. Mom tried hinting the same to my dad, but he threw away that suggestion with bitter sarcasm.

Mom had given up on the hope of getting the exorcist again, and my parents had resumed their normal behaviour to each other, after about a week. One of those nights, while sleeping between them, I overheard them. Mom was objecting to some proposal from Dad which I missed hearing but what I understood was he was adamant on something, saying that it was the only sensible and right thing to do. He said he had good references, and at least it was not a silly ritual of an idiotic god-man.

Two days later, my father took me to Kalimpong, a beautiful village in the lap of the Himalayas around sixty kilometres from Darjeeling. It took us nearly one day by bus to reach there from Calcutta. Dad had a chat with the tonga-wallah outside the Kalimpong bus stop. The tonga-wallah understood where we wanted to go. For the most part of our journey, Dad was quiet. He had told me that he would tell me the purpose of our tour once we reached where we want to go. After about two hours of rocky ride on that tonga, on the sides of the enchanting silvery river Teesta, we reached a huge mansion. It was still early morning when we reached there. The place was enveloped in a soft blanket of fog. Lots of trees, neatly trimmed, flanked the patio of the mansion. The morning coldness was not harsh; it was just delicate enough to feel good on the skin. The whispering rustle of the leaves and the low-pitched tweeting of the early birds was the only sound there after the tonga had left. The entire setting of the mansion was calming and peaceful. My weariness from the travel throughout the night, my apprehensions about where we were going had all taken a back seat. I was mesmerized by the huge colonial mansion and the serenity around. We went in through a big wooden door, as if we were expected.

A middle-aged person, in a long white robe, stood there in middle of the room. He gave a slight nod and a brief smile to Dad. He was taller than my dad. And many people around our place counted Dad as a tall person. Even though his arms were hidden in those robes, as a kid I imagined his arms to be strong like wrestlers', seeing how big his palms were. He had long blackish grey hair settling as thick curls on his shoulders. His forehead had three horizontal stripes, which I thought were made from sandalwood paste. Give him different clothes and he would look like Lord Shiva we have on our calendar.

'He is Jiten.' My father introduced me to the towering gentleman. He stood there silently looking at me, or rather I felt he was looking through me, probably seeing what I was thinking. As a kid, I felt he might actually be an avatar of Lord Shiva, and I should be careful while around him. After some hesitation, I broke into a slight smile. He smiled back and moved his huge palm on my head, ruffling my set hair. His name, my father said, was Narendranath Ghosh and he was a very spiritual person and would cure me of my troubles. He preferred being called Naren. Strangely my father did not believe in exorcists but believed that a person like Narenji could help me. For me, I didn't mind Narenji; he looked to be a hundred times better than the person Mom had called.

That day, I could say, was the second event of my life I clearly remember which made me what I am today. The horrific dreams stay as number one. I touched Narenji's feet and he lightly touched my head and blessed me, chanting a Sanskrit verse. He told us to have breakfast, after which he would talk to me in private. Talking to him in private scared me. As minutes passed, the empty enormous house was also getting on my nerves. Talking to my parents about my nightmares was one thing, but to discuss these with somebody else whom I didn't even know till a few minutes back was strange and an uncomfortable situation for me.

Narenji asked me to call him only Naren. It felt odd for me to call somebody so elder to me, and that too so big in size, by the first name. In those times, unlike now, calling somebody by their first name was not respecting them. But I thought it was wise for me to follow what he asked. After our breakfast, Naren took me to his study room which was overcrowded with books on various subjects, mostly Sanskrit and Bengali. He saw the awe on my face and tried his best to make me feel at home. He started asking me questions about my school, my friends, my likes, and other things, basically the usual things. And the more he was asking me about trivial things, the more uncomfortable I was becoming. His urge to know about my friends or what kind of books I read, I thought, was pointless. I was a kid, right? Now as I reflect on my spent life, those moments with Naren had a lot of significance. He slowly took me to the reason that I was with him there, in his study, with those imposing shelves of books. His deep resonating voice commanded authority. I dared not tell any lies to him, I thought. He asked me what I dreamt about, a bit casually. I felt he did not really understand how horrifying those were. Slowly he persisted with his questions here and there, and I didn't know when I started telling him everything, every little detail, those details which I didn't even tell my parents. I later felt that through his words, he had actually taken me in those moments. I don't remember exactly, if I was even fully conscious when I gave him the details of those walking figures that haunted me.

After he thought that he had heard all, he got up and walked to the window. He kept looking at those trees in his garden, lost in his reverie. After what I felt was a long, long time, he turned back and sat in front of me. He kept his heavy and big palm on my tiny shoulder, nearly hiding it and spoke in his usual resonating voice, looking straight in my eyes. 'Listen, Jiten, and listen to me very carefully.'

That double emphasis got me wide-eyed and attentive.

'You have a gift,' he said. He waited for my reaction, but on having none but a blank face, he continued. 'It is not about what you know or have experienced till now, it is about what you don't know yet. And though ignorance is bliss, but to free you of this torment, perhaps you should know about it. There is a good chance that these experiences may not occur after a few years, but if something happens to you in these few years, it will be a waste of a good gift. That is why I think you should know in detail about what is happening to you,' he said. I kept staring at him, gnawing my lip. I wondered why Dad should not hear about this.

'Many people spend their lifetimes, and at times a couple of lives, to reach where you are. The experience that you are getting can be explained to you only after you mature a bit. You cannot understand it at the age of seven. What you can understand though is that you are able to enter into a different world and you need to learn how to control yourself when you are there and how to stay safe. Be aware the realm you visit is very dangerous. This is no dream.'

As if I didn't know that it was not a dream. That night as my father waited outside the room impatiently, full of anxiety about what was happening to me, Naren taught me how to consciously enter that state. He said if I went there consciously, it would not be that terrifying. That night he told me to sleep in his room and practice the technique. I did that. After a couple of failed attempts, and Naren's patient persistence, it happened to me. I was out of my body. This place was absent from all voices, and for the first time, I felt great pleasure at being in that state. As I floated above my body, I saw my body lying on the mattress next to Naren's. To my surprise, in a few minutes Naren also floated out of his body. In that room both of us were floating. I could see that my father was sleeping in another room. Naren told me to concentrate and told me if I focused enough, I could see a silvery strand connecting myself with my body. He taught me techniques of how to go back to the body like a soft landing. We did that exercise that night a couple of times. After a couple of failed attempts, I was able to exit and enter my body very smoothly. He told me to beware that as long as the silvery strand exists, I am safe, but it may break, for reasons he said he did not know; death of the body was one amongst them. If it breaks, then anybody without the strand can enter into my body, after which I have to keep lingering on or take another body whose strand is broken. He taught me, in the event the strand is broken, what I should do to reach my own body. It was difficult and 50 per cent of the time it was not possible. The next morning, he insisted to my father to stay for a few more days which were necessary for my cure. I was also feeling happy staying with Naren in his regal mansion and practicing with him in the night. By the end of the fourth night, I was experimenting flawlessly. I knew how to fly to different places and come back to my body. Naren warned me about malicious entities I may encounter during my travels in the netherworld. He refrained from elaborating on that, considering my age. He had promised to coach me on this as the years passed. It was essential that I should not make friendships, commitments to people I meet in that realm. It was a dangerous realm and the entities there should be respected. Most important was to protect the invisible string that attached the floating body to the physical body. Some advice which he kept repeating during my training was that this out-of-body movement should not be done by me for the sake of fun or experimenting; it was a technique for meditation, for using the power of the subconscious mind, but he would coach me later. The reason I was taught this was now I would not move out of my body accidentally like I used to, and if I would ever, I knew how to return. However, I was very excited with my new learning. Dad and I started our journey back to Calcutta after around a week of practice with Naren.

After we came back, I wanted to try out the techniques he had taught me, but was afraid to try those alone. As I slept in my room after coming back, I remembered the old lady and others who had visited me. But the temptation to try it out, to check if it was something that I could do only in Naren's presence or I could do it at my wish. That night I made my first try for conscious out-of-body experience. The first thing that I saw when I was out was Naren. He knew I would try it and he was there calmly waiting for me. He had flown down from Kalimpong for me. After that he held my hand and took me around in the vicinity of my home in that parallel realm. He warned me again on the things he had said when I was at his place. This realm, he said, was much more uncontrolled than the realm where physical people stay. Here the people who are connected to physical bodies move with those entities who do not have connected bodies, or as people call them, either spirits or ghosts. A vacant body was always a target for malicious entities or ghosts. With Naren around me, those ladies with ashen faces and the one with a bandage did not come around. Naren told me the best was not to speak to them if I ever saw them. A few days went by, and I controlled my desire of trying out the new knowledge. Slowly,

I did it once or twice again. I started liking the tingling sensation which I avoided in the beginning.

As days went by, I became more and more confident. I was able to fly to the location I wished. I saw many others in that realm, mostly ghosts. Most of them kept to their own businesses; some tried to intervene but I knew the techniques how to fly away from them. I did not see the ones which I saw in my bedroom and my parents' bedroom before I met Naren.

Knowing the secrets of people is a very powerful weapon. I had not realized how to wield that power, though I am not sure that I know it yet. I never realized when I got addicted to this practice. I realized I could do this kind of travelling at my will, at any time of the day, not necessarily at night. I used to skip school and do this travelling in broad daylight now. I also found that by practice, this was coming more and more natural to me. I was getting better at it. My acquaintances at school and the place I lived feared me. I knew all their secrets and had always the power to blackmail them. At times during my travels, I found yogis, Sufi saints, and the like also in this realm. I got the opportunity to overhear what they said. I was amazed to see that in these realms, there were sessions conducted to teach and discuss matters. Yogis used to sit in a group and discuss; ghosts had their own groups and they had their own topics. Then there were Aghoris and novices like me. I was totally fascinated here. Ghosts didn't scare me anymore. I felt I knew enough about them to defend myself and make my escape if something untoward happens. Little did I know then how wrong I was.

As time passed, I made excuses about not feeling well to skip school or at times started from home to go to school but did not reach there. Roaming in the netherworld was like an addiction. My academic results were faltering, but I hardly cared for it. I kept mostly to myself in school. I did not have friends. I didn't need them. I had my biggest entertainment. I loved what Naren had said, I had a gift. I was convinced I was the most powerful and nothing could go wrong for me.

One of those nights as I was travelling, I got a terrible jerk from behind as if somebody yanked my hair. Though in the world there is nothing physical, and I had no material hair, the kind of tug made me jolt. I turned back and saw the furious form of Naren. He was not the calm Naren I knew; his face was seething with rage. He said that he was guilty of teaching me the techniques. Those techniques were to be used for spiritual advancement or the betterment of humanity and not to fool around the way I was doing. He said that if I would continue doing such travels again the way I was doing, he would cut the cord between me and my physical body, and after that, I would be dangling in that realm like many others I had seen, like a ghost. Though I loved coming to this realm, I still loved my physical body and the advantages it brought. Without it, the travelling I did would yield me no advantages. I don't know what he did to me, but whatever he did, it gave me jolts of pain like I had a few minutes back when I saw him. He pulled me, like the old teachers in school pulled the students, twisting their earlobes. He dragged me to a place where there were many yogis sitting. He showed me that place and told me that it was the only place I should be visiting. He would be checking on my activities; if I ventured anywhere else, the consequence, he threatened me, would be unfavourable to me. I was forced back in my body that night.

Two days later, my father received a telegram from Kalimpong telling about demise of his friend and my Guru, Narendranath Ghosh. They wrote he died in sleep.

Now I did the travels to the other realm freely. I had forgotten the rules of this realm as taught by Naren. I used to talk to people; I had all the confidence of a new learner that I could always come back to my body if I smelled trouble. In one such travel I met Arvind. He was nearly of my age. He was the one who gave me the term for this experience; he called it astral travelling. He also seemed to be quite experienced in this astral travelling though not as much as me. He started the first conversation with asking me about how I learnt all the techniques and how I achieved this fearlessness in that realm. I told him my story. Seeing that he was becoming impressed, I bragged more than what was real. Arvind told me he was an orphan. He also had accidental beginnings of out-of-body experience like me and he was spotted once in that realm by a fakir. The fakir, Arvind told me, was more than a hundred years old and an expert at this astral travelling. He taught Arvind how to control the experience he was having and the techniques for conscious travels into the subconscious realms. The fakir had also told him to stay away from ghosts, how to know which ones are vicious and which are not. He said that once the fakir got angry at him for misbehaving and had left him. Arvind never knew how to get back to him and had lost him forever.

Arvind said that he lived in Gujarat, which was around two thousand kilometres from West Bengal where I was. But in this realm of our rendezvous, distances did not matter. We started meeting regularly. We found good friends in each other. Arvind always had something to tell about what he had seen in his travels in the past. At times he used to take me there. He showed me the most beautiful landscapes. Sometimes he took me to some of the most menacing graveyards, to show how ghosts used to flock in those places. I saw that though Arvind used to praise me for my fearlessness, he was much better than me at that. The places which I feared he used to visit as comfortably as any other places. I still remember how he took me to some of the most dreaded ancient forts, the folklore of which gave me goosebumps; there he used to walk fearless. Many times we flew to the designated meeting places of yogis where they discussed spirituality. It was nice to hear how they discussed what they would be doing in the next few months or years from then. I remember seeing in that group one of the very celebrated saints of our time.

Time was going well with Arvind. As it turned out, he became my best friend. I had read that a secret's worth depends on the people from whom it must be kept. For me there was nobody better than Arvind to share secrets. Mutual sharing of secrets was fun. We had our nicknames, he was Tom and I was Huck, from the tale of Tom Sawyer and Huckleberry Finn. In the physical world, I was becoming an abnormal child, who slept most of the time and used to get very angry at people, including parents, when they disturbed me from sleep. I looked healthy so doctors could not diagnose the problem. Only I knew that there was no problem. After the visit to Naren, my father never took me to any other spiritual person.

But as I grew up, my academic results were going from bad to worse. The standing in school results was something that had finally started bothering me, because though my secret life was good, I was a subject of ridicule in the physical world. I was at the age at which, however desperately happy I was in those stolen moments, the fact that I was being ignored by people in the normal world was something that I did not like. Being teenaged is all about attention.

It was one of those chilly winter nights, thick with heavy fog, when I was waiting for Arvind at our usual spot. It was not unusual that Arvind used to be late. I was peaceful, lost in my thoughts. I was feeling guilty of not paying attention to my studies, not being of any help to my mother, who kept worrying about me. And then somebody broke my reverie. I felt somebody touched me on my back and I turned around to see, expecting to see Arvind. A silent, white scream came out of me. I saw the same old woman I had seen in my initial astral travelling days, the one with bandaged eye, just inches away from me. The shriek was faster than my recognition of the horror but the horror was way stronger and it persisted. She looked scarier from close. She was a ghost, not a travelling person like me. There were no attachments to her. Seeing her from so close, I had blanked out on all my expertise of running away from that spot; I stood rooted there, staring into her other eye: cold, stony, barely open, more like a slit in the middle of a dark pool on the leathery, wrinkled brown face. She looked like someone who had seen a lot of suffering in her life and was not able to forget it. The grey strands of her thin hair on her balding scalp were caught tight with the bandage. The face which was a nightmare for me for many nights as a kid was in front of me and I was staring at it. She allowed my fear to sink in. She stood there motionless, allowing me to looking into her eye.

In those few moments, I felt the face I was looking at was not really a malicious one. It was rather a very sad face. I remembered Naren had told me not to get close to pernicious nor sad souls; both can be dangerous, the later more so, he had said. I felt she was seeking my help or was trying to tell me something. She was trying to mumble something, but it was not coming out. She tried holding me, but I moved a step back. Just then Arvind arrived. Her expression changed when she saw Arvind; she was not angry, as I expected. She panicked! It was as if she saw a ghost—funny, yes, for a ghost to be afraid like that. But before she melted in that darkness, I thought she said something— something that I did not understand clearly. Later on, when I thought about it, I felt she didn't really say anything, only the left eye, the one which was not bandaged, gave an expression of warning me. We actually had a brief split-second eye contact and that made me think as if she said something to me or wanted to say. Though I always feared her and she was my definition of a nightmare, at that moment, I wished that Arvind shouldn't have arrived. There was something that held my attention, after my initial fears had dissolved. But why in the world did Arvind's presence threaten her?

I was disturbed and Arvind saw it. He also saw that I noticed that the lady saw him and panicked.

'What just happened, Arvind? Who was that woman? What did she want from me?'

Arvind stayed silent and looked away from me as if thinking about a reply for me.

'What happened to her when she saw you? What is your connection to her? Or my connection to her,' I continued.

Arvind looked at me sympathetically and kept his hand on my shoulder. 'You don't realize that I saved you, right? Instead of thanking me, you shoot me with questions?' he said softly, in a warm, friendly tone, something I had never heard. But I never had any friends.

I immediately felt embarrassed. Arvind had saved me from her, and yes, instead of expressing my gratitude, I was angry at him. He saved me from her sad soul latching on to me and being dragged in my body.

'I am sorry, so sorry, Arvind. I was scared, and that is why I reacted this way. Sorry . . .'

'Don't worry, friends are supposed to help. I would have cursed myself if I had come here late. The good part is you are safe and she has not latched on to you.'

That was the moment I thought I would do anything for Arvind. He had saved my life and I would stay indebted to him, forever.

Though, some questions lingered on. I didn't think that was the right time to ask. Who was she? Why did she go away, why did she haunt me? Why now? What was the connection?

Time went by, as it always does. Arvind and I were no longer teenagers. The craze for roaming into the netherworld had subsided; it had anyway started reducing after my encounter with the old lady. I was tall and lanky, with random hair here and there on my otherwise smooth jaw, when suddenly life came around. Slowly it was dawning on me that this life was full of possibilities and promises. There was so much more than just the travelling. I started focusing on my academics and managed to get respectable scores in my school exams. As this phase continued, I saw my parents seemed less worried; they seemed happier, especially my mother. And I was liking it. It was good to see her happy, her realization that after all her son was not really a weirdo, just an introverted guy. I could live with this image of introvert. It gave an air of respect about me. When most of the boys of my age are chatty, I came across as a thinking guy. Mirrors started fascinating me; like others of my age, I used to admire myself in mirror. I found myself becoming interested in the females around me. I started liking movies.

The change was in my realization about being interested in what people called normal activities. I didn't give up my out-of-body travelling, but restricted it only to nights. Arvind was not usually interested in my talks about girls. As we grew up, I found that our likes and dislikes were not matching as they used to be, earlier. While I liked to talk about my school and hot actresses from movies, especially the ones in adult Hollywood movies, he used to talk about visiting an undiscovered place in the astral realm or trying out some chant in a cemetery or how to take control of some easy ghosts. Not that our friendship was getting less, but the kind of 'Tom and Huck' thing we had between us was becoming less. I felt somewhere within me a guilt of not being able to like Arvind as much as I used to. The normal life also started to get me interested. At times I felt I ventured into that realm just because Arvind would feel bad about me not joining him. My guilt manifested in me getting unreasonably angry or nasty with Arvind on some trivial issue, and then we would not meet each other for a couple of days.

That year, it was a cold wave, an unusually cold and dry night for our city. There was hardly anybody on the streets. Arvind and I sat bored on our everyday spot. Neither of us spoke; there was nothing interesting to share. Also, it was some time we had discovered what got one interested, the other stayed indifferent to. So, we were getting used to the silence between us. Arvind finally took the initiative and suggested that we take a tour of the city, and the first place we found intense people activity, we could take a halt and watch them. We knew it would be difficult that night so it would be an interesting search. We decided not to go to the railway station, nor to the notorious brothel. What caught our attention was the city hospital. Watching doctors in a surgery would be an interesting thing, suggested Arvind. For us to see surgeons at work in our physical forms would be impossible, so watching while hovering above the operation theatre seemed to be an interesting idea to both of us. We flew into an operation theatre where we could sense a lot of activity.

It was a large room; in the centre, on a metal bed, was a frail-looking man with many tubes inserted in his body. There was a team of doctors working on him. Most of the body of that patient was covered in thick green cloth except the abdomen part, which looked as if dug up from where we saw. His internals were clamped and raised. It was far from interesting now that I saw it. But Arvind seemed very interested in what was going on, so I stayed on and did not ask to move out. The doctor whom I guessed would be the head doctor made a few incisions and there was a splatter of blood on those plastic gloves of the doctors. As one of the doctors controlled the blood, the other was watching the readings on the monitor. Something looked seriously wrong with the patient, the way the doctors were acting desperate after looking at the monitor readings. My sight followed a nurse who darted across the room and filled a vial with some liquid. She came back and the doctors injected that liquid in the patient's upper abdomen.

It took me a while to realize what I saw across the room where the nurse filled the vial. There in the corner of the room stood three free spirits, or call them ghosts. They looked like real material of which nightmares are made. Their eyes were full of lust, palpable evilness surrounded them, they were almost drooling looking at the patient. I could see them as we shared the same realm, and if this is what I had to see, I should stop travelling here. I turned towards Arvind to show him those, but Arvind was already watching them. And what scared me, worried me was, looking at those spirits, Arvind was not flinching at all. He was looking at them as if it was normal.

It was clear they were as if waiting for the patient to die. The patient's body convulsed a few times during that operation, and in these moments, I saw that one of the ghosts extended his hand towards the patient's heart but the ghost behind him pulled this eager one back and gestured him to be patient.

I felt sad to the core, to realize that the only difference between me and those evil spirits was my fragile-looking strand, my connection to flesh and bones, made me uneasy. What if it broke, what if I was reduced to one of them if my connection with my body broke? The thoughts scared me; just from being sad, I felt a mortal terror. I wanted to leave, but Arvind looked too interested and watched with the excitement of watching a cricket match's nail-biting finish.

In the next few minutes, the patient died, and the eager one pounced on it, trying to get in the body. But before he could do that, something strange happened. Something came out of his nostrils, something like I had never seen before. I cannot say it was like a thin smoke, but that is what I can say it was nearest to. And it happened in just a fraction of second. We all, in that realm, noticed it. And the ghost that tried to get in the body of the patient suddenly looked crestfallen as if he lost an important race by a whisker. The ghost who seemed to be the most mature of the three held the other ones and all of them melted away. I looked at Arvind, but he didn't grant me the pleasure of an answer. He looked equally dumbfounded. I felt I had reached a point where in those few moments, life took a pause, a solemn pause where it threw me something and judged me on what I would do. I didn't realize that then, as we came out of the hospital, both silent, intrigued, lost in our own interpretation of what we saw. Thoughts hung on the lips but were not falling out: the fragility of life and death, the body vessel, and the evil spirits. Questions without answers and nobody to go to, to ask. I missed Naren then.

After we reached our place, I told Arvind that I had not seen death at such close quarters, but that was the least reason for me getting disturbed. He said it was first time for him as well, but since we travelled in this realm, sooner or later we were going to encounter evil ones, as we encounter them in the physical world. I wanted to stop coming to that realm, but I knew that I was not serious. The kick I got from coming to that realm was addictive, stronger than any other addiction I ever had. Arvind said being uneasy about it was understandable; the only thing we should do is to understand it better. For the next few nights, we debated on whether we should stop doing it or continue. Arvind was sharply on not stopping and I was indecisive, and he won the argument.

We started staying around the hospitals to see what was happening and understand more of what we saw. I still regret it. I still had a chance till then to stop all that, but I didn't.

In most cases, the events happened the way we observed. There used to be ghosts around a dying person; after the person died, in a few seconds there was a strobe of light or smoke-like matter coming out of the body and the ghosts returned disappointed. The time of death and the smoky thing leaving the body varied, for a few it took seconds and for a few it took much longer. At times the patient could also leave his body with the cord attached a few minutes before his death. However we found rare horrifying instances where a ghost was able to leap into a dying person just at the time of the smoky thing leaving the body. If there was a delay, they were not able to get the entry. In some cases the dying person also re-entered the body. In none of the cases were the living people around the dying person able to make out a difference when it happened. I and Arvind started keeping the record of what was happening with people whose bodies the ghosts were able to enter; slowly as our data grew, we could see there was a pattern. We started validating our guesses, and most of the time, we were able to make a good guess in whose body the ghosts were able to enter and whose not. Our observations were becoming richer. Our guesses were becoming confirmations. Before a person actually died, we could spot a potential host for ghosts. We found out that hospitals were a good place for our observations and research.

It was Arvind's idea to test our knowledge. We brought with us a wandering ghost and showed him a person on the verge of dying, who, according to us, was a good host. As soon as the person died and his soul was about to exit, we gave the ghost entry into his body. The living people around the dying person felt that their friend had just defied death and had been saved. Only we knew what actually happened. Looking at the successful experiment at first stroke, Arvind was happy beyond limits. I was unsure though. I felt happy about our prediction, but playing with life and death and getting involved with ghosts was not a business I ever imagined I would be doing. Guilt. We repeated this transfer into another body once more, again with positive results, a couple of times after that and each time with success. We were convinced we were already good at that game. With word of mouth, our expertise was famous in this parallel realm. One of the ghosts offered that if we could make him enter into the body of a very rich person, he could transfer a lot of money into our accounts. We made it happen and he also obliged on his part.

That gave a kick-start to our new venture of body hosting. Doing business with ghosts seemed the beginning evil. But money gives enough reasons to put the guilt on the part of the brain; you learn slowly to ignore it. We crossed out limits, and we loved the easy money that came in. In the real world, I opened up a shop of selling mirrors and showed that I actually made a lot of money in that business. People around me thought I was born to sell mirrors the way I made money in the mirror business. Soon our business was expanding; we were selling handsome-hunk bodies, celebrity bodies, rich business persons, etc. The life, or whatever you call it, in that realm was very demanding with so many ghosts queued up. Like people, even ghosts had many unfulfilled desires about being able to look good, have an ostensibly rich life; some were after power, which was usual. We did not care how long they were able to sustain in that body or what happened to people around them, their near and dear ones. Later, I heard that some of those ghosts chose to enter into a living body to fulfil vengeance.

Far from realization of the consequence of my doings, I kept on providing the spirits a portal into the real world and was getting into the murky depths of viciousness. And then it happened. One of the bodies which we helped a vile ghost get into went on a bloodbath. He was vengeful and killed many people before being shot down by the police. All those people who died, I have their blood on my hands. Guilt. Guilt. GUILT in all capitals. I cried for many days and nights. I cursed myself many times for getting involved in all this. I cursed Arvind for having pulled me into the depravity.

But Arvind was steadfast on this business, arguing with me that each business has accidents. Even bridges fall down and many people die, but civil engineers don't stop building newer bridges. I was cut out for this business, to help wandering soul get a second chance. He made it look like I was a merchant of hope, from whom departed souls were getting a chance to do what they could not do in the one shot they got. Yes, apart from wicked and debauched souls, we also did business with a few gentle and righteous ones, who did well for the people in their second chance. They were spirits who actually repented when they got a chance to. Guilt and now confusion.

Whatever life I had made for myself in the real world was fading fast. Life passed quickly as I slept in the real world. Money was not a problem anymore. The mirror business was, as they said, a lucky business for me. But dealing with demented souls, souls with unfulfilled desires, with insidious intent had a toll on me. In my early twenties, I wore most of the time a melancholic expression on my face, looking like a person whom people would avoid starting a conversation with. At the age when my friends talked about whether they believed in ghosts and spirits and the supernatural and at times showed enough courage to watch horror movies, I was dealing with the real ones. Most of my waking time, I used to be in my thoughts, seeing those spirits even in my imagination, with eyes open. With the thought that people of my age were either watching cricket or chasing girls, I was chasing ghosts and going around the town with Arvind—guilty, confused, and depressed.

While all this was going on in my life, my parents and other relatives were convinced I should get married. Having a woman partner would infuse some happiness in my life. Probably I was suffering because of a lack of good company. Everybody except me made up their mind to get me married. And my being ready did not really matter. This is how it has worked so long in my side of the country, and I don't see much changing any time soon. So I was married to Rekha, one of the most beautiful girls I had seen in both the realms I travelled.

Soon after the wedding, I realized my parents and relatives were right. On the night of our marriage, when I saw her in full bridal dress and slowly as all those jewels fell away and her saree crumpled between us, I was transported to the pleasures I had never imagined ever existed in the recesses of two souls. I let myself be carried away with those kohl-lined, almond-shaped beautiful eyes. Her shy smile was worth so many words. I wished nothing, nothing ever should come to break the spell of that moment that happened to me, and only me. It was the happiest moment. It is so strange with these happiest moments, we never know when these happen; we are so much part in making it the happiest that we don't know how to cherish it. People said that meditation and out-of-body experience lead you to deepest peace; I felt, in those moments, they were wrong. With Rekha, in that hot humid weather, between those sweet moans, smelling those honey-hued arms decorated with henna, fumbling between her gold chains, I attained my highest peace. For many nights and days that followed, I forgot everything else and the only thing that I was focused on was the new female in my life. My parents were happy to see the smile on my face. I had stopped travelling to the other world. I had no interest left there. I was ready and felt I was already on the path to give up going into that world; at least this is what I thought.

I was happy that Rekha had given me my life back. It was already around three to four months I had not met Arvind or visited the other realm. I wished to forget those experiences as a bad past. But then as they say, you can choose to forget the past, but the past does not forget you. I knew my past would haunt me but didn't put my mind to when it would come or how it would come. I had a constant fear when I was not with Rekha, or at times even when I was with Rekha, that somebody was watching me over my shoulder. Now I was actually working as a mirror shop owner. In lull afternoons when there were hardly any customers or shop assistants, if I would walk in my shop, in those hundreds of mirrors, like a cliché, I used to see those ghosts, those spirits waiting for me, Arvind fuming over my absence, the people whom the rogue ghost had killed. I avoided leaving my cash counter and did not allow any relief to my shop assistants.

One of those evenings when I came home, Rekha told me somebody had come asking for me and had left a letter for me. The person, she said, did not say his name; he looked in some sort of hurry. Unusual, because nobody sends me mail.

The letter was from Arvind; he sent it through one of the persons he had transferred into a body, because as far as I knew him, he would not do such a kind of thing himself. The letter had just three words: 'Meet tonight. —Arvind.' I was very angry to see that. I had not expected Arvind to interfere in my physical world. It was an agreement, from his side rather, that we would keep our physical lives separate. I decided not to respond to it and avoid travelling into that world. A week after, again there was a letter, which said he was waiting. My wife was curious about the letters. I told her it was related to business and she should not worry. I could read her face; I knew she was not convinced and was still worried. She had seen me shredding the letter angrily.

There was a doubt about me on her face, though she did not probe, and I hated Arvind for that. I knew avoiding this any further would only worsen my situation. Also in all these years, apart from knowing that he was an orphan, I did not have any details of where he lived and what he did with all the money he earned. We were friends in that realm, but I did not know anything about his life in the physical world. That night, I decided to meet him.

As I floated out, I saw that Arvind was waiting for me outside my house. He was calm as I spat out my anger at him for sending his agents to my home. I told him that I would not like to meet him and that was the end of our friendship and the end of any business. I threatened him, saying that if he followed up on me in my physical world, I would forget that he was my friend and would do everything to cut his connection back to his physical world. He smiled when I threatened him. His being so calm frustrated me.

I knew my threat did not really mean anything to him. As I turned away to go back, he spoke. His tone scared me. It was neither angry nor vengeful; it was his best one, his smooth, balanced, warm, friendly tone. I knew he would make me doubt my decision, if I heard everything he had to say. But Arvind had that magic on me.

'Jiten, the world is full of billions of people, hardly anybody has the power we have got. These people make lives with their wives, kids, parents and eventually die off. We have a gift. After having this gift, to live a life at the level of those petty people is a crime. You were not made for this, Jiten. You have a higher purpose. Family, money, physical pleasures—leave them for those billions of people. Those are not for us. Maybe we strayed off for some time by making money out of our business in this world. Maybe we need to close that, but to give up this gift is a crime towards your maker, Jiten, don't do that. Don't be hasty. Think over it.'

'I don't care about the gift anymore. I used it for all I had to. My time to hang up my shoes was long due and now finally I have made up my mind, Arvind, don't stop me. If you believe we ever had good friendship, let us leave it as a good memory. Let us not interfere with each other in our physical lives. Our paths were together till here, but now they separate.'

'You are making a mistake, Jiten, you will regret it. Life as you know it is extremely unsure, God forbid you might get killed by a running truck or any other freak accident and then nobody knows if you will ever get a chance of this world. Once you get killed in your physical world you are gone—nobody knows how you can connect here—unless you turn out to be a ghost, which is even worse, and you don't have that in your control. We have learnt so many things together. People spend not just lifetimes but a couple of births to get to the stage you are, Jiten, don't throw this away.'

I looked at him; he was there, pleading to me with his eyes to be back to the good old days. 'Don't follow me, you are on your own, Arvind,' I said and walked away.

The last thing I heard him say that night was 'No, Jiten, *you* are on your own now.'

The next few days were very disturbed for me. I was not at peace, was becoming irritated at every little thing, nor could I focus on my work. I knew what happened between me and Arvind was not the last of our meetings. I can hide from anybody, but not from Arvind. The conversation from that night kept haunting me. I did not know what Arvind would do, though I very well knew what he was capable of. And these thoughts went on like an endless loop in my mind.

In that week, when I stayed most of the time alone, sulking about how to handle the problem of Arvind, my wife came to me, excited, saying that the pundit who had performed the ceremony of our wedding was in town. It was one of the silly traditions that we had: the person who would perform religious rites for marriages is considered nearly as God by the couple and they should seek his blessings whenever they can. My parents said his blessings of 'Bless you with a child' or 'May your spouse have a long life' or a similar kind usually came true. My wife insisted that we should visit him. He would also tell me some solution for my recent aloofness. I was not fond of meeting this guy, but who wants to get the newly-wed wife upset?

He was known by the name of Chhote Baba, which translates to 'the younger guru'. I am sure there was no logic in his name. He must have been called Chhote, which means 'the younger one' when he must have been a kid, and that name stuck around. Such things happen here; names stick. This time when I met Chhote Baba, he was not dressed in his traditional pundit dress, as we saw him in our wedding. He was in plain white cotton shirt and jeans. Well built, a tad taller than me, he looked young to be called a spiritual guru; he must have been in his forties when we met him. He was staying in a small apartment provided to him by one of his followers for his days of visit in that city. There was no fanfare of devotees, there were no flowers nor incense sticks around him, which is typical for these god-people. When I and my wife saw him, he smiled in a way an old acquaintance smiles. There was nobody there in that room other than the three of us. The person who had given the apartment sat in the room outside, allowing the close family friends to meet Chhote Baba. My wife poked her elbow in my ribs to prostrate before the guru and seek blessings. I obliged, I folded my hands, went on my knees, and made a bow.

'May the great god give you peace, my child,' he said.

As I got up, he kept his hand on my shoulder and looked in my eyes. There was something about his eyes that was not normal. He looked through my eyes into me, as if reading what I was thinking, or rather, he had power to know about everything that was locked in me. That look made me hopelessly dumbstruck, as if he hypnotized me, to a degree I felt frightened. With his one hand still on my shoulder, with the other hand he gestured my wife to go out and wait. I felt like a kid whose mother left him with a schoolteacher on the first day of the school. I wanted, rather very much wanted, Rekha to be there with me. But she smilingly went out of the room.

'Jiten, finally I get to meet you peacefully. It is time now, to talk about many things.' His voice was slightly hoarse, with a tone of authority. As I also kept looking at him, I felt I had seen him some place other than my wedding.

'I don't think we met before my wedding, but looking at you now makes me feel we have met before but cannot recall where exactly,' I said.

Chhote Baba didn't answer me, but walked to the door of the room and opened it slightly, craning his neck out, called out to Rekha and the person who had lent the apartment and told them to leave and nobody should be allowed to meet him till he said so. That made Rekha a bit worried and she wanted to ask why and what he wanted to talk to me about, but I could see she was afraid that Chhote Baba might get angry, so she left, with concern on her face. This Chhote Baba was now really freaking me out, more so with his demand for privacy. After a couple of minutes, after he ensured there was nobody around, he started speaking.

'Of course we have met, and I am not surprised that you don't remember me. Remember Naren? He took you once to the group of yogis and told you to follow them? You never went back to that place. You got distracted.'

I was surprised to hear Naren's name after so long. And him knowing something that was only between me and Naren was enough for me to understand that the guy I was talking to was not an everyday pundit. There was more to this man than I knew then. And in those moments, I felt sick in my heart, that the past had again caught up with me. My happy days were getting the ripples from the past and they would rock my soft present.

'You knew Naren?' I asked.

'Yes, very well,' he said in a mocking tone.

I remembered that night when he caught me wandering carelessly. He had that fatherly concern on his face. That was my last meeting with him. My eyes welled up as I thought about Naren.

'Then you also know that Naren died that night. I hope it did not have anything related to you,' I said.

'Yes, I know that as well. And no, it doesn't relate to me, but it is related to you. It is related to you, my child, he died because of you, he gave his life to protect you.'

Those words he said, I always feared them. It was a fear in my heart right from the time I heard my dad read out that damned telegram which announced Naren's death. The fear that it would be linked to me. Though you tend to throw out some feelings, make all efforts to forget, they invariably find their way back to you at unexpected quarters. They surprise you, throw you off guard, and you are left to endure the pain which you wanted to always forget. And mine came back to me after so many years through this most unexpected person who tied my nuptials, whom my wife thought is a kind of person I should meet, who had now me all alone with him. I could feel my wretched guilt palpitating in a form of anger.

'How dare you? How dare you say that? Who are you to comment anything on me or Naren? I don't know what you are up to or, for that matter, who you are! This talk should never have started—but now it is done. I don't want to continue with you, I am leaving!' I said angrily and got up to leave.

'See this, you are still behaving as a kid who needs a cane for making him listen. You have to mature with age, Jiten! Look at you, you are a married man, in a few months you will have a kid, do you still want to behave like this?'

'Having a kid in few months? How the hell you comment on my personal life?' I nearly pounced on this man, but he was a bit bigger than me and I controlled myself just short of taking any real chances of getting physical with him.

'Don't forget I am the one who blessed your wedding. You should respect me and not talk back in this tone. And, yes, you don't know yet, nor your wife, but she is already pregnant.'

I knew he could be right, there was always this possibility. He could be making a guess, though the worst part was that it didn't seem like he was. Somehow, it felt like he bloody seemed to know things. Just the mention of Naren's name had clouded all my judgment. One thing though, I was sure of: he had some evil touch about him.

I calmed myself. There was a reason why this meeting was happening. But why did it happen through Rekha? If I would fight and leave now, I might lose the chance of knowing who he was and why we were meeting. Another part of my mind, though, screamed at me if it would help me to know anything about this evil one. The earlier I got out, even at the expense of few unsatisfied thoughts, was worth it.

I stood there though, waiting for him to say something. But he didn't, he kept staring at me, mocking me with his sarcastic expression. That I was an idiot, not knowing many things.

'Okay, so explain to me, how am I responsible for Naren's death?' I asked getting a hold on my nerves.

'It is difficult, but I will try to make it as easy as possible for you to understand.'

'Thanks.'

'This realm of spirits is casual to you, which is not so for most, let us say it is not accessible to most the way it is for you. There are very few rare occurrences where a person like you stumbles upon this realm. For people who can come to this realm, have travailed for many years, many births to reach to this stage.'

'What you say, I've heard before. Why do I feel that there is a chance that you know about Arvind as well and you are talking to me on his behalf?'

The colour on his face became redder, his expression changed from being irritated to being angry. His left eye twitched and the Adam's apple bobbed up and down a couple of times.

Arvind and Chhote Baba together? Why I did not think about this for so long? Now that I thought about this, it made me suddenly hate this person. Fear even more. I was convinced he was more than I have understood him so far. I got the thing I was looking to cut the conversation and go away. 'You know what, this conversation is over, I am done. Thanks for your time, I am going.'

I started to get up but Chhote Baba, who was stronger physically than me, got up faster like an athlete and pinned me down on the sofa where I was sitting; his face was red with fury and he shouted loudly, 'How dare you insult me by associating with Arvind? I am here to deliver a message and not get insulted. Had people like us not protected you in those realms, by now you would be no less than an aimlessly rambling ghost. You wouldn't have lived to get married, leave apart thinking of children or family. So don't act smart with me, just shut up and listen.'

I was not going to wrestle him. And seeing Chhote Baba's avatar, I had lost my wits and could think of nothing but stare at him wide-eyed. There was silence for a few minutes and I could see his anger going a few notches down, his eyebrows relaxing, and his arms slowly falling down to his sides. He was calm and composed again. He kept his palm on my head, and in the moments those followed, we had left our bodies and were in the realm of spirits. I was here after a long hiatus. He took me to the place which somewhat looked like the place Naren had showed me. There was no one there when we reached it.

'This is a good place for us to talk,' he said, feeling contended with the place. 'Jiten, what do you know about Arvind? Have you ever visited him in his physical form?'

'No. Never felt a need of that. In fact he never encouraged talking about where he lived or what he did when he was not in that world. Why do you ask?'

'My son, as I said, today we are going to talk about many things, and most of the revelations today are going to be shocks for you.'

'Cut the suspense, come to the point.'

'Your friend Arvind does not have any real physical body! He is a ghost like any other ghost, with the difference that he is much more evil and intelligent than any other ghost you have come across till now.'

There are times when you know you have heard clearly but you wish to believe that what you heard was not true, I stood there speechless, motionless for a few seconds contemplating if I was betrayed all this time or this Chhote Baba was a hoax. 'Impossible! I have been seeing ghosts and our kind for a long time, I can make out a difference. What you say cannot be true.'

'A long time, Jiten? Do you even understand what a long time is? Arvind is a few centuries older than you. He is a master at this and you have not even started to scratch the surface of what power you are dealing with. He can easily fool you to believe what he wants you to believe.'

'Why would he do something like this? He has been craving money for a long time. Why would a ghost be greedy for money?'

'Arvind was never greedy for money. Didn't both of you earn money with this body transfers? You have your shop to cover the trace of the money, did you ever check what Arvind did with his money? Jiten, for Arvind money was just a tool, nothing else. Did he ever mention to you about his life in the physical form? The money he extorts he uses for his practices to gain more and more power. Many ghosts he has captured and used as his slaves to get things done for himself. Many like you he has been controlling to get his work done.' He kept quiet for a while, allowing the thing to sink into me before proceeding. His statements seemed convincing. Had Arvind planned for so many years? He was thinking of deceiving me all this while? While we shared secrets while we teased each other, while I cried before him, telling him about how my life in the real world was being shattered? The ego had shattered and there was no rage; it was worse than that, an empty feeling of being sucked.

'You were born with the power to enter this realm,' he said. 'This power does not come just like that.'

'How did it come to me, then? And why, why me? I never asked for this. I would have happily lived my life without this bloody thing that you call a gift!'

'Genes. Heredity.'

'You mean my father too had this ability.'

'Yes.'

'Thank God, I thought that whatever you were saying till now was true. But now I think you have mixed up a few things, what you say is absolutely not true. My parents never had any of this ability,' I said it, but with empty conviction. I did not believe my words, though I wanted to.

Chhote Baba smiled and said, 'Oh yes, Jiten, you carry it in your genes.'

'No, certainly not.'

Chhote Baba continued smiling. 'This is going to be another shock to you, Jiten, but I am sure you are getting used to it, there are few more on the way, so be prepared.'

I saw him staring at me. His smile dissolved, the contours of his face gave him a serious look, and I don't remember the transition. He took a characteristic deep breath that people take before revealing something very secret and important.

'You are not the son of whom you think you are. Your father, the one whom you think of as your father, was your foster father. Your biological father was Narendranath Ghosh!'

'Stop fucking my mind! This is impossible. I had no relation with Naren. I just met him through my father because of my condition at that time.'

'Did it never cross your mind, why would your father take you so far to meet Naren? With Naren, didn't you find anything special there? Did you ask your father how he knew about Naren?'

So many revelations in a day were getting overwhelming. I started being a sucker, a victim, and now an orphan raised by foster parents.

'Jiten, Naren was your father, a person of spiritual liberation, a great person who was dedicated to the well-being of mankind, a true Yogi. Your mother was his student. She too had reached spiritual heights. They were able to unite their energies and control their body and soul. Looking at you now, it seems difficult to believe that they expected you to be their biggest combined creation.'

That last comment felt like a tight slap. When he said that, there was no ridicule in his tone, it was stated as a matter of fact, more like an insult.

'Your mother though died at a very early age. After that, your father devoted full time to his spiritual advances and had asked me to find a suitable couple who can take care of you and act as your parents. Your so-called father was one of the persons whom we thought was a perfect fit. He stayed very far so the chances of him meeting Naren in routine life were minimal. Also, your parents were craving a son without enough money for adoption. They hailed from a good family, bore sound education and many other things suited them, which Naren thought were important.'

'What was that Naren needed so much that he had to leave me and go on his spiritual journey?'

Chhote Baba smiled and continued, 'Jiten don't think Naren was a normal human with a few extra powers. It will be difficult for you to fathom that Naren was not the usual everyday human being. His responsibility was much more than of his own child. Many saints have sacrificed their immediate family for the betterment of life around. Naren was one of them. Naren had been fighting with likes of Arvind and Arvind himself for a long time. The place where we are sitting is one made through his powers. Yogis meet quite often in such places and discuss ways to fight the rising evil in the society. In this place, nobody can enter without my permission, nor can anybody leave. We frequent many places around the world based on where we are needed. Arvind is the opposite of Naren, equally intelligent and a bit more powerful. He too has a place like this. Many yogis claim most of the troubles in this world are because of them. They are the ones who induce evil in minds and souls. Arvind was always a powerful nemesis of Naren. Naren knew that you would have this power of shifting between worlds. That was the reason that he wanted you to be away from him in a more protected environment. The power to roam in this space away from the physical world, to move any distance, floating through ether, is much beyond your current understanding. After you got the hang of the power you had, Naren observed that you were wandering off. It could have been dangerous. The spirits of the likes of Arvind, they can catch a wandering soul like you and can enslave you and get their tasks done through you. Naren was concerned and he made a mistake of coming himself to caution you. In doing that, he exposed himself and you. That night there was a big battle between Arvind and Naren. Arvind would have nearly entered your physical body by severing your connection cord, but Naren's power came in handy and you were saved. And, Naren lost his life. Naren told me before dying that I had to continue where he left and that I should take care of you. But at that stage or even earlier, I could not have compromised my position since Arvind is far more powerful than me. Arvind then approached you and you danced to his tune without you knowing that you were being manipulated. However, in the background I always kept protecting you. The business you were working on of renting physical bodies, I don't deal into. You went too far with that, beyond my powers.'

Chhote Baba was silent for some time. He thought it allowed me to understand the gravity of what he was saying. And I stood there listening to him, feeling that all this should end here, I should go back to the warmth of my wife's arms. This conversation never happened. But I knew I could not stop now. 'And so . . .' I probed him to go further.

'We cannot play God, Jiten. Allowing somebody to enter somebody else's body, giving false hope to the family of a dying person is not just a sin, it is interrupting God's business. We cannot spoil the balance of life and death. The repercussions of this game are extremely dangerous. The likes of Arvind do this and use people like you to get this done. Now do you understand why he stuck around with you? Your first experience of death in the hospital was a deliberate move by Arvind.'

'But, if he is so powerful, why did he need a person like me? He could have done it anyway. He could have entered anybody he liked. What did he achieve through me?'

Chhote Baba kept his hand on my shoulder (and now I was getting used to him staring in my eyes). He said, 'You still don't get it, huh? I told you that you were one of Naren's and your mother's best creations. You are supposed to do much more than what you have done so far. The digression in your path is because of the absence of a mentor like Naren. Had Naren been there to guide you, you were supposed to be the one for our salvation. Your body is much more than rest of the people, it acts like a bridge or a vehicle. Arvind with all the power he had was not able to transfer the spirits so cleanly into the dead bodies. Your presence was the kind of latch those souls needed. And that is your real gift, Jiten, not the accidental ability to move out of your body. That is why Naren had told you that it would be better if you never discover your real gift. There is one in a million or tens of millions like you. Fortunately for you, not many knew of your power. It was only Naren, Arvind, me, and the old lady you used to see, the one with one eye bandaged. She was pleading to you to transfer her. She knew about you because she was following Naren for a long time. She was waiting for you to help her since you were just a kid. But now she cannot trouble you. Arvind has taken care of it.'

'So what has kept Arvind so long away? Why is he not in my body yet?'

'Because he did not know how to disconnect you from your physical body. Disconnecting a vehicle of your kind, the one made by Naren and Chitra, your mother, could not be done by Arvind alone. And why would he do that before he achieves his purpose? You were like a goose laying golden egg.'

'And, is his purpose achieved now? Or rather, what is his purpose?'

'I am not as great as Naren or powerful as Arvind. I don't know what his purpose is, or what he is looking for. And that is not my business. I am an expert executor.'

'What is Arvind waiting for?'

'He was waiting for a perfect opportunity and a perfect place to execute.'

'What opportunity and execute what? Wait, you said you are an expert executor, so what do you execute? And what do you mean by he was waiting for? Has he left me for good?'

'Jiten, an opportunity like this one and a place like where we are right now. He was waiting for this,' he said sedately.

'I don't understand,' I said, becoming worried about what he was saying. His face and voice were freaking me out.

'I am sorry, Jiten, I am supposed to be your godfather, but . . . I am sorry.'

'I am completely lost now. What are you saying, sorry for what?'

'You've never understood anything by yourself. Arvind is far more powerful than I am, and I am not Naren and I cannot give up all my lifelong achievement for you. I am an expert executor at severing the connection of souls with their bodies. I have the power of keeping and trapping people in this place.'

I moved a few steps back. I didn't like where this conversation was going.

'This is not Naren's fort, unfortunately. I am sorry . . . very sorry, Jiten. I couldn't help you. This is Arvind's fort. You cannot come out of this place, unless I unlock. You are stuck here till I live. And that is going to be a long time, Jiten. And as you lie trapped here, Arvind will be Jiten who will be going back home after meeting Chhote Baba. He will be leading a life as Jiten with your wife and son-to-be. They have enough of everything, including money, to carry on their lives, at least for some time.'

Ignoring what he was saying, I made a few attempts to get out of that place, but he was right. I was trapped in that space, in that jail. In a jail between worlds, without chains and bars. I was yet to realize the full gravity of the situation I was in. But then, there would be many years to understand that.

'Why? Why tell me all this shit then? You could have simply taken me here and trapped me and gone back!' I asked angrily, but there was hardly any anger left, in the voice pregnant with sadness.

'I told you already that I am not as great as Naren. I want to live many years, since I want to practice many of these arts. Even greats like Naren do not have control of what happens once a person dies. I don't think my time has come yet to die, at least that is what I wish to think. I don't want to be an unsatisfied spirit in this realm waiting for eternity. Arvind found out recently my connection with you. He found out that I was protecting you. He threatens me, Jiten. He threatens me. I don't want to end up like Naren. I am on the verge of having few breakthroughs in my siddhis, my power in this paranormal world. Maybe I will find out a way to get over the likes of Arvind. But I need time, Jiten, I just cannot afford to waste all my years of relentless travail.'

'Naren must be ashamed of you,' I said, not giving any sympathy to his story.

'I know. I know I am being selfish . . . but if I can do something with what I am working on maybe I will release you, but if I die, Arvind will find one or the other way to get to you and then there will be nobody around to stand by your side. At least you know that I am there, or have a hope in me, that I will help you out.'

I wanted him to go away now, and leave me alone to think about what just happened. This morning, I was with my wife, having a breakfast with her, enjoying her conversation about meeting the pundit who blessed us on our wedding, made our wows sacred. Everything changed in just a few hours. Life is unfair; it made me sad. The gift, they call it, I call it a curse.

'There is one more thing that you should hear.'

'In the last few hours you have made me immune to any shocks or disappointments—just say it.'

'This will, Jiten.'

'Say it!'

He didn't say anything. Those few minutes of silence notched up the impatience in me. Was there anything yet to be unleashed in this hell that could be any worse that it already was?

'Say it!' The voice choked in my throat, and just a few ruptured wails broke out.

'Your son,' he said without looking at me.

'What did you say?' I had heard what he said, but forced myself into thinking that I didn't hear it.

'Your son, yes, it is a son and not a daughter,' he said, looking at me. His eyes were sorry, helpless.

'How dare you say anything about them!' I pounced on him, forgetting that I was trapped in that space and I could not lay a finger on him.

'Please . . . please keep my family out of this . . . please.' I fell on my knees and begged before him. I bellowed, I banged my fists on my chest, and he just kept looking at me.

'Your son . . .' he said, bringing my attention back to what he wanted to say. He gave out a loud sigh as if he could not come to what he wanted to say.

'Er . . . he . . . he slips in here, in this realm unknowingly, from your wife's womb . . .'

Those words were not made of sound. They jumped out his mouth with iron claws and leapt on me, ripped my heart out and pierced it with their talons and shredded it. My son was going to witness this hell? He was not going to get any Naren to mentor him; he would get evils like Arvind!

I was hopelessly impotent, paralyzed, pinned in that space, at the mercy of this creature. My son would endure all the ugly, sinister company in this realm and there would be nobody to guide him. Did that tender being deserve that? This was my final judgment. Hell for me is not as Dante said; it is here, in this forsaken space. Knowledge is the curse. Knowledge of your helplessness, of being a mute spectre as your loved ones endure an undeserved misery.

'Jiten.'

Chhote Baba broke my train of thought and brought me back to where I was.

'I beg you . . . I beg you, do whatever with me, but spare my child. At least do this for me, for Naren, and I will happily accept what I am going through. Protect my family, please . . . please . . . You were my godfather, do this thing for me, find out a way to disconnect my son from coming into this realm. Do whatever it takes.'

'Not that easy, Jiten. I will make a sincere effort. But I cannot do anything till he is born. And if something happens here, before he is . . .'

'Don't say that!' I leapt on him, but was thrown back in that invisible prison before I could touch him.

'I am not saying that something would happen to him, but you are well aware that there is a possibility. There is a possibility that I might die before he is born and then you are free. Even after he is born, I am not sure how I would do that, but I promise if there is a time when I can help, I would.'

'Please do, that is the last respectable thing that you could do to redeem yourself.'

'Once he is born, I will push this floating ability of his into his deep subconscious. This should take care of his moving into this realm unknowingly.'

'Yes . . . do that, please. I beg you.'

'But you must understand, I cannot take something away which is not given by us. I am just making him forget. And memory is a very unfaithful thing, I don't know what can awaken in him this power.'

I looked away from him; I knew what he was saying. 'Okay. Do whatever best you can. Take the curse away from my boy.'

'It is a mistake when parents try to indulge the thought that they can control the fate of their children. What he possesses or will possess is not given by you, it is against nature to interfere with such things.'

'It is a damn sickness!' I yelled. 'And when your child is sick, you have all the right in the world to get him cured. Don't teach me what I should do to my child. This bloody travelling in this realm is not natural; it is a disorder, a malady, a curse on us! I want it to stop with me.'

I fell on my knees and banged my forehead near his feet, forgetting that I was not in the physical body and no amount of banging would hurt me. He understood though, that I was begging. I was crying. 'Please make it stop with me . . . My tender child wanders aimlessly as a phantom in this realm, as close as one can get to the dead . . . oh my God . . . what have I got into?'

He did not reply, allowing me to cry.

After what felt like a long silence, he said softly, 'If this is what you want, I will put all the efforts to do that. I just don't know how good it will be. Such cases hang on hope. As I said, I cannot wipe this off, I am not a magician, Jiten.'

'Time moves slow here.' Those were his last words before he disappeared as a diffused apparition in the enveloping darkness.

'Time moves slow here . . .' I stood there, deep within this cavern of space, gazing out across at endless darkness, contemplating everything that I heard in the last few minutes. I knew struggling to get out would not help and I would get a long time to do that, but that could wait. This was the time when I should sink in the words I heard in the last few minutes, or hours probably. Soaking in the dark clouds of shame and remorse for all the sins committed, I lost track of the time. And it did not matter because the only thing I would have in abundance would be the thing I would like to burn to ashes. Time. Time—I will have lots of it.

In that isolated prison, I was losing track of the real world I was born into. Or was this the real world and all that was just a dream? Was reality so fragile? There were so many whispers, some soft ones, some louder, some were not even whispers. There were loud noises, clamour. And then suddenly everything would cease. Silence. Total silence. A screaming silence. And then softly, Chhote Baba would speak in my ear in his menacing voice, his narrative. A perfect torture. The story he told echoed in the hollows of that space, again and again like a stuck tape, and that sly and oblique laugh.

People believe that after a while we get used to the fear; our mind grows weary of the bother and it shuts off the feeling of fear. On the contrary, the mind just plunges deeper and deeper into the folds of the unfathomable anxiety of fear. You learn newer fears. When the first one ceases to be frightening, the mind generates a new one. Fear spawns fear, that one begets the other, more deliberate, more sinister.

Back home nobody would miss me. God! Why me? Why did you choose me? My wife would wonder why my behaviour has changed. She might start hating me. Arvind, that disgusting creature, would touch my wife with his dirty hands. And she will not know that it is not me. This space between worlds, in my confinement, for my crimes, I will have to endure. And I will, God, please just take care of my wife and my kid.

Time hardly moved. It was slow and painful. In this realm, time flows in an endless manner. I couldn't make out the boundaries of day and night. If years had passed or just a few weeks, I didn't know. Alone, isolated, not able to die, feel hunger, pain, or any physical need of the body. I kept on hoping that all this was unreal and I would open my eyes and find myself beside my wife. But it did not happen. The only thing I had were my memories. I lived and relived my life, sitting there thinking about it over and over again. The mistakes I made.

Slowly in some time, I tried remembering some of the things I had heard about soul refinement, some of the things Naren had taught me. I started contemplating over it. It was difficult in the beginning but then I had no worry of time shortage. Slowly I tried bringing peace to myself. The more I did that, I found there was eternal serenity in that eternal lonely space, in that eternal flowing time.

But the sadness in me ripped me from my peace. The feeling of hatred towards Arvind never subsided. I kept waiting, praying most of the time for either release or death. But neither came when I wished it should come.

I was in deep meditation when it happened. I felt there was no lock around me. I felt I was free. I tried moving out of that space, and I was able to do that. Probably, Chhote Baba found out something. Or he died.

I went to my home. There was nobody there. Arvind had relocated my family. There was no sign of my parents. While going around, I saw the date and realized I was trapped for around twenty-six years! Probably my parents had either moved somewhere or Arvind might have driven them out or they might be no more. I was seething for revenge on Arvind. And to do that, this time I needed a body. I had expertise in taking up the body, but I had never done it, I was never a ghost before, I never needed it. But now I would, I was determined. I had to select somebody with good physique, no health problems, and access to money and weapons if need be. My search went on for a few months and finally I found a vehicle that would suffice me—yes, a vehicle—the body is a mere vehicle. When I was prepared to take that body, I saw there were others as well. It was my test to check my expertise. And I did that. I beat others and now was in a body of a notorious criminal with good connections.

It took me a couple of years of searching for me and my family. Finally I found them. They had settled in a faraway city. When I saw them after so many years, I was not able to control my emotions and I remember I cried like a baby in that hulk of a body. I saw how graceful and beautiful my wife looked with slightly greying hair. Just by looking at her, I could feel her soft touch and the light aroma which enveloped her. I guessed the man next to her was my son. How handsome he looked. In fact, quite like me when I was his age. As for my body, it looked good as well, with a beer belly though. I could not see if my wife had any other children after me. But those three people looked happy. Somehow Arvind did not make their lives miserable. He was living my life honestly. I kept following them for some time, thinking if I should forgive Arvind and let that family be happy while they live or take my revenge.

I kept a vigil on, I kept an eye on Arvind. Though he was not a bad family man, not a wife beater or of that sort, he was still Arvind. Under the façade, he still contacted many spirits and his insidious activities were in full swing. He had heightened his ability to connect to spirits through my body. Keeping him alive, I was never sure when he could harm my wife or my kid or many others. A kill was necessary, even if it meant that my family would get a setback. But my son was ready; he could take care of my wife if it came to that. I was determined.

On one of those nights when I kept following Arvind, I saw him coming back from the infamous brothels. He seemed to be enjoying my body to the fullest. I had decided that it was time; if I killed him in his physical form at that time and made sure his soul leaves and nobody enters, I would kill him for good. But to kill him meant killing my body.

That night as he walked trying to avoid the pits that were dug for the road repairs, I suddenly jumped in front of him, startling him. I looked into his eyes and he looked into mine. Both of us felt we could see each other's soul. He recognized me in the new body as well. But before he could leave the body, my finger on the trigger moved faster. The last sound he heard was the sound of the bullet that pierced his lungs and he fell in one of those pits with a muffled thud. There was shock on his face; he also felt betrayed probably, or he never thought that I would come back and destroy my own body. It hurt to see my body lying in the pit in the gruesome state. I made sure the body was damaged to an extent no spirit would take it up. Finally, I killed myself.

I did not care for this new body; I knew it would anyway wither out soon. I was thinking how I would break all this to my wife and son about this. Would they ever believe in what I would say? Or should I just let it go, never tell them about this, let it be the sad ending of her husband and his father?

I did not realize that somebody was following me. That somebody gave out heart-rending cries, and as I looked back, I saw my son. I did not realize that Arvind had inducted my young son already in his bad vices. In keeping an eye on Arvind, I had not looked at my son at all. I realized then that my son was also coming from the same red-light area. Before I could say anything, for me too, the last sound was of the bullet that was came out of my son's gun and made an entry in my forehead.

'You should have not killed my father!' he said as he cried.

I landed on top of my very own body; in the few moments before I died, I looked into my son's eyes, felt like I probably made a connection, blessed him, and closed my eyes, knowing that I did not know about the journey from here on.

Looped

Pratap trudged slowly towards the bus stop. Carrying his laptop backpack, both thumbs locked in the shoulder straps, head down, he watched absentmindedly the little clouds of dust he made as he kicked the pebbles on his way. A bit underweight with an average Indian height, Pratap had all the qualities to disappear in a crowd. People like him were not uncommon in Pune since it had gained the status of upcoming IT hub in India, followed by Bangalore and Hyderabad. Many people coming from idyllic remote cities or villages, following the dream of affluence, urban lifestyle had lost their own identities in the infrastructure jungle of metro cities like Pune. Pratap was one of them. Coming from a small village, Udhana, in the state of Gujarat, which was hardly bigger than one of the sectors in Pune, he did not seem to get the hang of the local culture or language of Pune. This morning as he walked to the bus stop, he looked weary, sleep deprived, with dark patches beneath his eyes.

A Monday morning, it is 8 a.m. and his day has begun. Standing there, he waits for the company bus. In that half-asleep, tired state, somewhere he feels pride that he has a special bus and he no longer has to cling to the bar of the bus door as he did before getting his job. He mildly scoffs at others on the bus stop. He usually kept to himself most of the time; he was not a conversation picker, more so because he did not know the local language and people around him looked to speak only that. It was already ten minutes past eight, and the bus was still not there to pick him up, making him impatient and mumble a few curses under his breath.

Half-sleeve checked light-pink shirt with black fitted trousers a tad shorter than what could be a perfect fit, a black backpack with his company name and logo in orange, he stood out to be different from the rest of the people waiting at the bus stop. Of the others standing there, waiting for the bus, two men who seemed to be in their seventies stood there patiently, in spotless white kurta and pyjamas, with a bright fluorescent pink-coloured turbans. One of them was busy rubbing the dried tobacco flakes on his palm and the other person looked expectantly to get a share from the wad of that tobacco. A lady in traditional saree stood with her back pushed against the railing of the bus stop, carrying a kid around a year and half. The kid was naked save for the black thread on his waist. There were a bunch of kids in school uniform waiting for their school bus. These kids were looking at Pratap, whispering to each other and laughing. One of those fellows, who had his front teeth gifted to the tooth fairy, was just not able to control his laughter. He tried covering his mouth with his two little palms, but the spray through the missing teeth was unstoppable. Wiping his hands on his shorts and the pole of bus stand, he continued laughing.

This irritated Pratap. He looked around, very consciously, but tried showing as if it was natural, touched his face to see if there was something funny there. He moved towards the shiny tin sheet that was nailed on the left of the bus stop to look at himself. The sheet had a poster of a voluptuous actress in red blouse from a recent movie. People had torn the face and few more areas from that poster. When he stood before that shiny greyish tin sheet and saw himself, it looked as if he stood there in red blouse with plump midriff and his tight black pants under that. For a few seconds he stood there and laughed at his own image. But the next instant when he saw his black pants, he realized to his utter embarrassment why the kids were laughing. His zip was open and the corner of his pink shirt was peeping from the open space and looked like a bold pink triangle on the black pants!

His face turned red with embarrassment and he quickly looked around to see if anybody else was also watching him. He was suddenly feeling hot under his armpits, with the feeling that the entire world around him was looking just at him. It did not feel right to zip it up there, so he moved his hand there making it look very casual and walked few steps behind the bus stop. He could hear the roar of laughter from the kids. He ignored them and focused on zipping up, but the damned zipper was stuck in one of the threads from the protruding shirt! He was cursing and praying under his breath, as the drops of sweat on his forehead rolled onto his sideburns, his underarms were getting wet as he frantically made short slight squats and tried pulling the zip up. In this mental mayhem, from the corner of his eye he saw his bus coming. Come on, come on up . . . up . . . up . . . No! Damn, the pink loose thread from the shirt was now all entangled there. As the bus came near the bus stop, it honked a couple of times, but he could not get in the company bus in that position. Finally the bus came at the bus stop but did not halt completely; it just slowed enough for one or two persons to get in.

Finally, Pratap managed to pull the zip up and he quickly rushed in front but by then the bus had moved ahead and had picked up the speed. Pratap ran behind the bus for a few meters but missed it.

He did not wish to go back to the bus stop to catch the city bus, especially with the squeals of laughter coming from the kids echoing there. He thought of catching an autorickshaw, but it was not very regular in this part of the Pune outskirts. After walking for about five minutes, he saw a *tempa*. *Tempa* is a local name for a vehicle common in this part of Pune; it looks like a black machine pig, has five wheels, has space enough for six people to sit comfortably but is usually crammed with at least ten people. He signalled it to wait and the tempa obliged. In the tempa, his hands still checked his pants to ensure the safety of his zippers.

He was cursing the day, the city, and the office. Nothing in Pune was good. The morning episode he conveniently blamed on the new city, something like this would never have happened in Udhana.

Finally after a couple of hops between the tempa and autorickshaw, he reached the office.

What now? He asked himself. The first email of the day was a reminder mail from his manager to fill his time sheet for last week. The same email also reminded him that progress of his work done was not updated in the system. 'Wow, thanks. Nice start of the day,' he thought. Along with Pune, he cursed his manager, Chandrakant Patel. One of the words he hated in IT was ASAP and more so because this was probably the favourite word of his manager. Each email from his manager ended with this word.

What followed in the day was the daily routine of team meetings, targets, more work / less time, the so-called Monday motivational speeches (which were nothing more than a 'eh!'), and the usual blah-blah which went on. Afternoon came earlier than he thought. It was already lunchtime. The office had a cafeteria at the ground floor. He never took lunch with his friends. He went alone. The fact was he didn't have any friends. Before entering the cafeteria, he looked at the menu and gave a sarcastic 'humph' kind of a grunt. Like always, lost in his thoughts, he was eating his lunch slowly. A bowl of lentil soup, spicy eggplant curry, curd, rice, and extremely red pickle, and there was absolutely nothing new about it. He was feeling sad and beaten and he did not know why. This as well was not was not new to him. He knew something was wrong. He never felt good in Pune. Probably he was missing his own small happy village, in this metro city, he thought. He did not realize when he finished his lunch, put his tray on the dishwashing counter and slowly dragged himself back to his desk.

At his desk, he kept fiddling with the stationery there, still drifting in some other parallel worlds conjured in his mind. Not many people disturbed the trance of Pratap. They had learnt to leave him. As per them, Pratap was boring. He did not have any real work since he had joined. Had read a few manuals, had a few trainings but no real work. In his recent appraisal, his manager had told him he was not proactive. 'Proactive, my ass,' he said to himself. 'Pratap, you are not focused' was his manager's next line in the appraisal. 'I am focused, you buffoon, but what will I focus on, your fat ass? Do I have anything real to focus on?' He kept on talking to himself. 'See, you don't even heed what I say.' His manager continued his own rant. And Pratap continued his own to himself. On the surface he was calm. His eyes were fixed on the edge of the table, peeling off the mica from the corner with his fingernails. He had walked out of the conference room with the lowest grade and a message of no bonus, without any fight. After Pratap had walked away, his manager kept staring the door for five to six minutes without realizing how to react, then exhaled with a big audible noise, bobbed his head sideways a couple of times, and left the conference room feeling even lower than Pratap. He had come prepared to give a pep speech followed by warning to Pratap, but it seemed as if he had failed miserably.

Today after lunch, Pratap was going through those moments again. He didn't realize that his eyes were wet. He suddenly felt he missed his mother. His mom—he wanted to rush back to her, leave this fucking slavery of men and machines and go back to his own small peaceful village. There was no special reason that day, but a trickle went down from his eye. His wiped his eye and went to the toilet. He cried there. Probably he cried because it was Monday. Probably because of the way the day had unfolded. Probably because of his recent appraisal. Probably Pune. Probably everything.

After he came back and slumped on his chair, then something happened. Something strange moved within him. His body went lose, his muscles were as if not in full control. He closed his eyes and took a deep breath. He felt relaxed and he felt in those moments, he slipped into something rare to him: a few moments of peaceful sleep.

After a while, he got up, didn't care to look at the clock, packed his laptop in his bag, and just went out of the office. Nobody noticed him leaving. Everybody was busy in their work or gossip. He got into a running bus, surprisingly easily. The bus was so full, nobody came for tickets. At his stop, he just got down. Reaching home, he did not feel hungry as usual. He went and crashed on his bed.

He fell asleep, a long, peaceful one.

He got up feeling fresh as never before. He did his usual chores with more speed and by 7:30 a.m. he was already at the bus stop, neatly dressed, though in the same type of clothes. But more important than the clothes was that he was wearing a big smile today. The bus was supposed to come at eight, so he was waiting patiently, not restless like usual. The Pune breeze was cool and relaxing this morning. In a few minutes, the lady with the kid came to the bus stop. Today, the lady did not laugh or smile. She just stood there. Pratap looked at her kid; their eyes met. The kid gave a slow gentle smile, showing his front two teeth. That smile made Pratap happier. Then the schoolkids came. Probably it was their exam day; they all were sombre. One of them was reading from his schoolbook, the other two fellows were discussing a mathematics problem, something related to the price of a diamond being proportional to its weight. He got onto the bus and had the best day. Nobody shouted at him and things went very smoothly. He just sailed through all the troubles. He was not able to believe what was happening. Suddenly, the city of Pune, which he considered rife with misfortune, misery, loads of work, angry people was seemingly a perfect place. The evening was happy. That night he slept early.

When he got up, he saw that he was up early, again pretty fresh. He reached the bus stop early. The weather was nice. In a few minutes, there was the lady with the kid. The lady was in her thoughts and did not react to Pratap's presence. Pratap saw the kid and gave him a smile. The kid gave a slow gentle smile, showing his front two teeth. Pratap felt something familiar about it. A few minutes later, a bunch of kids came. All looked in a serious mood, as if it was their exam day. One of the boys was reading his schoolbook. The other two were discussing something. Pratap had a feeling of a longish déjà vu. He went near them to hear what the boys were saying. He knew what they should be speaking but could not exactly recall. Then he heard them speaking about a mathematics problem about the price of a diamond being proportional to its weight.

'Aha, exactly, yes, I knew it.' Then the bus arrived like it came yesterday. And slowly the day unfolded exactly like yesterday, but each time, he only knew about the thing after it had happened. He felt how good it would be to know at least two minutes in advance. He would be a hero then, saving the world. But it did not happen. He knew he had seen the thing only when it happened.

He went home and slept; it was a bit slower day than yesterday. He got up at 7:00 a.m. and rushed through the chores and managed to reach the bus stop in time. He boarded the bus, waved at the bunch of kids who were probably reading science textbook for their next paper in exams. One of the kids was reciting in a very poetic way the definition of 'density' over and over, enough to make everybody around him learn it. The day was fairly okay. He got a task to call up one of their clients and get the necessary information for the problem they had. He was able to note all the info correctly and fill in a blue coloured screen with loads of information about the call. He thanked the client before putting the phone down. He sent the information to another team to solve it as he waited for another call. The day finished early; Pratap went home and slept. After getting up, he realized he was late, and he acted faster to reach the bus stop on time. There he saw the kids reading a science textbook. One of the boys was reciting the definition of 'density'. The day again followed the same scheme which he had lived through, including talking to the client and filling the information again. Even this time he was unable to predict; the events struck him only after those had happened. What was going wrong with him? That night he went home and did not sleep.

He kept on drinking mug after mug of tea. It was very late and it did not register with him when he fell asleep. Getting up was really painful. He barely managed to reach the office. He looked tired and was not focused on his work. His manager came and gave a look of contempt, let out a husky grunt, and left. The night followed, the day followed, in the pattern which he knew there was a husky grunt, but only after it was let out.

This routine went on for a few days or weeks or months; Pratap had lost the count. It was just double days he had been facing. He looked wearier and wearier with each passing day. He was carrying a blank expression all the while. This morning, Amar, the boy on the other side of his cubicle in the office, came up to him and said in a low whispering voice, 'It is time that you visit Dr Kapadia.' Pratap just gave a nod without looking at Amar.

Pratap followed the advice and went to Dr Kapadia, the psychiatrist who had his clinic in the campus of all those IT companies. The stress from the work probably demanded a shrink to be around. At Dr Kapadia's clinic, at the reception there was the familiar face of Geeta, the doctor's receptionist. Seeing Pratap, she said he had to wait, since Dr Kapadia was tending to one of the patients.

Patients—Pratap knew she was going to say this. With Dr Kapadia, the session was an echo of events he knew would happen.

'So, Pratap, the dreams?' Dr Kapadia's question was more like a statement.

Pratap looked at Dr Kapadia as if he was looking through him towards the switchboard on the opposite wall, as if he was asserting his own thoughts. 'I don't know. I just get repeat telecasts.'

'Pratap, what do you feel, are you dreaming now or are you awake?'

'What do you mean? I am awake right now, of course!'

The last thing he remembered from the conversation was that his sight blurred and he could see the doctor's smiling face blurring into bright light that shone into his eyes.

'Mr Patel,' Dr Kapadia said, 'your son is a case where we have to be patient, rather very patient. Neither I nor any other sleep specialist can bring immediate results. The psychologically induced sleep disorders that we are discussing with the country's top neurologists and psychologists are all telling us to wait and see the effect of medication.'

'But, doctor, he has been in this condition for a few weeks, since he came to Pune for his job. Doctor, he is our only son, a boy in his early twenties, we need to do something. I cannot face his mother, who blames me for pushing him to come to Pune. This is why we have moved him to your care!' His father broke down as he said this.

'All these threads are related, Mr Patel. As per my recent talks with Dr Udwadia, the best psychoanalyst we have, the condition of Pratap is largely because of both of you. You were extremely strict and your wife was extremely light on him. I am sure you knew very early on that he was a more sensitive kid then many of his age. Every time people made fun of him, or you ridiculed him, he used to find solace only in his mother, nobody else. Every encounter Pratap faced in this new place, a strict, tough person was always a representation of you in his life, with all your good intentions when you had compelled him to come to Pune so that you can toughen him. But in doing this, you robbed him of his only mental shelter, his mother. This drove him to extreme depression. As I know, he had been crying many nights when he reached here. Slowly he got into the condition called narcolepsy, in which he had attacks of sleep at various times of the day. He used to drift into long dream spells. His office staff was supportive and used to allow him to sleep. We don't know yet how his narcolepsy moved into hypersomnia, where he is now having long sleeping time. We also don't know why he is in REM phase, that is, in layman's words, dream state in this condition. Usually in hypersomnia, patients don't dream so much. This makes the case of Pratap stranger. But I assure you, Mr Patel, we will have a breakthrough very soon.'

Chandrakant Patel with tears in his eyes was seeing his son on the hospital bed; his wife, sitting near the pillow, had one fist clenching Pratap's hand and the other hand she was moving through his hair. Amar, Pratap's school friend, was standing near the bed, looking at something outside the window. He closed his eyes and allowed the tears to flow as he prayed.

Next day, Pratap got up feeling very low. He took a slow shower, lost in thoughts. He dressed himself absent-mindedly. He was in his usual black pants and pink-checked shirt. He did not realize that his pants zipper was open and his pink shirt corner peeped out. He walked slowly to the bus stop, carrying on his slender shoulders the weight of his backpack. He was ridiculed at the bus stop by a bunch of kids and he missed his bus. He knew that kids were going to laugh at him and that he would miss the bus. He knew the day was going to be terrible and he just waited for it to unfold.

Jack shall have Jill;
Nought shall go ill;
The man shall have his mare again,
And all shall be well.
            —Shakespeare, *A Midsummer Night's Dream*

Mismatchmaking

I wished to die.

Suicide, yes. I was not sure though, which would be the best way to. I picked up the razor blade to slice my wrists. I gently pressed my thumb on the definite hard edge of that sharp and cold metal blade as I kept staring at left wrist, my target for the cut. I softly traced the blade over my wrist with the lightness of a butterfly and realized blood gushing out of my wrist was not the way I would like to die. My favourite and the costliest bed sheet would be stained. I would not like to see it that way, even after I died. I did not have any good strong rope to tie a noose around my neck. And I didn't like the sight of the way the body hung after a person died. There was a railway station about 300 metres from my home, so there was an option of dying under a speeding train, but to have my guts cut and splattered for an ending would be such a gory and horrible way to die. I dislike even the Final Destination movie series, and to do something like that to myself was unthinkable. With poison, I might throw up and land up in a hospital.

I was indecisive here as well, as I had been for the most part of my life. I didn't wish to live in those moments, and dying felt like an easy option. But I didn't have enough stomach to go ahead and kill myself. I felt how good it would be to just walk out of my body. All the philosophy said that the body is a mere cloak for the soul. Then why couldn't I just take that cloak off, without pain? Have a new cloak without any stains from my old cloak—how convenient that would be. God cheated. God has been cheating me for most of my life. Destiny (yeah, easy to blame that bitch) wanted me to live, see many nights and days, face more disappointments, endure more pain, go through few more insults. I cursed myself, I cursed the situation, and I cursed her. (*Her* is not destiny; *her* is she who ruined me. I cursed her.)

I cried. I cried at everything. Why did she say that ours was not a relationship yet? All this while, she was just checking if both of us matched. Matched? How can someone say that so casually? I felt as if a heavyweight boxer punched me in my guts. There was a searing pain in the hollow of my abdominal cavity when she said that. Who said there was heart involved in love? My pain was in my guts and not the heart. I would have preferred to die in front of her with a heart attack (painless though). And then my soul would have flown over her and enjoyed seeing her scream and shout and people gathering around her and blaming her for my death. That would have been such a perfect way to die. But I did not die. I did not say anything to her. I did not shed tears. After she walked off from Coffee Café Day, our usual meeting spot, I sat there for a few minutes, paid the bill, and then left. She did not even wait for me to come out with her. She called me like an hour before saying that she wanted to talk about something important. I had thought that she wanted to fix the date of our wedding. I was excited to meet her; I wore the special perfume, the one I had kept for parties and weddings, my silk shirt as well. I thought I looked good. I thought she liked me like that. I waited for her in the café. When she came, I stood to greet her; she smiled and sat down. I did not know that in the next two minutes, my world would come crumbling down. How does this happen that just moments before, we have no idea that our life is going to change forever, even end? We are enjoying, we are dreaming, we are seeking nothing more from God, thinking our life is perfect, and in just a moment, everything is poof! Gone! The entire dream of future life you daydreamed is gone! Buh-bye! How unfair is real life. I like the soap opera life, where before the change, they take a commercial break and they show a sneak preview of what is coming up. There is bloody no sneak preview in real life and that is so mean of God! God cheated. He has been cheating me for most of my life!

I was thirty-two already, where was I going to find another girl? Six weeks back, my parents had put my profile in an online matchmaking site. My job in IT maintenance was put as handling and supporting international customers. Everyone does that. Nobody's job profiles you see on matrimony site are for real. My salary was stated a bit more than what my boss makes. After a few rejections, four weeks back, my father had received a call from her parents. They all came to meet us. I fell in love with her at first sight. Or whatever they call it when you lock your eyes with somebody and you feel how great it would be to spend a lifetime with her. As she sat on our black rickety spring sofa which squeaked every time somebody sat or moved on it, she looked as if she came right out of my imagination. She looked like a goddess to me, a bit on plump side though. Blackish brown flowing hair curled just around her shoulders. It looked as if the dangling earrings were too heavy for her soft and small earlobes. I marked it when she tucked the loose tendril behind the ear. Once, the manager in our office told me as part of my annual appraisal that I did not have an eye for details. Bullshit! Look at me now! I still remember all the details of that day. She wore a yellow tight-fit salwar showing all the necessary body contours, and red tights, with sleek red Bata sandals.

Our parents said we could go to my room and talk to each other, get to know a few things about each other before we made a decision. Seems weird that in these times of Facebook and other social networks where we share everything, right from the insignificant facts as colour of the underwear to life-changing milestones like getting married, that too in real time, we had to be 'allowed' by parents to go a different room and talk. However weird it seems, when parents are involved in finding your match, this is how it is. And if I think about myself, it is not a bad system. The talk with her was great. Most of the time, it was me who was talking and she was responding with different tones and lengths of 'hmms', all the while with her eyes looking at the floor and her fingers playing with the corner of her yellow salwar. What lovely, slender fingers she has (or should I say, had). I never knew before that moment, that talking about nothings could be so intoxicating. It was around twenty-three minutes of talk with her, when my father called me from the living room downstairs, saying that her parents were leaving. In those twenty-three minutes, I had made a decision of the rest of my life. She was the one made for me and I was made for her. Thirty-two years' waiting was worth the wait. Before she left the room, I asked for her email ID. She smiled and blushed; the reds on her cheeks made her even more beautiful. Or maybe I imagined that red colour there, but there was no doubt that she looked beautiful. She scribbled her email ID on the scrap of paper and made a smiley below her ID. I still have that piece of paper in my wallet. I felt people like me inspire Karan Johar.

Our first meeting flashback is finished and I am back to reality, the hard reality of being rejected. I took out that piece of paper from my wallet and kept staring at it; tears rolled freely now. I crumpled and tore it apart before throwing it on my table. I had my happiest days in those four weeks and now suddenly everything seemed like a distant dream. On the night of our first meeting, I had emailed her and added her as a friend in Facebook, which she had accepted immediately. We chatted throughout the night. She worked as a schoolteacher. She taught mathematics and science to seventh-grade kids. Her school supervisor was a jerk and the principal was a good person who understood her. The vada pav in her school canteen was delicious. The other teachers, including the supervisor, were jealous of her, because the principal favoured her. The kids also liked her. They made a ruckus for all other teachers, but for her they were well behaved. They never hit her with pieces of chalk, crumpled bits of paper or hooted at her when she turned to write on the board. Except once, last year on Teachers' Day, when she had her hair untied and wore a sky-blue saree with a sleeveless blouse, according to her and some staff members, she looked very good and sexy; a few of the senior boys whistled at her. She confessed that though she glared at them in anger, she liked it. To know so much about somebody, and that somebody could be a beautiful girl, was like defining heaven for me. Whosoever said that it was difficult to know a person in a lifetime was dumb.

But now, as I sit here contemplating suicide, I realize how wrong I was.

At the age of thirty-two I was still a sex-starved virgin. While all my friends told me about their victories around their carnal experiences, I kept my desires in control. Her coming into my life made me feel my life was coming out of Karan Johar's movies—all colourful with romance at its best. I had her photo as the wallpaper on my office laptop. When people asked me about her, I acted as if I wanted to avoid the conversation around that topic and then with pride told them that she was the one, my life, and that we were soon going to get married. I also carried her photo in my wallet. They might be laughing behind my back, but I did not really care. I thought they would be jealous soon when they saw me married with her. Many nights, I would imagine our wedding night, exactly like they show in movies, to the details of me drinking the almond milk and slowly removing jewel by jewel from her bejewelled body as she blushed and looked away from me. I also read her poetry from Rumi that night. But all that came crashing down, suddenly. I wondered how a few curt words can destroy everything, shatter all our dreams. How was I going to go to the office again, face the people around when they would ask me about her?

Her name is Pria. She did not use *y* in her name like other Priyas. 'We are not a match' keeps reverberating in my heart. What should I do, should I write my frustration about her on Facebook, before I die? Should I make her responsible in front of the world by using Facebook as my suicide note? Should I tag her?

I thought about it for a few minutes and knew I would not do any of those things, nor would I die, not tonight, not like this, not suicide. To chew on the thought of suicide is one thing but to go ahead and see yourself dying needs more willpower and I lacked that throughout my life. And as I sat there on my bed, looking at the pieces of her photo, slowly the thought of suicide diffused. I realized what a fool I was to think about such a step. Thankfully, I did not go through with my thoughts in that moment of madness. Good God, I thank my wobbling knees and indecisive mind that I could not kill myself. Though, I still want to get married to Pria. And in that moment of realization, what floated in front of my eyes was my true inspiration. *Hindi desi Bollywood* movies! A montage of movie songs flickered through my eyes, pumping confidence in me, the girl saying no should not be taken as a no until . . . I don't know until what or when. But I deserved a try.

I sat in my room, thinking of my next moves. The good thing would be to meet her again. Not by asking her on the phone or email, but by directly surprising her. I opened her resume the matchmaking site had sent us and noted her residential address. I wondered why I never looked at it before. The plan was to go and wait outside her house and keep an eye on her activities. Wait for next good moment. In the meantime, build some impression on her family. I quickly became the Hindi movie protagonist, imagined that outside her house there were a few goons harassing her and her father, and I come just in time to beat the hell out of the villains. My punches and flying kicks land them twenty feet away after I do three somersaults. And I become the lover boy turned action hero. By the time I get up from the fight, there would be a small stream of blood from the corner of my lips, and Pria would come running and tear her dupatta and clean my face, and then hug me with all her sweetness. Her father would be blessing us, standing a few feet away, looking with pride at what a hero his daughter has chosen.

Her house is a small house with one floor up having a large window and a balcony facing the road. I should be careful not to be spotted from that window and make myself look like a stalker. I am the hero and not the villain here. The floor down has three sides open and one side shared with their neighbours. Most of the houses here were similar. I could see a car, a blue Maruti Zen parked in front of their gate, and a white scooter at its side. I did not see her black scooter which she rode when we met. She must be out, meeting that new person who was creating a love triangle in our story. I chat with the paan- and cigarette-wallah on the opposite side of the road, keeping an eye on her house.

It is 9 p.m. as per my watch and I do not see the black scooter coming back, though I see light and silhouettes of others in the home. The cigarette hawker is getting restless with me, so I drive around the block, pass around a few narrow streets to kill time till she comes. After about fifteen rounds around the block, I come around the front of her house; I still don't see her scooter. I take a U-turn and came back to check the house number; it matches with the address I noted from the site. It is now around 10 p.m. and she is still not back. I was concerned and jealous, which was more I was not sure, probably more jealous. When she was with me, she stayed with me only till seven and now it is 10 p.m. and still she is going around. I wait, burning petrol going around the blocks at least twenty, thirty times.

My watch shows twelve o'clock, and still no sign of her black scooter. I take out my cell phone and log in to Facebook. I should have thought about this earlier. I see her status as available. I wished she was like that in life for me. I knew she did not make her status available through her phone, so she must be at her home, then why was her scooter not here? Against all the warnings from my brain, I sent a hi to her. In the next minute, I see her status turning into 'away'. Weary, I drive back home. It is late for me as well. I get the suspicious looks from my mother when she opened the door for me.

'Lots of work,' I reply to her questioning eyes and walk straight into my room.

I knew what I should be doing tomorrow first thing in the morning: call up my office and call it a sick day.

This morning, I get dressed as usual but make the call to office as planned. Parents believe I am going for work as usual. So far so good. I drive straight to the hawker opposite to her house. For you all, reading my story, don't worry. I am not a psycho, I am not going to harm the girl, I am just an everyday, unmarried male, who is in love with a girl. A male, rare species to be a virgin at the age of thirty-two. I say this in my mind to make myself feel whatever actions I am taking are justified.

I still didn't see any black scooter. I asked the hawker if he knew who stayed in that house.

'Vinod sahib', he said.

I did not remember her father's name, so I asked if he knew if there was a young lady living there. He looked at me with suspicion, but since I had bought the pack of Gold Flake cigarettes, my price for getting the information (though I don't smoke), he was okay to give me the information I asked.

'Pria memsahib.'

So my location was correct, then what the hell happened to her scooter? I did not wish to go into the details of her vehicle with the hawker. So I waited. After waiting for an hour, I saw a girl coming out, must be between twenty-five to twenty-eight years old. I wondered who she could be.

'So now you see your Pria memsahib,' mocked the hawker, smiling at me.

'No, no, I am asking about Prriiaa, not her sister, or whosoever she is, she is not Pria,' I said.

'Sahib, I am here for many years, I know who Pria memsahib is, she is Pria memsahib,' he replied.

While we talked, that girl passed us without acknowledging my presence.

I was confused. I directly went home, told my parents I was not feeling well so I came back early from office. I went straight to my room and opened the matchmaking site and searched for her first name and last name. Three candidates came up, and one of them was the girl I just saw, the girl to whose house I went like a stalker, but *my* Pria, or the Pria I was searching for, was not listed there. Then who was the girl I was talking to? And I also knew now, that omitting *y* from *Priya* is not unique as she claimed.

I checked the helpline number on the site and called them. After I had a brief altercation with the girl on the other end, probably from some remote call centre, about the issue, she finally transferred my call to their supervisor. It took me nearly one hour to actually talk to the supervisor; every time somebody connected me to the supervisor, it went on in a long wait with the irritating Bollywood wedding number.

After every thirty seconds, they thanked me for holding and invariably after hearing three thank yous, the phone was disconnected. The last girl I talked to on the phone, I was so infuriated with her explaining the same situation again and again, I was downright verbally abusing the girl on the other end.

I felt like killing the supervisor when he blurted out his rehearsed first few sentences: 'Sir, how may I help you? Did you have a look at our newly uploaded catalogue and also we have a new app for Android phones.'

I take pride in the way I controlled my anger and cooled myself down, nearly like a professional. I wanted to understand what happened and not vent out my anger on him. After explaining to him my story, the line went silent for a while and it took me three blank hellos for him to respond.

'Sir, we had a problem two weeks back. We had thought that we had cleared everything up. But looks like not everything was rectified,' he replied.

'What problem? And what is not rectified?' It was too much for me now to control my anger any more.

'Sir, some weeks back, one of our clients was refused by another of our clients, and the rejected person felt we were somehow responsible for it. So he hacked into our site and messed up our databases. He mixed the people with same names and their addresses and created havoc. It took us around two days before we understood what was going on. We connected with our clients and already apologized and sent them the correct profiles. But since you did not get back to us and we missed contacting you as well, your case fell through the cracks. We have also filed an FIR against the person, with the cyber police. Sir, we sincerely apologize. We will refund your money and also provide you free service and the new app for Android phones free of cost. Please do not post against us in social media.'

When I asked him about the Pria whose profile they sent me, they told me that once a person confirms that she got her match, they remove the profile from the public permission area and don't provide her information to anybody else. Since she had requested to remove her profile, it would be unethical and illegal to say anything about her. And he hung up.

What the fuck! Ethical, my ass! My case fell through the cracks and they give me the ethical bullshit! And yes, don't forget to shove that bloody app for Android up your ass. And all this while I was speaking to some other Pria!

I immediately logged in to Facebook to check about her. To my utter dejection I found out that after last night's unwanted hi, I was blocked from her friend list. So I called her number, but that number was unreachable. I finally settled for sending her an email—email that said I would like to meet her once. I respected her decision but requested her to meet me once more. I would be going to our meeting spot, the café, at six every evening till she decided to come and meet me.

After I wrote that mail, something changed in me. I prayed after that. I actually requested God that her decision would change and she would meet me. And that she would accept me. I did not pray when I was rejected, just became dejected when she said that we were not a match. But with this goof-up, things changed. I feel it was not accidental. There are no accidents, my teacher once said. I conveniently put that philosophy here. I feel Pria will realize my love and come back to me. Now that I recall our meetings, I remember the twinkle in her eyes when she talked to me. She cannot betray me. The problem in the site was meant for me, so that I can meet my real soulmate. I would not have liked the 'real' Pria, had the site worked well.

My life till now was plain, no story, and this search for my love has given everything a new meaning, a new excitement. Pria was a gift from life to me, the one I or my parents did not plan. If I get her, it would be a hell of a story to tell our kids; if I don't get her, well, I have not thought of that part, at least not yet. I vow, if I and Pria meet again and she accepts me, I would put whatever money is needed to bail out that crazy fanatic who hacked the site. I would thank him. As Paulo Coelho says, when you want something, all the universe conspires in helping you to achieve it. I pray to God, make sir Paulo Coelho right. Or like in

Hindi movies, if it is not a happy ending, the movie has not ended. Till I meet her, I will not be at ease. Wow, I feel energetic, something to look forward to, I feel indeed like a desi movie hero. My story starts now!

How I wish to live!

Club Turquoise

I was staring at the person sitting on the aisle seat diagonally across, two seats ahead of me, on my flight from New York to Mumbai. The shiny bracelet dangling from his sleeve arrested my attention. Maybe it was just a coincidence. I kept telling myself that, but was not able to take my eyes off that shimmering stone hanging on his wrist. The flight had just taken off and the seat belt sign was still on so I had to stick to my seat for some more time before I could ask him about it. I had seventeen more hours in the flight to find a good time to chat. I knew that the next few hours would be restless till I talked to this person.

I touched the amulet under my shirt and felt its delicate warmth between my fingers. Slowly, I took it out and held it with my fingertips. The translucent blue stone dazzled the same way as it did many years back when I had received it. I closed one eye, focusing the other eye on it and gently rotated it in my fingers, following the bluish hue it made on my palm with the tender morning sunlight shaft that came from the flight window. I realized the person sitting next to me was staring at me, wondering at my kid-like act. I gave him a nod, a short pursed smile and slid back the amulet under the shirt. I felt it took some sun and passed it in me. Its warm touch felt comforting on my chest.

The seat belt sign was off; I reclined my chair, eased my shoulders, extended my legs, took out my U-shaped pillow, and tried to relax. I had no intention to sleep, but putting on the eye mask would help me concentrate. I did that, and just as they show in movies, the scenes from the past started flashing. Me, seven years old. My native village of Khavada, in Kachchh near the India-Pakistan border, a small desert village, hardly known then. My school. My friends. And that serene face, the most beautiful I ever saw.

Her name was Kasturi; people called her Kasturiben. Every lady—well, nearly every—is given the tag 'ben' as a mark of respect for a sister-like lady. She had come to our village with a group of pilgrims. Her group had gone back but she lingered on. She settled herself in the temple of Ashapura, the goddess who fulfils hopes. It was not new or unnatural that people would stay in or around temples. Many travelling pilgrims would stay around the temple for a few months before they left Khavada. She must've been in her early fifties at that time, but that is a guess I am taking now. At that time, estimating her age never crossed my mind. In my mind, her image is still fresh, especially the one when I met her last time, sitting with her back resting on one of the pillars of the temple, her eyes lightly closed, clad in thick brown saree draped over her head. Her slightly wavy, thick, long black hair neatly combed, unbraided, coming out over her left shoulder. A sandalwood-paste dot on her lightly creased forehead.

Every morning, an hour or two before the sunrise, she would make herself comfortable in the centre of the temple, facing the deity. She would close her eyes lightly and allowed the divine voice to flow through her. She would start her devotional songs with the morning ragas. I came to know much later that each of those ragas had names like 'Bhankar', 'Kalingada', 'Nat Bhairav', and others. The world, which was still dark, melted away for her and for the listeners as well. Her voice was as delicate as a thin strand of smoke curling gently from the incense sticks in the temple. Slowly, taking its own time to rise above, the thin strand of her voice rose and expanded over the listeners, shrouding them from everything else. That was the sound with a lot of heart in it. It was like all the wonders of the universe had been transformed into sounds, sounds of hundreds of colours and form, light as a gentle breeze, cosy as the winter sunshine, quick as the rain, intimate as a mother's lullaby, and subtle as the presence of the divine deity she aroused with her sound. The listeners would close their eyes and allow the sound to drift them to the divine place they imagined. The birds around would stop chattering, the breeze would stop rustling the trees, even the wicks in the oil lamps seemed to burn slower to enjoy the sublime sounds. The entire place would be enveloped in the feeling of peace, serenity, and wonder. Even after she would stop singing, people would keep on swaying with their hands clasped near their chests and their eyes closed. That's how people got to know her for the first time.

Her face, now I can put words closer to what I felt about it then, was therapeutic. Whatever little problems I could have had as a teenager, those vanished the moment I saw that face, the eternally blissful and unearthly, without any trace of worry. It radiated happiness. Her almond-shaped kohl-lined eyes were arresting if you locked yours with them, and kept you there for long. Maybe over the years, thinking about her, I might have created an exaggerated image of her in my mind. Sometimes if you adore somebody and don't see her for a very long time, you start building a mental image of that person which is probably more than what she would be in reality. The memory holes are, over time, filled with elastic imagination. What you end up remembering may not always be the same as what you might have witnessed. Maybe this is my case with Kasturiben. Maybe, but it doesn't feel like that; she really held that charisma.

I had celebrated my sixteenth birthday just some days back, when I last saw her.

She told wonderful stories—stories which were earthly, of people who were like us, of gods who were not vengeful but bestowed grand wishes on their devotees, of demons who had changed their dark ways and had become saints. The evenings in the temple after her coming there were different. Temple regulars spent more time in the temple, occasional visitors became regulars, and many new people joined the evening temple club. They came to listen to her stories, her simple narrations of everyday life, her songs, and some just came to soak in her aura. People thought she was some saintly person, but strangely enough, she never gave any particular religious discourses; in fact she was a big proponent of science. She kept emphasizing the importance of seeking logic in every religious or traditional practice we followed.

Nobody ever said something like that with so much clarity and still did not lock horns with the religious practitioners of that time. She had a way of convincing people, a way to negotiate in a subtle and non-offensive way. People loved her. I in particular found a mentor in her, though I did not know the meaning of the word *mentor* then, I just knew that we had a connection.

She loved children and children loved to be with her. Her stories for us were full of riddles and puzzles. She wove a world of stories in which each of us filled the characters, and each of us dreamt of a somewhat different story. Each time we would have to make a choice, and based on the choice we made, our stories proceeded. We were the characters in her story as well. Nobody had told us such stories. Now, after so many years later, after studying in India and the US, I understand how much she was ahead of her time, using the cognitive teaching skills which were still undiscovered then. I felt pride each time I was first to crack the riddle and shouted the loudest to grab her attention, just to make sure that nobody else was heard. I started feeling that amongst all, I was her favourite kid. Probably the way she was, every kid must've thought like me.

The Ashapura temple, where she stayed, was on the route to school. Once on my way to school, I heard her singing. I entered the temple and stood listening to her. I lost myself in that sweet voice and forgot that I was supposed to be at the school. I just stood behind her till she finished. After she finished, she turned back and smiled at me and gestured me to go near her. 'Don't miss school for the sake of songs or stories. There are many interesting things that can be learnt each day in the school,' she said in her soft whispering tone. I felt as if it was the end of all my efforts to make a good impression. I would now be out of her good books. The boy who was not interested in school! I smile at my innocence every time I recall that incident. I stood there like a statue, staring my feet, feeling ashamed.

'Don't worry about being late, there is still a lot to catch up at school, we will talk on your way back from the school, now run!' she said, and holding my chin lightly, she lifted my face to look at her. She gave that smile, which told me I had lost nothing and things were even better. I would get her exclusive afternoon time! I ran to school with a spring in my feet and was impatient for the school to be over. That afternoon, after school hours, I went back to the temple. That was probably the time we could say was the first point where my life started changing.

She was there with back resting on a pillar and eyes closed as if contemplating on something. She sensed my arrival and I felt mild guilt at breaking her trance, but her warm smile and gesture to go and sit beside her made everything right. We talked about what I learnt that day in school, what I liked, about my friends and many other things. She listened and I spoke. She just indicated her understanding with nods and eyebrows raised and occasional pressing of her lips, with a few whys and whats. I attempted in vain to answer with whatever I could, but there was another why followed by yet another one. The other kids were back home getting ready for afternoon play, and for the first time, I liked that I was not part of that. I loved my time with her. As the afternoon evaporated into evening, she told me to stop. I felt there were many stories left to be told; there were so many secrets which I could give away, but I would have to wait for the next day. As I was about to leave, she told me to inform my parents that I would be with her, so they wouldn't be worried about me. I smiled back, nodded, and ran home. There was a lot to share with my mom that evening.

I was not the academic topper in class nor did I excel in any other field. I was not bad either. In our school, where a class with maximum strengths had hardly eight to ten students, where in the empty classrooms goats and camels came in to cool off from the desert heat, where we learnt 'A for aapal, B for baall . . .' in fifth grade, being the topper didn't really mean much. But that I say now, after so many years; at that time, being the best amongst the eight students meant getting the bit of extra attention from teachers and, most important, extra respect from fellow classmates. Since that afternoon, I was a regular visitor at the temple. I was fortunate enough to have found my gentle teacher. I don't know if I found her or she spotted me, but it worked for me. She neither praised too much nor criticized; she was just listening and still telling many things. She changed my destiny. The one thing she taught me then and I practiced regularly with her is something that I still do: the different ways of contemplating. On the day that went by, on the learning I had, on what I read and what I thought about it. I had to take to her any piece of printed paper; it could be in English, Hindi or Gujarati, and it could come from anywhere, right from the pieces people used for wrapping vegetables to abandoned magazines at the scrap shops. I had to read it to her and discuss on that. She was filling in where the school fell short, right from academic subjects like science and mathematics to arts and history. She knew everything. Fortunately in my time then, the parents were not crazy for competition; otherwise, Kasturiben would be compelled to start tuitions. I got exclusive attention from her. Her way of teaching was simple to understand; her examples were connected to me and my friends, the science was from everyday life, the mathematics was about games we played, and before I realized, I was way ahead, not only of my class but a few classes senior to me.

Nobody could guess that she knew so much about so many things. I don't think we had people in our village to appreciate who she was. But then, I don't think she was in our remote village, in a small temple, looking for any recognition. As time passed, I got more of her unwavering attention. And getting better in academics was the least part of what I received from her. She was a live example for many virtues, modesty being the prime. A few others were being focused, mindfulness, following the breath, and being in the state of silent awareness. She taught me how to look deeply at people, at our own actions, to develop empathy, and to love and be loved. Be courageous, she said, in thinking and in actions. None of those things were said in our books or taught in the school.

Three years passed. And those three years changed everything for me. I was certainly a different person. My perspective to look at things had changed. Everything was promising. In those three years, Kasturiben stayed as she was, a lovable mentor; she never became close to our family or to any other family in the village. She limited herself to her songs and stories in the temple. Nobody knew about her personal side or anything about her before coming to our village. She remained the gentle, mysterious recluse. Nor did I tell anyone much about her, with a selfish feeling that I might lose her if others knew about her. They would flock around her and I would get less time.

It was one of those hot summer desert afternoons. By now stopping at the temple after school was a subconscious affair. She was sitting in her usual position with her back resting on a pillar, her eyes closed, in her silent awareness. But that day, she had her cloth bag kept next to her. It looked to be packed with her belongings. She hugged me in her usual loving way. Her eyes were wet and red as if she had been crying or trying too hard to control her tears.

'Are you going somewhere?' I asked.

She took a deep breath and held it for few seconds. 'Close your eyes and listen to me,' she said very softly, her voice nearly choking. She did not answer my question though.

I closed my eyes and anticipated a surprise.

'Ram, I am giving you something, keep it always with you. Always. Keep it guarded like the most guarded treasure. Don't give it to anybody. Not even when you grow up.'

'Okay . . .'

'Promise me.'

'Yes, I promise. But what is that?' I tried opening my eyes to see what she was giving.

'Close your eyes and just listen to me.' She caught me peeking. 'You will take care of this.'

'I promise,' I said sincerely.

'This will bring you lots of luck and fortune. When you are in doubt, hold this one and remember me, your troubles will melt and you will have an answer to whatever you seek. Never forget that you are cut out to do something big, and that there is no short cut to practice, there is no alternate to having the right focus, and there is no world for you if you are not humble.' Saying this, she placed something warm in my palms and closed my fist.

'Keep your eyes closed and focus on what you have in your hands. Feel it.'

I don't remember how many minutes I must have been sitting there with my fist and eyes closed. When I opened my eyes, she was not there. That was the last time I saw her. She disappeared. Just like that, suddenly. I looked around but she was nowhere. At that time, I did not know that it would be the last time I saw her. No goodbyes, no farewells, no tears, no drama—she just vanished. Nobody from the village also saw her leaving the village. I still feel sad that I didn't get to say a proper goodbye to her. Thinking of it now, had I known, I would have made a big drama then, making it difficult for her to leave, and brought on the attention of many others which she probably wanted to avoid.

After she left, I ran around the temple and nearby places to look for her. I didn't even look at the gift she gave me. After I felt that she was not around, I came back to her usual spot, with a hope that she might be sitting there and I was unnecessarily worried. But she was not there. I saw then what she had given me. It was a turquoise translucent stone. Just under an inch long, it was a perfect smooth oblong. In the centre was a black horizontal line etched, running across the stone. Under that line there were three dots made horizontally. It looked as it had light of its own.

My mother made an amulet out of it and since then I have it around my neck. And I still guard it as a treasure.

As she had said, it was indeed my lucky charm. I excelled in academics. My parents received income from unexpected corners. I kept on getting scholarships and gold medals. I changed cities for further education and finally landed in the US in a premier management college on scholarship.

Today after completing my post–graduation, I am on my way back to India. The shimmering bracelet dangling on the wrist of the person sitting diagonally from me, two seats ahead, held the same stone, at least it felt so. Same color, same line, and the three dots.

******

It is eight years since I met Kabir on the flight back from the US. Kabir was coming back, after completing his stint as a junior scientist at a university-affiliated atomic research institute, to join Bhabha Atomic Research Centre in Mumbai, more so to get closer to his family. I cannot forget the expression on his face in the flight when I showed him the amulet I held in my hand. Neither of us went to our destinations from the airport. We went to the nearest coffee joint. We were there for five to six hours with nearly fifteen coffees each while we told our individual stories about the blue stone to each other. Kabir had nearly the same story as mine. He was also gifted the stone by his mentor. He had his childhood spent in a town of West Bengal, called Guptipara. It was a small town then, known for its terracotta temples. His mentor had come just like Kasturiben, to a temple known as Brindabanchandra, with a group of pilgrims. Her name, as she told him, was Chhaya Devi, and kids called her Chhaya Mashima or just Mashima, which means a maternal aunt. Chhaya Devi had the same style of dressing, and the way he described her, both Chhaya Devi and Kasturiben looked the same. Neither of us had any pictures of our mentors, because it was the seventies, and taking a photo was not a common thing. For Kabir too, she had disappeared one fine day, suddenly, after giving him the blue stone, with similar promises of fortune and luck. The years we had spent with Kasturiben and Chhaya Devi were the same years. So they were different ladies with similar features, dressing, style, the way they spoke, the way they taught. Many of the stories were also similar. It took us some time to believe in each other's so similar stories.

Who were those benevolent ladies? Why were we meeting? Why now? What was the common link between us? What was the motivation of these ladies? Could there be others? Finding answers to some of these questions brought me and Kabir near to each other. As we started drawing links between our lives, it was also important to understand if there were others like us. The investigations started with the most obvious media, newspapers. We created a fake company and gave an advertisement for it in nearly all the leading dailies. The advertisement carried a photo of the blue stone and the skills we asked were weird and abstruse. The intention was to check if the photo in the newspaper could attract the attention of the people we wanted. And it did. We had to answer around eight hundred calls from people who wanted to apply for our company, but after scanning for a few weeks, we found three people we wanted to find: Ashwini Deshpande (a lady from Pune who had just passed the Indian Civil Service exam), Lakhshmi Nair (a lady from a village near Cochin who worked as a journalist in the local newspaper), and Rubin Patel (a small-time business man then from Gujarat). The link or the pattern was getting clearer. All of us were nearly of same age, we all met the mentors of our lives nearly at the same time, we all had a modest childhood, and all of us had great academic life and a career-launching platform. All of us knew we owed our lives to those ladies; had they not come into our lives, we probably would have had a different course of life. And indeed the stones that all of us were given brought us lots of luck. None of us had any photos of those ladies. Some of us went back to our native villages to start the investigation about those mysterious ladies, trying to check patterns amongst them. But it didn't help. Everybody in the villages just had good stories to remember, but nothing came out which could lead us to those ladies. It was clear that there were more people like us were spread around the country and probably our task was to find them.

In all these eight years, we came closer to each other and so did our families. We were not in the same town, but we made a point to meet in person once a year at least. Last year we came across one more person, Mirza Abid from central India, an artist by profession who was also a blue-stone member like us. Our investigation is still going on. We have also set up a few institutes around the country to help people with modest beginnings like us.

******

Renu was over the moon when she saw her post-graduation results. She was first in her division and had secured the university gold medal. That state of elation however was very brief; she was disturbed by the note she had received yesterday. The contents were personal and yet enigmatic; she wondered who would know all those details about her. She was intrigued to meet the sender. There was no demand and the note did not seem like blackmail. She did not talk to her boyfriend about it as the note instructed and went to meet the sender at the place she was told to. As she stood there waiting, there was a soft tap on her shoulder. She turned and saw a beautiful lady with a beaming smile.

There were many meetings between Renu and the lady after that.

******

It was a big room of an average, inconspicuous hotel in a small, non-urban city of India. The hotel was specifically chosen because of its averageness, its location in middle of nowhere. A place somebody would hardly come to stay, the twenty-room hotel probably never saw even ten rooms occupied since it was built thirty-three years back. It was clear this hotel had a purpose, and clearly it was not of hotel business. The old but strong walls of the hotel had some secrets safely for many years. Today it was going to add a few more and it was ready for it.

The room was hot and stuffy and it smelled of old, but rich furniture. In the far corner of the room, a small pedestal metal fan whirred and rattled its metal blades throwing hot air around. In the middle of the room, there was a long solid-mahogany table, lit on the ends by the two lights hanging overhead. The light was just enough to light the two ends of the table; the rest of the room was dark. The suspense hung thick, almost palpable. On one side sat a frail old man adjusting his bifocals on his button nose as he looked at one of the eight young ladies sitting in front of him. The eight ladies sat in the semicircle at the other end of the table, with light illuminating the face of the one in the centre. They did not know each other. But the one thing they knew was the language of anxiety, the language of fear. They could sense the same in the other seven ladies in the room. The beads of sweat trickling down the nape of the lady under lights were shining and gave away the hard throbbing vein underneath. Were they tricked or it was indeed what they had been told? They were told to reach different locations on their own and then had been blindfolded for the last three hours of the journey.

There were eleven more people in the room, five and six flanking the old man's right and left side. They stood in the darkness. Only their borders on the side of the light were visible. One of these eleven people was a young man, and the others were ten middle-aged ladies. The old man gestured the young man. He came and stood behind the old man, with his head going just above the light, making it completely dark.

'Don't be afraid. But I can understand if you are.' His voice was deep, rich, and smooth. And it seemed to be a known voice to all the eight ladies. The lady in the centre quickly flicked her head around to see if the others had the same reaction as hers, to feel as if the voice was a known voice.

After the pause, allowing his voice to settle in the room, he continued in his resonating deep voice. 'Coming here was probably the most difficult decision you have made. Good choice. Thank you. To select you all, my team has done immense hard work for more than a couple of years, observing you, relentlessly. You have been combed out of the entire country. You are the best of the best. And we would take you higher. You will be the best psychologists in the world.

'As briefed to you by your mentors, who are here as well, you will have to undergo five years of complete hiding. Money will not be a problem. But you are not here for that. We have checked that on our end. Your motivation is to do something for the nation. And to that, I promise you will all get a chance to render great service to the nation. And that is the only thing I promise. You will not get any recognition, people will not know about you or your services, not even your families. For people outside this room, you have jobs in foreign countries which require extensive travel, with hardly any or poor communication. From the money you will be sending to your families, they will be thinking you are really making handsome money. You will be allowed to talk to your families from time to time. Your communication will be recorded. You will not reveal anything about your work, location, or any other thing related to your operation. You have been already given a fair idea about this by your mentors, but I felt it is important enough to emphasize.'

There was a long pause after that. One of the ladies from the dark spot tried asking a question, but the old man gestured her to be quiet by moving his finger over his lips.

'Questions will be answered to individual members by their mentors. Each question is different and so will be the answers. For now you just have to listen,' he said.

'Ahem,' the person behind the old man cleared his throat to get the attention back to him. 'You are not dealing with soldiers or terrorists but with our own people. The only weapon you carry is love.'

'Yes, love. For the last sixty years, my mentor has been experimenting and running this model. And now it is my and your turn. The power of picking the right people from different parts of our nation, particularly the parts which are not having the focus of the nation and connecting them is the key to the kind of nation we want to build. I am not talking about you. The kind of people you will be connecting, I am talking of those people.

'Many names you hear in the news or read in newspapers are the people assisted in their initial years by your mentors. People in key positions do connect to each other regardless of us, but they connect only for their professional give and take, or for a specific need.

'We build a kind of a secret club where we connect them through something obscure, something they feel indebted to and that makes the bonds between them much stronger and sustainable. They feel natural connectedness. These people, the chosen ones, will be at different positions in the society in a few years, and when they connect, they would become an insurmountable strength. The strings we set now, we invest in people so that they become the kind of game changers we want them to be and plan for their connection when the time is right. You don't have to believe in the system to start with. The system has a proven track record. Just follow the instructions, and with time, you will be the best believers of the system.'

He gave a pause and looked around. The old man looked up at his face and nodded. There were many questions bubbling in the heads of those ladies, making them uneasy and distracted. This pause allowed them to settle down. The speaker knew about this. He had seen it before. For now, his pauses were filled by the rattling blades of the pedestal fan.

'You all will be given a new identity. We are in the digital age and anonymity has become near impossible. We have friends in key positions who will keep on deleting your presence from the digital media; however, to remove complete traces will be impossible. So you will have to stay low, inconspicuous and not attract unnecessary attention, stay away from the media, including no photographs being posted on social network sites. You will report to your mentors if you make even a blip in the social network. You will be trained for one complete year by your mentors before you actually take the field. We have the list of candidates ready whom you will start watching along with your mentors.

'My mentor and I have more than enough money to make you all very rich in these five years, as long as you abide by your oath to spend this money only after five years. God forbid, if something bad happens to you on the way, your families will get the money. Once the mission has already started and you cannot quit before end of your candidate's training, if you land up in any trouble with people, we will transfer you from that place and wipe out all possible proof of your existence. If you quit and leak the story, you will not have enough proof and we will have to take an extreme step which we would not like to. Now let us take the ceremonial oath in blood. Jai hind!'

As the young man came around to the ladies for the oath, they saw his face; for the next few seconds they felt choked and breathless. They looked at each other and then again at him. They were looking at the recently elected prime minister of the nation.

Mea Culpa

The roads here never sleep. And this is my routine one, in its usual deplorable state. Night-time, no street lights, and forever under construction. The 'under construction' sign, bent sideways, safely hidden from view. Roadsides dug up and littered with boulders, pockmarked with craters big enough to swallow half the bike's wheel. Blinding lights from oncoming traffic. Gravel spread all over the roads. General symptoms that tell you either the city is expanding or the city elections are approaching. Of course, there is a natural way, of rains, but that was not the case now. The advantage is, whenever you are late for anything, you can always blame it on the roads; nobody can really challenge you. Everybody understands and has learnt to live with the fact that the condition of the roads is completely unpredictable. It has ceased surprising people anymore. We all just bitch about it. As far as bitching is concerned, it is done for every other thing, so it doesn't really matter. It is a sport we resort to address our work pressures or general frustrations.

The main part of the road is jammed with cars always, thanks to the easy instalment car loans. As the office time (from seven to around seven thirty) is over, these cars, bikes, scooters flow out of the multilevel parking of those imposing offices and then flood the roads. The bikes and scooters flow around these cars, flank the sides and every little space they get between the cars and trucks. Trucks are always there; wonder where they keep on going, but they are always there. The bikers, I suppose, are made to take an oath when they are given the licence, that every little space on the road can be taken and should be taken. Another thing is about honking. I am sure I use honking and cursing more than the clutch and accelerator. And so does everybody else. The traffic moves in slow speed and the accidents are more like kisses between the two vehicles, lips of one car giving a peck on the butt of the car in front. As people are used to the road condition, so are they used to the usual thump on their cars; they draw the windows down and spill out genuine expletives aided by finger gestures. Life goes on in the metropolis.

I have been driving on these roads for so long that this road has ceased to exist for me. It is an oblivious conduit. I am so preoccupied most of the time while driving on this road that I never realize when I start, how I drive, till I get to the driveway of my apartment or the parking of my office. I sit in my car and pop up in the office or home. I would say there is a strange silence in this chaos. The honking and cursing is part of the subconscious; it doesn't bother us anymore.

That evening was different though. My life was going to be changed. All of us wonder, from time to time, how we start our day completely unaware of how that day might turn out. Some days just take you by the scruff of your collar and throw you in completely different world, through a portal of no return. That was one such evening.

It was nearly seven thirty, dark enough to be blinded by the oncoming cars. I was in traffic, very much of it, and still cursed it. I was not comfortable that evening, rather very uneasy. Something in me told that things might not turn out well. Lata Mangeshkar's haunting melody played on the radio. It was one of the songs I liked, but if someone would suddenly switch off the radio and ask me about the song, I had no idea. It just went on as a background something. I kept looking at the rear-view mirror, looking for the side on the left to move ahead. I knew it was a futile try.

While I moved in and out of my attentiveness and looked at the traffic and the damn road dug up on the sides, all of a sudden a bike overtook me from the left side, two people, one male and one female, both without helmet. Fuckers! There was hardly any space between my car and the crater-sized holes on the sides, but whatever it was, the biker had discovered it and had pushed his bike through. I gave out a few expletives and shouted, 'Go die, you idiot!'

The biker turned to look at me and he took off his eyes from the road. What happened after that is etched in my memory. I still am disturbed every time I think of that moment. It happened in a few seconds, but it runs in slow motion in my head since then. When that idiot took his eyes off the road, he missed looking at the hole that was dug out and the boulder on the left. He lost his balance when his front wheel got into the ditch and he bumped hard on the boulder. He was thrown over the boulder in the mud. It was followed by a scream. The lady sitting behind fell off and hit her head on the road and then rolled to get hit again by that boulder. But just before that happened, the strong light from a car coming from the opposite side flashed on her face, and even though the last part happened in a split second, I saw her face, her surprise, her agony, and she saw me as well. When her head hit the boulder, I felt I missed not one but several beats; something in my chest gave a sharp pain. I didn't know then that the accident would haunt my memories so long.

I rammed brakes and brought my car to a screeching stop. The car behind me hit me hard, and for the first time, I didn't get back with a barrage of cuss words. Thankfully, I did not hit the car in front of me. I didn't bother about the traffic jam I was creating by stopping on the road or the chaos from people or the honking or the hit I got. I came out of the car from the passenger side. I could not open my side of the door because the car next to me was too close. Before I could get to both those people, they were already surrounded by onlookers. I felt enveloped in shouts and shrill cries. From where do these onlookers suddenly materialize? There was nobody a few seconds back on this side of the road and now suddenly I had to shout hard and elbow a few people to penetrate the crowd and reach the couple. It was my luck that they did not hit my car and landed up in the ditch; otherwise the curious onlookers wouldn't be merely curious, they would have busied themselves in beating the pulp out of me. For now they were surrounding the couple and analyzing what exactly happened rather than helping.

The lady was already unconscious by the time I reached them. I had to back off the people by literally pushing them to allow her to breathe. I told a few people around me to help me, and another guy picked her up and put her in my car. Her male companion was panic stricken and obeyed what I said. He did not realize it was me who was responsible for his fall. I told the people around to take his bike and park it at the side of the road, and I and the biker would take the lady to the hospital which was five minutes from where we were, and it was in the direction I was going anyway. She was not bleeding when we brought her in the car. She was unconscious and her body felt stiffer; it was difficult to fold her legs. It took us several minutes before we could get both of them sit behind me. But at that point, I was a better choice than an ambulance. For an ambulance to reach this part of the road would have taken a much, much longer time. Now was the time to show my driving skills. People had already seen us bringing her in my car, so a few cars ahead of me had already pressed themselves to the left, giving me way on the right. Through lots of cuss words, finger gestures, and blaring horns, I managed to overtake many cars in front of me. Driving faster than most, I reached the hospital in about ten to fifteen minutes.

Thankfully there were not many people in the hospital, in fact only the hospital staff other than us in the waiting room. We got immediate attention. I waited in the waiting room after the hospital staff had taken her to the emergency room. The waiting room smelled like the signature smell of most hospitals here, strong disinfectant and something else. I don't know what that something else is, but you get that in most of the hospital.

I saw the chubby receptionist behind the desk was waiting for us to fill the hospital forms. I gently squeezed the biker's shoulder and gestured him to move towards the receptionist. The noisy corridor was silent again; the hospital staff had taken the lady into the surgery room, and the chubby receptionist was patient. I saw the biker's face for the first time then. He was bleeding from the concussions on his forehead and there were a couple of bruises on his cheek and arms. He was scared, restless, shocked, and panic stricken. He kept peeping from the glass windows of the closed doors of the narrow corridor which led to the operation theatre. The receptionist raised her eyes over the rim of her glasses and looked at him. She didn't tell him to stop being frantic or to relax or to come and fill the forms; instead she busied herself with the monitor in front of her desk. I was sure she was playing solitaire or something of that sort. I had some eye contact with her; we were both looking at this biker who was unaware of his own injuries, clasping both his hands in a tight squeeze, digging his nails into the back of his hands. Both of us, we felt we could understand him.

He didn't seem to notice the thick trickle of blood wetting his collar. I gestured the receptionist to call somebody to dress his wounds. The receptionist pushed a few buttons on her phone and in an inaudible voice spoke to someone. She gestured me back with her open palm, which meant I should expect help in about five minutes. There was a middle-aged nurse with us in less than five minutes. She looked gentle and slowly led this guy to a small room through his brief resistance and insistence to stand there and keep looking through the windows in that silent corridor.

As they nursed him, I lingered on, and so did my guilt. *Go die, you idiot . . . Go die . . . Go die . . .* Had I not spoken those words, nothing would have gone wrong. I knew the idiot was wrong to overtake me from the left side, where there was as good as no space, but if I had controlled my anger, he would have crossed that patch of the road without this fatal accident. And of course I hated them for not wearing helmets. *Go die*—why, why did I say that? Something in my chest still kept squeezing, twisting. The girl would have been safe had I not said that.

Finally, the hospital forms. The biker was Vinod. With tears welled up in his eyes, he must be seeing the forms double or maybe triple. I didn't ask him, just took the pen out of his hands and moved the forms near me. He gave it as if expecting me to do that. The lady companion in the operation was Sheetal Patil, age: 24, no known allergies or surgeries in the past year. *Sheetal Patil*—the moment I wrote her name and age, I had the cramp of ache in me again and my hands were trembling as well. She was so young. God, please . . . please let her survive this, the guilt would be too much for me to live with. The hospital form took much longer than I expected; it was difficult to console him and understand what he said. He said they had no insurance cover, but they had enough money to bear the hospital expenses. The hospital should only worry to make sure that she was taken care of.

It was nearly eleven thirty when the doctor and his assistants came out of the operation theatre. I and Vinod both rushed to them to ask how Sheetal was holding.

'Under observation,' the doctors said with glum faces, without looking at either of us, as if there were secret cameras, and any doctor who was spotted smiling with the patient or with their friends and family would be imposed a penalty!

The doctor walked briskly with an entourage of his assistants through that corridor and the white expanse of the waiting room. Of course, the entourage did not acknowledge the presence of the receptionist who might have killed her game of solitaire when she must have seen them approaching. As we ran behind them, keeping pace with their fast walking, we got the attention of one of the pretty assistants and she stopped to talk to us, as the rest of the group silently moved into the doctor's office and the door closed behind them.

'So, what do we expect, when can we see her?' I asked. Vinod was unable to make his questions audible.

'She is still not completely out of danger. We will have to monitor her vitals for next twenty-four hours before we can say anything on this. There was severe internal haemorrhage, but you came in time. Any delay would have cost her life.'

I liked this assistant. Vitals—I liked the sound of it when she said it. It was like I heard in an American doctor series. Not that I liked that series, but it was the only one going on when I used to come back from office late hours and switch on the TV. Compared to the Indian soaps and melodrama, I liked that American series far better. My drifting into the pretty assistant and the sound of the vitals was interrupted by a strong hold on my shoulder. Vinod leaned on my shoulder, and I felt his tears, warm and moist on the sleeve of my shirt. I saw the pretty assistant as she too entered the doctor's office. I wonder what they would be discussing there. Probably the vitals.

'You came in time,' Vinod said, barely coherent. 'Thank you, thank you . . . thank you,' Vinod said and clung even tighter to my shoulder, with muffled sounds of crying. The only reaction in this situation, I suppose, is to use the other hand and hold him firmly, rub his back, and then stroke his hair. Nobody teaches this, but I suppose this is the one reaction that anybody might do in this situation to make the other fellow comfortable. And it did comfort him, when I followed through with the action. His breath smelled of fear, so did mine. As I stroked his hair, I felt my fingers shivering. The chubby receptionist looked at us. I saw her watching us, before she went back to stare at her computer screen.

We were not allowed to see Sheetal. I asked Vinod if he would like to freshen up at my place and have some dinner. He just shook his head and gestured that he was comfortable there.

I had a modest apartment at about four hundred meters from the hospital, in the suburb Manjri of Pune. I had no one waiting for me at home. I had just moved to Pune six months back when I switched my job. My parents were still in Mumbai. My apartment was small, like most other apartments in my area, where software engineers flocked. One-bedroom apartment with minimal furniture, a typical setting of a bachelor's apartment. A drawing room with a TV and set-top box but no sofa, just a mattress with a few cushions thrown in, which were the only luxury in the room. Bedroom with a single cot and mattress, a table littered with a few USBs, a wireless modem, my tablet, and a personal laptop, a bookshelf on the left side of the table with hundreds of books. I had changed my location for first time in my life, so carrying most of my books from Mumbai to Pune seemed to be a good idea in the absence of any friends in a new city. I knew I could always depend upon my invisible friends cast from the dusty old covers of my faithful books. My bedroom was my man cave. Reading a good thriller or browsing aimlessly with a Scotch after dinner was the best part of the entire day. And yes, a minimal kitchen, just enough for one person.

I went home, and though he said he was comfortable, I knew he was hungry. I reheated the rice that was made the previous evening along with some dal and took it to the hospital. I also carried a thermos with ginger masala tea.

'You don't need to bother so much, you've already done much more than I could wish for.' There was overwhelming gratitude in his eyes.

'No worries, I don't have anybody at home, you are company tonight.'

Both of us had our dinner in the waiting room of the hospital. He was indeed hungry. After the dinner, we had a cup of tea and I could see him relaxing. And my mind once again reminded me how culpable I was for this happening: *Go die, you idiot . . .*

'Don't you want to call somebody at home regarding this accident?' I asked him.

'I don't want to call my parents now, they will be tense. Anyway, they don't stay in Pune, they are in Nashik and they don't expect us for the next two days. Once she is okay, I will call them tomorrow morning, telling them there is nothing to worry about,' he said. 'There is nothing to worry about . . . nothing to worry . . .' he repeated.

A trickle came down his face, as if he had just said the password it needed to unlock the tears. He wiped his eyes with his shirtsleeve, which was dirty after the fall. 'I really wish to tell them that there is nothing to worry about . . . she is my little sister . . . you know . . .'

I saw the receptionist sneaking at us. I moved closer to him and patted his back. 'She will be okay, I am sure,' I said reassuringly.

'I pray,' he said with pain in his eyes. 'I will never forgive myself if anything happens to my little sister . . . it was all me, my fault.'

'Don't blame yourself, it was an accident.'

'Yes, but you don't know . . .' he said, and then he paused to suck in air.

A sudden sound of shrill beeps startled us. Panic attacks for both of us, as if both of us anticipated that there would be some bad news to come, and finally it came. The receptionist was startled as well; she sprang from her chair, leaning over the reception counter, watching in the direction of the sound and then ducked to see her monitor. The pretty attendant came rushing out. I didn't see if she came from the same room she had entered. I wondered if she was still with the doctor and other people. She had a clipboard with a few forms clasped to her chest as he came out from the other side of the corridor. She looked towards the receptionist and nodded.

'Room one oh three,' the receptionist told her as if it was obvious.

'What happened?' I nearly shouted at the receptionist, as if it was her fault that there was a beeping sound.

'Nothing for you to bother about, we have one ageing patient in one of the rooms, he gets sudden fits, it demands our immediate attention a few times every night.'

Vinod stood looking at the receptionist, wearing a shocked expression, as if he did not believe what he heard. 'It's because of me . . . all because of me, the poor girl is suffering,' he mumbled as he dawdled back to where we were sitting before the beeps interrupted us. It must've been two hours after midnight when we eased ourselves in the waiting room chairs and dozed off.

There was a river, deep red. And it stank of death. I stood looking at the figurine near the cliff, precariously balancing herself on the edge, just few feet away from where I stood. And then our eyes met. Her mournful eyes looked expectantly at me. She looked for help, and extended her hand to hold mine. I moved towards her, a bit afraid. I felt my feet were cemented, and each step I took was an effort. I extended my hand to hold her. I could see on her face a glint of something along the lines of a smile, or maybe I just felt it. She still looked terrified, but it seemed she knew I would extend my hand and help her. When our fingers touched, I felt a jolt of electric shock in my body, and instead of holding her, I pushed her. And the last thing I saw of her was the horror on her face, the lost confidence in her eyes, and the shrill cry as she plunged down the cliff in the churning red river of blood. I woke up with a shriek. I was sure I made the receptionist miss a beat. When I woke up, she looked startled and came running to me. She put one hand on my back and the other on my shoulder. I saw Vinod was still sleeping, undisturbed. He looked sad in his sleep as well. I shook my head to deny the offer for a glass of water from the receptionist and changed my side to get back to sleep. Just before that, I saw again the sad face of Vinod. *Go die . . . die . . . Go die, you idiot . . . It's not Vinod, it's me.*

The sound of the cleaning ladies and the vacuum cleaner woke me up. It was seven thirty. Vinod was not where he slept beside me. He was near the window, staring out at the traffic. I knew he was preoccupied and not looking at the morning traffic. The receptionist was not there at her desk. I got up and walked to Vinod. It felt strange that I had slept an entire night in hospital with Vinod. None of us said anything. I joined him in looking at the traffic on the road.

'The doctor will be on his morning rounds in a few minutes,' announced the new receptionist. Probably the one we met last evening worked for the night shift. I liked her, the one from last night. My mind could not help comparing this new lady with the chubby receptionist we met last evening. I thought had it been this lady last night, she would have shushed us a couple of times when Vinod was animated. How judgmental of me! I had just met this lady, and I had already formed my opinion. Just then we saw a doctor coming in from the other side of the corridor, followed again by the pretty assistant. He walked briskly and the assistant behind him gestured us to stay calm and wait till he came back from the rounds to ask anything.

'Any time you get so close to a head injury, there is always a cause for concern,' the doctor said with a solemn face. Finally we had got his time after he came back from his rounds. And he didn't look like the snob I took him as last evening.

'I would say we have to wait and pray for the best, it is too soon to comment,' the doctor continued after his brief pause.

'But she is out of surgery, right?' Vinod was clearly not buying the clichéd doctor statements of *pray for the best.*

'Yes, and on the way to recovery. But unfortunately you cannot meet her just as of now, we will have to wait till she stabilizes.'

'How long will it take?'

'I can't really say that. Could be a couple of hours or maybe a day. We will let you know as soon as you could see her.'

'But, I am family, I am her brother,' Vinod demanded as if he was talking to a government officer who denied his basic right.

'I understand, and what I say is best for your sister.'

He didn't wait for my thank you and started walking towards his office. By now there were many other people flocking to the hospital waiting room. The new receptionist didn't have time to play solitaire; she was busy with somebody right from the time I saw her.

It was time for me to get to my day's job. Vinod profusely thanked and hugged me as I started to leave. 'She'll be okay, I am sure,' I said as I left.

The day passed slower than usual. I was unable to take the accident off my mind. The whole thing repeated in slow motion again and again as I sat staring at my computer screen. I already knew I wouldn't be able to get myself off it. I would drop in to check on them on my way back home. I bought some sweet limes and biscuits. I don't know why, but everybody who visits a hospital buys sweet limes and biscuits, at least in this part of India. It is so taken for granted that if you spot a person carrying this combo, sweet limes and biscuits, you can bet he is visiting a hospital. In a few cases, some people add green coconut with pink, blue, or white straws.

Five to seven in the evening were the visiting hours. When I reached the hospital, I expected to see Vinod in the waiting room. He was not there, and the shift of the chubby receptionist had not started. 'Your friend is with the patient in the ICU,' the receptionist from the morning shift said, recognizing me and knowing what I would ask.

'Thank you, may I visit as well?'

'Only one person allowed and that too direct family members while the patient is in the ICU.'

There was no tone of 'sorry' from her. Bloody officious—I knew my guess was right about her.

Vinod walked out with bloodshot eyes, carrying a shadow of an invisible floating cloud of sadness on his face. He looked at me and then at the flimsy white polythene bag in my hand carrying those trademark sweet limes and glucose biscuits. His looks told me without the need for words that his sister had not recovered yet to eat those things. As he walked towards me, a trickle flowed out of his eye, involuntarily. He dabbed it with his cuff. Then the other eye, and the dab with the wet cuff. He looked at me again and walked the next three steps to me hurriedly and hugged me tight. Tight. I hugged him back slightly bewildered, looking from the corner of my eye whether that officious little receptionist was looking at us. She was not, she was busy writing something. Vinod was like a hot potato out of the oven. I could feel the strong heat from his damp shirt sticking to his back. The back was throbbing and I could feel my shoulder getting wet.

'You are God . . . sent to us . . .' Vinod said as I eased him into the nearest chair. 'I will never be able to repay our debt to you,' he said, taking my hand in his. I was now feeling indeed uncomfortable, and I felt though the receptionist appeared to be writing something, she was able to listen to us. There were two more people in the waiting room, one of them reading a Marathi version of *India Today* which was five months old. I could see that from the cover page. The other was listening to some music from his portable music device.

'It is so painful to see her like that . . .' he said, voice trembling, barely audible. 'My little sister . . .' he said. After that there was no audio to what he spoke, but I guess he was blaming himself for that event. I closed my eyes and the scene flashed once again. *Go die . . .* Slow motion now, the biker takes his eyes off the road, strong light from the approaching truck illuminating the girl's face. For a split second, my eyes meet hers, the face of shock, and crash. *Go die, you idiot.* Mea culpa.

Later, I understood that she was still unconscious and the doctors had told Vinod to be patient. 'Vinod, you need a good warm bath, something to eat, please come to my place, it is two, three minutes from here.'

'I am fine here, I don't want to move, I don't want to leave her alone.'

'This is hospital, Vinod, you are not leaving her alone. Getting fresh will help you. I insist, please come.'

'You've already done so much, so much that a close relative would not do . . . I know this is a debt that I will die with, you are a godsend to us. I don't want to bother you any more.'

'You can thank me on the way to my home' I said and smiled. It looked like he smiled. He agreed to come with me. He took a long hot water shower and ate like he was really hungry. We hardly exchanged any words. He looked exhausted, and lost in his thoughts. I didn't want to probe about any details. They tell that when a person speaks his heart out, it relaxes him, but at that moment, in my house, I didn't feel it was a good time to burst him. That night after dinner I dropped him back to the hospital. That night, again the same dream: the river of blood and me pushing her to her death.

Next morning, I made my tea and filled a thermos for Vinod, packed a pack of biscuits as well. But just before leaving the house, I thought, am I overdoing my role of doing good? Probably yes. I left the thermos and the biscuits on the shoe rack near the door of my apartment and went off to the office. I didn't visit the hospital. The day at the office remained disturbed. I was not able to focus. I didn't do any work, but hung around in the office. Finally at eight in the evening, I left for my home, slowed my car near the hospital but did not stop. Disturbed night, disturbed sleep. The scenes of the accident, the sad face of Vinod, the chubby and the officious receptionist, the glum doctor, the pretty assistant—they kept on appearing as a never-ending montage. I thought I was going crazy, and then the words *Go die* . . . Next morning again, I avoided going to the hospital, avoided making an extra cup of tea as well. And I knew I was doing it very consciously, as if trying to break a routine. That evening, I thought Sheetal might be already okay, so I stopped. I had mixed feelings, relief, as I walked towards the hospital waiting room and, at the same time, was uneasy to face Vinod. I found myself hoping that I would see Sheetal today. It was the chubby one at reception this time. She gave a full smile on seeing me. She remembered me!

'Room one oh six. Your friend is well and recovering,' she said, smiling at me. As I smiled back at her, I knew things will be better.

I softly knocked on the door, twice, and then pushed the door, allowing my head to peek in. The bed faced the door directly. I could see Sheetal propped against the bed, which was raised at about sixty degrees. There was a tube in her wrist, which was connected to one of those hospital clear plastic bottles hanging inverted on the stand at her left. Her head was covered in white bandages, which looked like a rough-cut bandana. Her feet were under the blanket, and when I noticed it, I had this urge to look at her feet. I felt like going in and raising the blanket a bit and seeing how her feet were. And no, I have no feet fetish. I don't know why I felt that urge. Then as if I was watching a movie, and the camera panned from the blanket-covered feet to her slender and delicate fingers and then her neck, I saw her face.

It was beautiful, but sad. So sad that after that I noticed everything in that room, she looked sad. The flower pot with plastic rose, the inverted bottle, the bed, the blankets and probably the hidden feet looked sad. A teardrop, like a rheum caught on her lower eyelid, like a spot of varnish, made her eyes sparkle. She had nice brown eyes. I couldn't make out clearly, but I felt I saw her lips trembling. Beautiful, but sad.

'Ahem,' I announced my presence finally. I didn't notice Vinod sitting on a chair beside her. He was probably in one of his reveries.

Vinod saw me and jerked himself up from the chair and nearly sprinted towards me and hugged me tight. What is with his hugging? 'Thank you, thank you so much. We are indebted to you for the rest of our lives!'

Oh please, go easy on those thank yous, you just remind me of things I want to forget.

'Sheetu, he is the one I have been talking about. He is the one who saved you. You owe your life to him.'

'Please, Vinod, don't say that!' I was annoyed now.

Sheetal looked at me and nodded and then the droplet which hung so delicately on the eyelid came down and took with it a stream. That's when I noticed she had bruises on her cheeks and near her chin. I am sure, I could not stare at a girl like that in any other situation, especially with her brother around, but hospital gave me this opportunity to dare in front of her brother. I stared at her till she lowered her eyes and looked at the wrist where the needle punctured her vein. I didn't know what to say, and the best was to keep my mouth shut, which I was good at. I wanted to take a step towards her and brush off the tears from her face with the back of my palm. But I stayed there, unmoved.

It was evident that it was not the accident which made her sad. She looked heartbroken, as if unhappy that she survived. I remembered her illuminated face just before the crash, the agony in her eyes. The silence before I walked into the room was laden, heavy with lot of unspoken words between the brother and sister.

It was becoming uncomfortable to stand there in that silence. I would have probably choked in that. 'I am happy to see you recovering,' I said, looking at her, realizing I had forgotten the essentials, the sweet limes and pack of biscuits.

'Vinod, I will wait outside,' I said, and without waiting, I walked out. I gave out a big sigh after I came out; the air was certainly lighter and breathable here. There was better light as well, less gloomy outside than inside. I sat on one of those chairs facing the receptionist. She smiled at me. And it helped me, when I smiled back at her. I should have asked her name, but I didn't. Vinod followed me in a few minutes.

'I thought that I might not see you again.'

'Sorry to disappoint you,' I replied, making Vinod smile a bit.

'I informed our parents. They are worried. For them to come here all by themselves is difficult.'

'We will move to one of the hospitals in Nashik,' Vinod continued.

'What? Why?' I asked, almost in a fighting tone, as if it was not his decision to move. How could he not discuss it with me?

Vinod looked at me with a surprised expression. 'I have spent whatever money I had here. This is Pune, a costly place. She is also out of danger and now recovering. Even the best local hospital there would cost lower than here.'

I knew he was right about this.

'I will also get some local help there,' he said.

'What? You say you didn't get local help here?' I felt a stab in my heart. I got up and started walking towards the door. Did he think me insignificant?

Vinod also got up and held my hand.

'I didn't mean that! You have been like a god to us, but I have bothered you too much. In your two days of absence, I felt very lonely, I missed you, terribly. I wanted to talk to you. You, a complete stranger in this city, came along and extended help when most needed, to the point that I depend on you here much more than you can possibly imagine. I felt the loneliness unbearable, with her in ICU and me alone outside, I was going crazy. I thought at a point in time I would just walk in the ICU, rip out the tubes, and shake her violently to wake her up . . .'

And he started crying suddenly like a baby. He didn't cry like this even when we brought Sheetal here. I have no idea of handling crying adults. I became very aware of the receptionist and other hospital staff around us.

'There is a cafeteria downstairs, let us go there,' I said to escape from that room. The presence of that chubby receptionist made me conscious of our melodrama. The officious one would have been better; she didn't so much as bother to look at us.

'And please stop calling me God and thanking me,' I said in a slightly irritated tone as we walked the steps down to the cafeteria.

He was crying when we got down to the cafeteria. Fortunately there was nobody in the cafeteria, except the person at the counter. Vinod settled on one of the chairs and banged his head on the table and resumed the intensity of his crying, which he had reduced on the way down.

'I don't understand how money can be a problem. You told me Sheetal works for one of the major IT companies and I know they have a good insurance cover, especially for accident cases. How is money a problem?'

'Because she will not work there anymore.'

'What do you mean, what has happened to her? I thought that she was all well!'

'That is not a problem, she is getting better. But she will leave the job. Rather she had already left when I was taking her to Nashik.'

'She had resigned from her job?'

'No, it is complicated . . . I don't know how to explain to you.'

'Try me.'

'I will,' he said. 'You, I can trust and I am sure you will understand me . . .' he continued.

'First have a glass of water.' I got up and brought him water in that thin, cheap white plastic cup hung in a stack in a dirty worn-out plastic bag on the filter. Halfway, I realized one glass would not be enough, so I went back, filled one more.

He gulped both of them and looked if I had brought one more. He took 'no thank yous' very seriously.

'Two days before the accident, Sheetal had called me late evening,' he started as if narrating a sad play to an audience. He closed bleary eyes and allowed two streams to flow down unhindered. 'She was unhappy, I could sense it at the other end of the wire in Nashik. I could understand when my little sister is not happy. And this time, I felt there was a serious problem. She didn't speak much. She said she wanted to meet me. The very next day, I took a leave at my office, and early morning I stared for Pune. That evening, when she saw me, she hugged me like she used to as a kid. How can somebody not love her?'

A gulp of air and he continued. 'She told me something that completely took me by surprise . . . In my worst imagination I would not have imagined something like that . . .' Gulp. Suck air. Wipe cheeks with dirty cuffs. Continue.

'She told me she was in love! Can you think of it? She said she loved a boy from her company!'

I had to run again in my mind what he said. I was not even sure what I heard. This person I was talking to was freaked out because his sister, rather his 'lit-tal' (the way he pronounced 'little') sister was in love? Was I spending all my time with an orthodox freak? If you ever wondered if a person can change opinion about somebody in just a second, I vouch for it, you can! I just started hating this guy whose tears now meant nothing for me. But I felt I should hear the rest of the story.

'We are respected Brahmins in our locality. We would be gossip material if people come to know that she has chosen her partner herself who in most probability might not be of our high caste and might not even speak our language! I and my family would not be able to face our neighbours or relatives!'

Was this guy really saying this? Or was I on a TV show to see my responses when a person says something like this? Was I transported back to the eighties? Was this guy for real? Would I be penalized by the court for killing an orthodox fucker like this one? I will be probably saving the world if I get rid of these kinds of guys. I was not even looking at him now.

'I raised my hand to slap her but could not do so . . .' he said. 'I asked her the unthinkable . . . a brother should never get in this condition. I should have died before asking this, but I did. I asked her if she had already sold her dignity to a pig, and slept with him . . .' He started wailing at this point, but I didn't offer any sympathy, I was furious.

'She didn't say anything . . . and I fell vulnerable to my anger and slapped her. For all these years, I have never even scolded her, she was the apple of my eye, and even raising my voice at her was out of the question . . . and I slapped her . . .' He buried his head in his arms and cried.

I felt like banging his head on the table.

'I didn't even know if this guy she spoke about would take care of my little one like I did . . . and she didn't even think of me before falling in love . . .'

Right! Look at me; I am talking with a freak who has reached a height of overestimation. His sister should have thought of him and called him before falling in love, asked his permission, and then probably he would have got the pleasure of denying it! His sister robbed him the right to deny!

'Did you check with her, who this person was? His name or his background? He may not be that bad,' I said, trying to control the urge to loathe him.

'I lost all my control to my anger. Anger consumed me completely. I said she had turned into a slut after coming to the city, that I was wrong in supporting her to change the city and stay alone by herself, against our parents and relatives. I should have never supported that. In that moment of heat, I wanted to slap her a few more times!' he said.

In that moment, I wanted to kill this person! He was not even listening to me, he was vomiting his rant.

'I told her to leave the job immediately and leave with me for Nashik. There was no reason why she should be in this city, the city which poisoned her mind.'

Cry. Cry more, I don't care. Die crying!

'She begged, she fell at my feet to allow her to go on with her life with her bloody boyfriend and this city. She wanted me to meet the boy! Look at the audacity of the little girl, she is asking her elder brother to meet the idiot she had chosen! She said leaving her job was not easy, she had to give notice and all that. I said if she would not accompany me to Nashik, she would find me dead the next morning. I made her cry . . . I made her cry . . . but I don't understand how my little sweet sister got into a trap of that bloody boy, whom I deny to even see!'

More crying. I banged my fist on the table with a frustrated thud, to have associated with this person.

'The last words I spoke to her before the accident were that she should have died before bringing shame to our family! I didn't'—heavy sobs—'mean any of those words, I swear to God, they were just my anger, my shock that my little sister went and did something I find wrong, but I would never ever see anything happening to her. I would die ten times before something happens to her. And my last words to her were that she should have died. And when that accident happened, those words hit me. They kept ringing in my ears, that she should have died . . . that she should have died . . .' He cried for the next few minutes and I allowed him to. I didn't coax him, nor did I put my hand over his head or shoulders.

'You must go to her, she is alone,' I said breaking his state.

'Yes, and you must be getting late as well. Thank you once again and you should go.'

I left the hospital that day with a very heavy heart. That poor girl received curses about her death twice, once from her brother and once from me. *Go die, you idiot!* Just before leaving, I gave him unasked-for advice. That he could make his sister quit the job, but since there was no resignation, nobody knew that she had quit. Ask for insurance. Get her a good treatment. If he really loved her, he should do this at the least. I said that and left.

I didn't go to the hospital for the next three days, not in the morning, nor in the evening. I hated his face after that evening. But on the fourth evening, I visited again. I didn't want to, but I did. On reaching there, I understood that they had checked out of the room that afternoon.

'Checked out? Are you sure?' I asked the receptionist, the officious one.

'Yes, sir. They checked out this afternoon,' she said and she was back to work or whatever she was typing on that computer.

Something in my chest cringed tight, very tight. I felt betrayed. The fact that they didn't feel it was important to inform me before checking out of the hospital was painful. They just walked out as if I was one of the hospital attendants? That's what you get when you do good for people; in the end nobody cares. I quickly came out of the hospital. I stood near my car a couple of minutes to contemplate on what happened. The shady restaurant on the highway, just at a stone's throw from the hospital came in handy. A couple of pegs of Indian whisky helped me come to terms with reality. I must have looked like one of those silly idiot Hindi movie characters who sulk, probably even cry silently when they drink. After about two hours of lamenting and being drunk, I started for my home.

In my inebriated state, I saw some dark shadows moving around the stairs near my apartment. Short, quick-moving shadows in that singular fluorescent tube light hanging outside the building. I could see the security guard comfortably, snugly sleeping in his blanket. Bastard, why did we pay him? I cautiously moved forward.

'Hey,' the shadow said and moved from the dark passage in front of the lift into the light.

'Hi, Vinod, what are you doing here? Didn't you check out of the hospital?'

'Yes, we did, Sheetal was discharged today by the doctor this afternoon, but we could not have gone home without meeting you, could we? And I didn't want to disturb you in your office work, so didn't call you. We have been sitting outside your building since afternoon.'

Sheetal also walked out in that light. I could see her face. The bandage was still on her head. She still looked sad. I cursed myself for thinking they had left. I understood from their expressions they didn't feel comfortable to see him drunk.

'I am sorry you had to wait, very sorry. Let us go to my apartment and have food,' I said that and I realized there was no food at my place. And we give so much bloody importance to food. Come and have food! Why do I have to bring food? I was guilty of thinking that they left without telling me, and then I got drunk and now I offered food when I knew there was hardly anything.

'I have got my bike ready, it was not much damaged anyway. We will start for our home, so we will reach well in the early morning.'

I looked at him and knew even in that mild fluorescent light, he didn't really mean what he said. Maybe my being drunk made him say that.

'Come up,' I commanded.

And he followed like a good boy and so did Sheetal. I didn't have much to offer as food, but I knew they must've been hungry since the afternoon. While I poured in alcohol in my bloodstream, they were starving here waiting for me. For now they had to be contented with coffee and stale bread with some strawberry jam I found in my refrigerator. Sheetal slept on the mattress, me on the sofa, and Vinod slept on a thin bed sheet spread out on the floor. I felt some kind of happiness at the fact that Sheetal was sleeping in my house, though I hated the fact that her orthodox psycho brother was here as well. The next morning, he told me he had taken my advice and Sheetal would continue with her job and she was covered in the insurance as well. He thanked me again, with the same intensity. He left the bike at my place on my insistence. I dropped them at the bus stand and both of them went off to Nashik.

Vinod came a couple of days later for his bike. Sheetal was recovering faster than doctor's expectations. Her parents also called me a couple of times, telling how lucky they were to have me around when the accident happened. *Go die, you idiot* echoed in my ears.

Vinod kept in touch. He called me regularly telling me how Sheetal was doing and about his business, about his wife and kids and their family, many things. He liked speaking on the phone. A month after, Sheetal came back to Pune and slowly started with her work. Sense prevailed. Vinod used to come to Pune many times now, maybe to check on his 'lit-tal' sister! Every time he came, he came with a box of sweets to my place. After the initial few minutes, when the questions related to Sheetal's recovery were done, we didn't have much to talk about. But he used to sit for an hour or two, fiddling with a newspaper, or ask about my work or curse the roads of Pune. Idle gossip sometimes, not worthy of any serious consideration. At times I sat with him swapping channels. It looked like he wanted to tell me something, but he struggled at that. The dilemma was apparent on his face. But my opinion about him had not changed much after knowing how he reacted to his 'lit-tal' sister's need for finding her own partner. I didn't want to encourage him to talk about anything.

But in one of his visits, he finally vented out. He looked vain that evening. An overwhelming and unbearable sorrow weighed him down. Crushed. I couldn't resist, and I asked him what was bothering him. This was the signal he probably wanted. He looked at me through his rueful eyes, and mumbled something.

'Well, say it. I know something is bothering you.'

'Sheetal may have gone on a wrong path. But she does not lie to me. She says she will not go against my wish . . . she is a good girl . . .'

'I know that, but why we are talking about it? Did her boyfriend make contact or something?'

'No . . . no, rather the opposite . . . looks like she has forgotten him. He was like a bad dream and it is over now. I am happy about it.'

'So, what's troubling you?'

'Er . . . who will marry her . . .'

Again! Who is this guy? A relic from the last century? Or maybe he and I exist in different worlds. Maybe I am too urbanized.

'Vinod, that doesn't matter . . . she is a good girl. As long as she is good now, she will find somebody good . . .'

'Will you . . .' He clasped my hands and looked at me, searching for an answer in my eyes. 'Will you marry her?' he asked me.

Funny to be proposed to by a girl's brother.

Nearly a year has passed since then. Sheetal is pregnant, not heavily, just in her second month. We both are happy. I do still have to deal with her brother many times.

Some things are better unsaid though. Vinod doesn't know, not yet. And I hope he never will. That I was waiting below Sheetal's apartment on the night of the accident. That, in that bloody Pune traffic, they got stuck and I moved a bit ahead of them. That I was following them to Nashik. That my comment on the night of the accident was to an idiot overtaking me from the wrong side. I didn't know it was his bike. Bloody, fucking coincidences. And he kept telling me he was guilty! On some nights, the accident still haunts me. I and Sheetal laugh about many things from that episode, but I thank God for saving her. I wouldn't have been able to live without her. Vinod will never know that I am *the* Ajay, the boy she talked about to him a year back.

The Game

That night it rained. Finally! It rained in sheets, as if the sky was throwing up, belching out whatever was stuck in its throat for so long. After that, both of us, the sky and me, felt relieved. For the last few days, the city stayed glum under the shroud of dark, low-hanging, and bulbous clouds. People looked sad, suffocating under those pregnant clouds. Bad moods floated and wrapped everyone. I too was contributor and victim of that hovering bad mood. I was fired three days back after working for five years at the same place. They told me business was down and the clients were not paying enough. My salary was not affordable. I got a severance package of three months plus all leaves paid. That gave me three months of pay and no work to do. I did not speak about this with anybody. The fact is I don't have any friends to share. I am not a freak though; I did talk to my colleagues, my ex-colleagues now, but I didn't feel anybody cared about my job status. Except the bank where I had my mortgage and the landlord, it made no difference to anyone if I held a job. For my parents, I didn't really felt the need to talk to them about my job. It did not really matter to them what job I did as long as I wired the money to their local post office. I called them a few times a month and that was enough. As for me, after getting sacked, I realized getting another job was not going to be easy. My company had converted me into a complete dummy. Straight out of university, I was made to work on a tool they sold to clients which created reports, invoices, letters, and bills. In the last five years, I got an award twice for using that tool the best. After five years and out of job, I realized I knew nothing of the industry other than that silly tool. I had zero market value.

Lying lazily in my apartment this afternoon, my stomach gurgled and shouted it was hungry. The refrigerator was stone cold and empty. There was nothing in the kitchen. I could have eaten anything at all. After I was fired, I had locked myself at home and kept either staring at the ceiling fan or flipping through the TV channels. Everything that was eatable in the house was already scraped.

I took out my car and drove out. Outside it did not feel like afternoon; it was more like late-evening weather. Bloody deceiving weather! My house was just beside the highway; driving around one hundred meters, I got on the highway. I decided a pack of noodles from the nearest grocery store would be perfect. But instead of driving in the direction of city to grocery store I turned towards the outskirts, and kept driving. Preoccupied with myself, I drove on. Knowing that the direction I was going, I was not going to get any kind of noodles for the next fifty kilometres. I saw on my left Doshi Vade, the popular chain of cheap Indian burgers in my part of the city. I stopped and stuffed myself with those spicy potato balls stuffed in the dry bread overflowing with red garlic paste, gulping it down with the local sticky and overly sweet mango drink. I got a few more of those burgers packed for my road ahead.

I did not know where I was going, but driving felt good, so I drove on. I had diverted myself from the highway and had taken an off road. There was less traffic on that patch, particularly not of those annoying trucks and speeding buses. The road was rough and it went up and down and curved suddenly, but the best part about it was, it was empty. A few houses were spread here and there, and far fewer people. I wondered why I never did this kind of driving before. It felt therapeutic.

After about three hours' drive, I covered a distance of a bit more than one eighty kilometres. I was in a zone of nowhere, right in the middle of cities, villages, just somewhere on the road. I rolled down the windows and took a deep breath, filling my lungs with the air from the zone of nowhere. But it tasted the same. The weather had followed me here. I realized it was time for a break. And before I could process the thought of taking the needed break, I saw a small makeshift shop on the left of the road, as if it just sprang out of mind. There were three people around the shop and one more sitting behind what looked like a counter. The shop was decorated with multicoloured potato chips packets and a few cheap biscuits, tobacco pouches and cigarettes. The person behind the counter was stirring, already boiling tea. The pan with the overflowing tea was black with the soot from the stove.

It looked like the spot where I could rest for a while. I parked and walked to the shop. On the left, there was an old, worn-out bucket of water. I splashed some of the water on my face. But it did not bring any freshness; it just made me realize how tired I was. I went behind the shop to take a leak and asked for a cup of tea as I walked behind.

There were a few wooden benches and I took the one in the furthest corner. I sipped the brown sugary syrup which was supposed to be tea. The scalding liquid stung my tongue. The tea disappointed me. Spotting the tea shop exactly when my body needed it had made me anticipate the feel and taste of it. I wanted to feel good about it. I wanted it to freshen me up, rejuvenate me, lighten me, but nothing like that happened. It was just hot, sweet, sticky liquid burning my gut pipe. Though the drive till then was good; it made me forget what I wanted to forget: the fact that I was jobless. That I had no idea of what I would do once these three months would be over was not bothering me.

After what must have been ten minutes of sitting there, I felt strange. Strange like mild but long spurts of shudders went through my spine and head. Was it the tea or was I hungry for too long and my body was unable to cope up with the shot of sugar? I paid the person behind the counter for two cups, allowed him to keep the change and came back with the second cup and sat on the wooden bench. Maybe the second cup might make me feel good. As I sat there, holding the cup with a slightly broken rim, I felt as if those people standing there were staring at me in a weird way. I looked around, not directly at them but more in a casual way. The three people around the shop looked to be engrossed in what they were discussing, and the person behind the counter in the shop seemed to be looking elsewhere. I dismissed the thought out of mind and focused on my attempt at making that tea make me feel good. But as soon as I took my eyes off those guys and focused back on the tea, I felt the four heads turning and looking at me. I was not sure if I saw that from the corner of my eye or I just imagined that. The feeling reminded me of a girl from our office, who told me that females have the sense of knowing when somebody stares at them. I remember laughing at it. She said the intent of the stare made the difference. As I continued slurping, the feeling just became stronger. After about ten minutes or so, it started making me uncomfortable.

Maybe it was the annoying weather, maybe I was tired. I had no rush to reach anywhere, and that was the good part of the day. I came back to my car, opened the windows slightly, pushed back my seat and the backrest to maximum tilt, adjusted myself in that space, and closed my eyes, wishing I could get a good sleep. I am bigger than most of the average Indians. Six feet one inch is pretty tall for Indians, and for that reason, I was never really comfortable to sleep in my hatchback car, but hope is a big thing.

I don't know how long I slept, but I got up from a horrible dream, most of which I don't remember. In the last scenes, I was being buried in the ground. I was not sure I was dead, because I could see people throwing gravel on me. Dead people don't see anything, so it must have been a dream and I am still alive. Or maybe people do see even after they are dead, just that they cannot speak back to the living that they can see around. It was that kind of dream which mixes up our realization of the boundary between what is a dream and what is not. Lying in that pit, I saw some of those people around were leaping to get hold of me, to eat a part of me, while the others were pushing them away. I tried to remember those faces who were so enthusiastic to bury me, eat me. I remembered. They were faceless. There were no faces, just blobs of flesh above their necks, smooth and round, no eyes, no nose, no lips— nothing, just a plane smooth, featureless ball. I tried to remember their bodies. I somehow was unable to give a shape to that as well. There was no delineation. I realized there were no faces nor did they have any bodies. So then what was that which kept throwing cold stones on my face? Cold gravel kept hitting my face; it continued for some time before I woke up startled, and realized raindrops were hitting my face from the slightly open window of the car. It was dark outside. I checked the time on the cell phone and was shocked that it was eleven twenty-six; it was already late night. It was still afternoon daylight when I slept. What happened to me? Was I so tired to sleep for so many hours? Was the tea drugged? As I moved my legs around, I realized my knees were paining from staying in the same position for long hours. I looked around, it was raining hard and the visibility through the windscreen was not even beyond a few meters. I tried to see the shop on my left, but it was all dark and I could hardly make out anything. It seemed to me I was in the middle of nowhere all alone. I switched on the car headlights before starting it. In that light the raindrops glowed, showing the path of the light. Apart from some glowing raindrops, I was unable to see anything; somehow I remembered a few trees around this spot when I stopped in the afternoon, but at that moment, it seemed to me there was nothing around, just a big plain earth with me alone on it.

I fumbled in all my pockets before I could find the car keys. I gave a shot of ignition to my car. It didn't start. I gave one more shot and then followed it with a few quick ones. The engine made a dull coughing noise, hardly audible in that pelting rain, and did not start. I took out the keys with a hope that if I put it back again, it might just start. People in IT think that starting things once again from the beginning would set things right. The concept of restart is unconscious to most of us. I wiped the keys on my shirt before I could put it back, and in doing so, I dropped them in the darkness somewhere near the accelerator. I cursed myself for being clumsy. I tried to feel the keys with fingers, without looking down, but could only feel the wet rubber mat. The internal lights in the car were not working. I was waiting whenever I could give the car for full service, could get that fixed as well. The car was due for service six months back already. I took out my phone to have some light. There was no network connectivity in that area. Bloody telecom companies, they show advertisements in which even the remotest part of the African jungle is covered but they leave out parts where people actually live! Thankfully it had battery and it threw enough light to spot my keys. It was just under the clutch shaft. I had to bend down completely with my head bumping the dashboard to pick it up.

Those who are not above six feet may not realize the difficulty of getting down there under the dashboard while still sitting on the front seat fumbling for the key. I smiled to myself when my fingers felt the cold touch of the keys. It felt like a small achievement. I bumped my head for the second time on the dashboard as I got up. I wiped the key again, holding it tighter this time and was about to push it in the slot when suddenly I gave a blood-curdling ghastly cry!

There was a person, or looked like one, peeping in from my side of the windshield! I almost died of shock. In that light of car headlights with everything dark around, a person was banging his fist on my windshield! What the fuck, I cursed enough loudly but it was contained in the car. From where did he suddenly appear? Probably I must've startled him as well. He must not have seen me in that car bent down, without any lights in. He must be a local ragpicker; an abandoned car in the middle of nowhere is a good place to scour.

He came to my side of the door and started tapping the window; now it was even more difficult to see him. I lowered the windows and saw him. Drenched to the bone, severely shivering, he stood there with clasped fists as if pleading. 'Sir, please let me in, or I will die of this rain and cold,' he begged.

A middle-aged person, must've been around fiftyish, begged me to save his life. I had no idea from where he suddenly appeared, but that was not what I was thinking, rather I was not thinking anything at all. The small shop was closed; at least nothing was visible in that darkness.

'Come on in,' I shouted so that he could hear me.

I don't think he really had to hear me; he was on his way already to sit beside me. Wet and dripping, he came in and sat next to me. I looked at the mess he created on the seat with the pool of water around his feet and on the seat. He did not say thank you, nor did I expect him to. He didn't even look at me. He was looking straight ahead through the glass somewhere in the darkness. He had light white moustache and uneven grey stubble. He wore an expression of shock. I wondered why he was in shock; apart from being momentarily startled, it should have been me who wore this shocked expression. And what did I think, why did I just invite a roadside bum in my car? Idiot! I cursed myself. In a few seconds of awkward silence, I was composed. I saw he was still shivering, his fists, jaws tightly clenched, his face, neck, shoulders, arm muscles tensed. I wanted to tell him to relax, but I did not say anything, just kept staring at him. Water was still dripping from his head. For a moment, I felt it was not just dripping water on his cheeks; he was crying. But I know better than to get into unnecessary conversations with strangers.

For those few moments, I had forgotten that I was trying to start my car. I looked at the key and then at him and mumbled, 'Let's see if you are lucky.' He looked at me, his eyes still not relaxed, as if ready to jump out of their sockets. 'Lucky,' he repeated in his thick hoarse voice. The car started in the first stroke and I revved up the engine. I asked him where he wanted to go. He didn't say anything, just raised his finger up and pointed straight ahead. I had no rush, nor any direction to catch up. I had time. I had my sleep as well, so I was good to drive. Though in that pouring rain, with hardly any visibility, it was difficult to drive normally. I was extra cautious, extra slow.

For the next hour, neither of us spoke. Then I heard slow and soft snoring; he had made himself comfortable. But even in his sleep, his face didn't seem to relax.

The time must've been around two something when he got up. He did not acknowledge me, nor that he was in my car and that he might have missed his way. His eyes still looked at something distant. He reminded me of what my mother used to tell me, if I made funny faces and if by chance I sneezed, my face would stay in that expression. Something like this must have happened to this guy. Even after he was in my car, comfortable and protected from the rains and cold winds, he still had his jaws clenched, tightened cheeks, creased forehead, and popping eyes staring something that shocked him.

'You okay?' I asked, trying to start a conversation. He did not reply. I repeated the question but he didn't bother. We were quiet again for a few minutes and then I spoke again. 'Where do you want to go?' He just raised his finger pointing straight, like he did earlier. 'Right.'

I did not have a good feeling when he came in my car and made himself comfortable, and now it seemed so convincing. 'Who are you?' I asked, keeping my patience.

At this, he looked at me. For the first time, our eyes locked. The expression in his eyes changed; it seemed they became darker. He held his connection with me for a few seconds and then resumed his staring beyond my windshield. I had nowhere to go and I had thought that he would be good company, but his strange expressions and silence, though they were intriguing, were also annoying.

'If you are not going to say anything, I will not know where to drop you. I can stop my car here and you can please get down.' Those eyes again looked at me and I felt they were darker briefly again.

'I am a ghost,' he replied.

Exactly! This was what I needed. A lunatic!

I thought for a moment, to stop the car and force him out. The rain had stopped as well. It didn't look like he had to be anywhere; maybe he was just like me. But he did not look to be harmful. He hardly carried anything. Most likely the way he was, he was not carrying a gun or knife or something with which he could inflict harm on me. Nor did he look like a fugitive. He was just a senile old man. Maybe he would be company in the night so I could drive without becoming sleepy. I could drop him anywhere and he wouldn't mind. And he had ignited an interesting conversation by saying he was a ghost. If I kept probing, he would make up interesting stories. So, I kept driving, accelerated a little since it was not raining, nor could I see anyone on the road, a completely deserted patch of road. Neither of us spoke for the next few minutes, as if I was digesting the fact that I was driving with a ghost.

'Hmm, a ghost,' I said.

'Yeah,' he replied.

'Tell me more about yourself, I mean what kind of ghost are you?' After I asked that, I realized, what a silly question, and to start with! As if I believed there were kinds of ghosts and I knew their types.

Maybe there are the bloodsucking vampires, werewolves, sinister apparitions—sure there are. Thanks to my knowledge from movies.

He turned to look at me for few moments as if telling me, don't ask me stupid questions.

'Okay, I suppose you don't want to talk about that. But I understood ghosts are just some lost souls, probably unsatisfied when they are within the bodies. They can fly around. But you are made up of flesh and bones. You don't look like a ghost.' I tried a completely silly, idiotic attempt at showing my knowledge of ghosts. I thought he would give me the same stare of 'don't be foolish'.

He cleared his throat and said, 'The less you know about the soul thing, the better it is.'

'If you are a ghost, why do you need a lift, why do you care about being wet? What, are you going to die of pneumonia?' I thought I cracked a good joke. In fact, I thought at that moment, it was so good that it should be posted on Facebook: a ghost who feared he would die of pneumonia. I was sure to get comments like ROFL and many likes.

He didn't even acknowledge it. Maybe he was a kind of dumb guy, who does not get jokes. I made my conclusions. It is not me, it is him, I convinced myself.

'I am travelling in this body,' he replied.

'And my car,' I thought. At least this was a good joke. Same reaction from him though.

'Inside this body of flesh and bones, as you say, I am a ghost,' seemed like he cleared his status.

'So am I and so is everybody else, no? We are born and die, we are travellers, as many philosophers claim. Our soul keeps going from one body to another. For now, I am travelling in my body.' I acted a smart-ass here.

He did not answer. I thought that I got the better of him.

'Hmm?' I probed.

'You will die, between changing bodies. You will die. You have to. But for me . . .'

'Yes, and for you?'

He remained silent, and kept staring outside beyond the darkness. 'You were saying something about yourself. You don't pass death?'

Silence.

'Hmm?' Same attempt at probing.

'No, I don't.'

This person was getting interesting. He had piqued my interest; if I kept kindling, I was sure that the night was not going to be boring.

'What happens if I kill you here? Will you die then? Will you still get to change your body?' I asked.

He looked at me and scoffed, mocking me. If I had the stomach to do anything worthwhile, leave the killing. There was something strange about his eyes, especially when he looked at me like that. The facial expressions were different, a sad face, but his eyes had a different story. They looked mean to me; they scared me. We again had a spell of silence. This person had started to seem spooky.

'What is your name?' I asked.

'I don't have one. Names are for identifying bodies. I don't really know what this body is labelled as. I just found it, like a temporary vehicle. I don't understand how knowing my name is going to help you. In this car, you are going to talk only with me, so you don't need my name and beyond this car, we will not meet unless I wish so, in which case you still don't need my name.'

It was certain he was not a case of an unstable mental condition, and on the contrary, he seemed quite smart. After his wisecrack on the importance of names, he saw my unease and made a sarcastic grunt and spoke.

'I know you will not understand the nameless part, you cannot get out of names. For your sake, one of my names, which stuck for a long time, was Arvind, identify me with that.'

'You think I am a twelve-year-old kid to believe in all the ludicrous shit you are saying?'

'What you believe is hardly of any significance. Your understanding does not change anything. The sun was still rising when people did not believe that earth is round and goes around it. You may choose not to believe and for that I hardly care. I said I am a ghost, so that you can understand that I am not exactly like you, otherwise the concept of ghost you understand is far from what I am. Your understanding of ghost is limited to what you see in your idiotic movies.'

'So then you explain me what is a ghost according to you?' I asked, irritated.

'Nothing. As I said, I just used this word as something that you might understand. That I and this body are different. I can leave this body at my will. I am a professional body shifter. I can do for myself as well as for others. Which is probably different than your definition of ghost, I suppose,' he answered.

'Body shifter?' I laughed mockingly at him.

But my laughing didn't bother him. He wasn't irritated. His eyes just became a notch darker and meaner.

'So did you die before become this body shifter?' I probed him further, trying to align my definition of 'ghost'.

'Body dies eventually. Do you care for what happened to the clothes you wore ten years back? Apparently, no, same with me, I don't care what happens to the bodies. For instance, even this body, I don't like this, it is old and is a carrier of many diseases. But I hardly care,' he answered.

'How do I know that you are who you actually say you are and not some dummy building a silly story, can you prove it to me?' I asked.

'You are being stupid now. I am in this body, in this shell, so while I am like that, I am limited to what this old body can do. If I come out of this body, you will be driving with a corpse. And if at all I wanted to come out of this body like this, I would not have got into it in the first place,' he said.

I felt his sudden arrogance extremely rude. His absence of any manners to show me any kind of gratitude for the lift I gave him in his moment of distress was something I overlooked but now he was not only acting smart but also ridiculing me. How dare he call me stupid? I slammed the brakes and brought the car to a jerk halt.

'You know what, please get down from the car. Get some other lift. I suppose you really don't want to go anywhere, maybe you are a criminal getting away, maybe you are just a homeless person wandering around. I don't wish to get involved with you, please leave. Thank the rain you got my sympathy, but that is about it,' I said rudely.

'I don't understand the problem with honesty. I am being as honest as I could be. What do you want to hear? Had I said I am a sad old person carrying a lot of misery in my bosom, would that make you happy or more reasonable according to you?'

I was silent for a few minutes, my irritation subsided. I realized I did not have a problem with his ludicrous take on himself being a ghost or not having a name. I had a problem with the way he was acting smart, not respecting me and absolutely no acknowledgement that I was the one who had helped him in the rains.

'You think all this while you are helping me?' he said this as if reading my mind. 'Do you even know where you are? You are driving for few hours, not knowing where you are going. You think I don't realize that you have been driving aimlessly? All you see outside is just a plain road with all darkness around, no milestones, no houses, and no trees, is it usual? Did you realize there is absolutely nobody else on this road? With a population like our country's, do you think there would be a road where you travel for so long and you don't see anybody at all?' he said wickedly. His eyes twinkled with a glint of malignity.

I looked outside; it was indeed nothing else. The plain road stretched only till it was lit by the headlights of my car. There was nothing around us, at least not visible in that absolute darkness. There was no moon in the sky, or the stars. Where were we? Why didn't I think of this earlier? But if I was on the off road, it was possible that there are no people around, maybe tonight was the cloudy new moon day, so I didn't see the moon and the stars. Yes, could be, but this person sitting next to me, who looked a poor miserable fellow who came begging for help, now looked way smarter and sinister. And now with what he had said, I wanted to get down from the car and walk a few paces around to see if there was anything beyond the road we were on. And the way he said it, with his conviction, he forced me to think. It was an absolutely normal road, just the time and area was making it feel lonely. Everything was perfectly okay, I told myself. But my face was shamelessly exposing my fright.

'Mister, who the fuck you think you are? Get out of my car right now,' I shouted.

He laughed at me but did not get out of the car. 'Check the time, we have been driving for a very long time, maybe from the time you will know how much further we are,' he said.

I took out my mobile from my pocket and saw the time. I kept on looking at it as if I didn't understand what I was seeing. My mouth froze and hands shivered, unable to hold the mobile properly. The time it showed, eleven twenty-six, was the exact time when I got up from the rains near the makeshift shop where I had met this weirdo. Was the watch gone bad or it was something else? What the fuck?

He looked at my face and laughed, now even louder. His laugh still reverberates in my heart.

'Do you think you can make out a difference between a dream and real life? I bet you cannot. What do you think are you dreaming right now or you were dreaming before? How will you ever be sure what realm you are in, a real life or a dream state?'

I felt suddenly everything around me became cold. My teeth chattered and my entire body was violently shivering. My vision started becoming fuzzy. The car, the surroundings, this fellow sitting next to me were becoming hazy. Everything started mixing in each other, like everything was made of smoke; the only thing I could see were his lips, and what he said was the only voice I heard.

He kept on saying 'Guess where you are—are you in a dream state or are you actually driving?'

Everything around me was grey now, made of smoke. I was being buried again, slowly lowered in earth. I was surrounded by faceless people who were throwing gravel on me, gravel cold as ice pellets. I was looking at them from the hole they were putting me in. I saw there was a person who moved behind the faceless people. He was the only one who seemed to be like a regular person. I was not able to see his face. I wanted to call out to him, but I was choked. There was already lot of gravel in my mouth to open it and speak. I tried moving my hands to call him to save me, but I had no control of my limbs. And then I saw this person's hand on the shoulders of the faceless people; he was moving them away. And then he came ahead and looked at me. He smiled. I recognized him immediately. He took a fistful of cold pellets and threw it on my face. His eyes had the same malice.

I was looking at myself!

I mustered all the strength in me and shouted, spitting the gravel in my mouth and throat all over.

Suddenly it was daytime. There was light all around. I was confused. I looked around me. I saw the same makeshift shop. There were two or three people there. I was sitting on the ground and my car was like twenty feet away from me. What was I doing here? What the hell happened to me, I thought. I looked at the people near the shop. They were staring at me; maybe I shouted very loudly. I stood up and tried walking towards the car. I felt kind of weak in my knees. I walked a few paces, and to my utter shock, I saw a reflection of the same old man in the window of my car. I gave out a death-defying cry and looked behind to call people from the shop to help me. But behind me there was no old man whose reflection I saw and the people from the shop were again staring at me as if I was crazy to shout. I looked at the window again, and again I saw the reflection of the same old man. Then it felt like as if my car started! And I was right, it did indeed start and started moving away and just before it joined the highway, the driver opened his side of the window. I saw the person driving. It was me!

There was a loud cracking sound of lightning and suddenly the rains came down like a cloudburst. I heard the murmur of people behind me running away and closing the shop. I did not turn around and see. It made no difference. I heard somebody shouting from behind; he was asking to get the old man inside from the rain and storm. I stood there crying in the rain. In a few minutes, there was a pool of water around me. I saw the reflection of the old man in it. There was no sign of my car or me. I did not shout. I just cried.